35

28

Assume every agent is a double agent.

31

Never leave a fellow agent behind. You're in this together. Go team Secret Agent!

AMANDA HOSCH

STONE ARCH BOOKS
a capstone imprint

Mabel Opal Pear and the Rules for Spying is published by
Capstone Young Readers
A Capstone Imprint
1710 Roe Crest Drive, North Mankato, Minnesota 56003
www.mycapstone.com

Cover illustration by Ira Sluyterman van Langeweyde
Book design by Tracy McCabe
Design elements: Shutterstock: Anelina, Attitude,
Christopher Brewer, EsSueno, My Life Graphic

Library of Congress Cataloging-in-Publication Data
Names: Hosch, Amanda, author.
Sluyterman van Langeweyde, Ira, illustrator.
Title: Mabel Opal Pear and the rules for spying / by Amanda Hosch;
illustrated by Ira Sluyterman van Langeweyde.
Description: North Mankato, Minnesota : Capstone Press, [2017]
Summary: Fifth-grader Mabel (code name Sunflower) wrote the Rules for a Successful Life as an Undercover Secret Agent, so when her parents leave town abruptly she is not too worried—but when her beloved Aunt Gertie is arrested, and her objectionable Uncle Frank and Aunt Stella (Frankenstella) and her annoying (but clever) cousin Victoria take over her house and the family's private museum, Mabel begins to smell a rat and she is determined to find out what her suspicious relatives are up to.
Identifiers: LCCN 2017000422| ISBN 9781623708054 (paper over board) | ISBN 9781496540515 (library binding) | ISBN 9781496540522 (ebook (pdf))
Subjects: LCSH: Museums—Juvenile fiction. | Family secrets—Juvenile fiction. | Aunts—Juvenile fiction. | Cousins—Juvenile fiction. | Detective and mystery stories. | Washington (State)—Juvenile fiction. | CYAC: Mystery and detective stories. | Spies—Fiction. | Museums—Fiction. | Secrets—Fiction. | Aunts—Fiction. | Cousins—Fiction. | Washington (State)—Fiction. | GSAFD: Mystery fiction. | LCGFT: Detective and mystery fiction.
Classification: LCC PZ7.1.H667 Mab 2017 | DDC 813.6 [Fic] —dc23
LC record available at https://lccn.loc.gov/2017000422

Printed and bound in the United States of America.
010664R

For my mother,
whose love of books shaped my life.
I miss you every day, Mom.

Preamble to Rules for a Successful Life as an Undercover Secret Agent

Life as an undercover agent can be stressful, lonely, and dangerous. These rules were written by an agent-in-training to help guide you when you feel out of sorts. They're not meant to replace your Academy training. Use Rules for a Successful Life as an Undercover Secret Agent *to remind yourself how to act in difficult situations. Like Rule Number 15 says, "Be in control."*

All the rules are important — some more so than others, depending on the situation. The most important rule of all is Rule Number 3: Trust your instincts. Unless your instincts are often wrong. If that's the case, Number 29 is a good rule to keep in mind: Anticipate surprises.

Also remember that Murphy is always correct and you'll be fine (Rule Number 17). Rule Number 12 will get you out of sticky situations: Always have an escape plan.

Your country thanks you for your service. While your name will never be known, your actions reflect upon all of us secret agents, for better or worse. Sometimes, you might feel a bit dreary, toiling away in anonymity. On the bright side, no one will ever know if you make a mistake. Unless you start a war. Don't start a war, unless explicitly directed to by your commanding officer. Then double-check to make sure he/she is not being controlled by the enemy (Rule Number 4).

Trust no one and have a great day!

Compiled and written by Agent-in-Training Sunflower, age ten.

1

Live in a quiet and remote small town where everyone thinks they already know the real you. Don't give them a reason to change their minds.

— Rule Number 1 from *Rules for a Successful Life as an Undercover Secret Agent*

The first hit on my window was tentative, like maple leaves tapping against the glass during a gentle rain. The second thud was harder. The third sounded like someone had thrown a rock wrapped in a sock — soft but with force. Since it didn't seem like the barrage was stopping anytime soon — *thunk* — and might actually crack the glass, I dropped my book, *The Fulton Sisters' Adventure,* Number 87, and got up from my bed. Samantha and April Fulton would just have to stay stuck swirling around their mysterious wormhole until I got back to them.

I pushed the window open and a pinecone whizzed by me. "Who's there?" I called as I looked through the branches of the old wild apple tree. The gold and red leaves blocked part of the view of my backyard, but movement on the left caught my attention.

"Mabel, what are you doing?" Stanley Brick stepped out from between two huge Douglas firs and dropped a pinecone.

"What are *you* doing?" I said before I remembered exactly why he was using my window for target practice. Recently Stanley had gotten tired of knocking on my front door, since no one ever answered it. It was hard to hear the knocking from my room, and my parents weren't home often, so I'd suggested we try something new. "The signal! You're doing the signal."

He nodded.

"And I'm supposed to give the counter-signal."

"That was our plan." Stanley picked up a different pinecone and tossed it from hand to hand, as if testing it to see if it was ready to launch.

"Sorry. I was reading Adventure Number Eighty-Seven," I said.

"Have you gotten to the part where Samantha and April meet the waitress who is secretly a ninja who rescues lost children?"

"No." I covered my ears. "Don't say another word." Stanley nodded again, this time in understanding. A clean-enough hoodie was on top of a clothing pile, so I put it on. "OK. Ready now!" I called out before closing the window.

Stanley threw the next pinecone. *Thunk.*

I flipped the lights on and off twice — my counter-signal — and headed downstairs. Six giant cinnamon buns sat on the kitchen counter. I sighed and thought, *Pity buns for breakfast. Again.*

I know — most people would be happy to find homemade goodies in their kitchen on a Saturday morning. And I was — sort of. Aunt Gertie made the cinnamon buns because she knew they were my absolute favorite treat. But it was the third time she'd baked them this week, and the fact that she'd made them again meant that my parents were still away, saving the world on one of their top secret missions. Good for the world, lonely for me. There's a limit to the amount of self-pity that can be wiped away by sugar and cinnamon. I hadn't reached it yet, but if my parents didn't come home soon, I might.

I was lucky to have Aunt Gertie stay with me. That was our family's protocol whenever my parents were away (protocol: rules for how to get things done in certain situations). Aunt Gertie had left hours ago to open the Star's Tale, her café and knickknack shop, where she served coffee and pastries to the hordes of day-trippers and hardcore backpackers making their way to Mount Rainier for one last fall hike.

I ran through the kitchen, sliding across the wooden floor, and opened the back door to let Stanley in. He was in full hiking gear even though we were only going to our favorite tree grove, about a forty-five minute walk from here. Though he'd never been a Boy Scout, Stanley was always prepared. The pockets of his forest-green vest bulged with maps, a compass, and a tube of sunscreen. In his backpack, he kept a variety of items like sunglasses, snacks, water, extra clothes, a flashlight, a first-aid kit, matches, and a pocketknife. Before I could join him outside on the porch, the rich aroma of cinnamon and sugar had lured him inside.

"Are your parents awake?" Stanley whispered as he made a beeline for the buns. I'm pretty sure I heard his stomach growl.

Dodging Stanley's question, I shrugged, grabbed a bun, and started eating. Though it was a pity bun, it was warm, gooey, and made with love, and that made my belly happy. I zoned out, thinking about what my parents might be up to at this very moment.

The truth was, I had no idea whether my parents were awake, or even what time zone they were in. My parents worked as top secret agents, a special type of spy known as "Cleaners." They would go into really bad situations around the world to clean up messes made by other spies. One time my parents had to erase video footage of the original spies sneaking into a forbidden area and walking out with documents clearly marked "Top Secret." Sure, the actual Cleaners' work only took twenty minutes or so — my mom was a whiz at hacking video surveillance systems — but my parents had to physically remove the hard drive containing the back-up video. According to Dad, he was in and out in fewer than seven minutes. The real time-eater was the flight to the other side of the Earth: sixteen hours and five minutes — each way. My parents never gave me too many specifics, but spy work of any kind sounded dangerous and fun, and more exciting than their cover stories.

On the surface, my parents sounded boring. Even their names were snore-inducing: Fred and Jane Pear. My father maintained old telephone lines that run through Mount Rainier National Park and Mount Baker-Snoqualmie National Forest. He also repaired cell phone towers. Sometimes Mom went to keep him company. At least there was one exciting thing about his cover job: He got to pilot small planes. Mom could pilot too — just not for her cover job. My mother was the curator for our family's private museum, Le Petit Musée of Antique Silver Spoons. She spent her days looking at old stuff — mostly spoons — and filling out paperwork. Lots of paperwork.

Why a spoon museum? It'd been in our family for generations. My great-great-grandfather used to travel a lot. He would bring my great-great-grandmother a commemorative silver spoon from wherever he was. When the kitchen drawers were stuffed with more than a thousand spoons, my great-great-grandma bought the house next door, put the spoons on display, and charged admission. She called it Le Petit Musée because she thought it sounded sophisticated. She didn't know the French words for "old silver spoon."

"Is it OK if I have another bun?" Stanley asked, breaking into my thoughts. I nodded as I continued to uncoil mine, its sugar and cinnamon melting on my tongue with each bite.

The spoon obsession was odd, I'd admit, but it was a harmless enough hobby. My great-grandparents collected spoons until they died. Then my grandparents added to the collection. When Mom and I did inventory last summer, we counted more than two thousand spoons on display. Some of the spoons were rare, some had gemstones or gold handles, and all had to be dusted and polished on a regular basis. And when Mom and Dad were out saving the world, who do you think had to clean all of those spoons? I only got a measly five dollars for the job, even if it took all afternoon.

At least when I help Aunt Gertie, she pays me in pastries and *cash,* I thought as I savored my last bite. I decided against another bun and washed my hands.

When Stanley finished, he took two cups from the cupboard, opened the refrigerator, looked inside, and said, "You're out of milk." He continued to poke around the fridge, behind the yogurts and take-out containers from

Mai's Diner. If we hadn't been best friends since practically birth, I wouldn't have noticed his grunt of irritation. He was used to my kitchen being fully stocked at all times. We had an unspoken agreement. He never mentioned my parents' bizarre schedules, and I never mentioned that he'd practically lived at my house ever since his dad had left and his mom had to start working two jobs.

Stanley closed the fridge door and, with his pointer finger, tapped the photo he had given to my parents of the red-winged blackbird. The bird was perched on a nest of woven reeds and cattails, his scarlet and yellow shoulder patch standing out against his sleek black feathers. Stanley had shot the photo on a camping trip we'd taken in late spring. He smiled every time he saw it on the fridge door, which was practically every day.

I couldn't very well tell him that my parents had been gone almost ten days, much longer than anticipated. While Aunt Gertie was a marvelous baker, she totally flaked out on normal grocery shopping.

"We can get milk from the café," I said as Stanley put the cups away.

We went out my front door, past the spoon museum, and walked into Aunt Gertie's shop. The three buildings — my house, the museum, and the café — took up an entire block on Main Street, which was only four blocks long. The only other buildings of note were the old jail, which now doubled as a tourist info station, and Mai's Diner.

The Star's Tale was packed. Stanley and I elbowed our way to the front of the line, flashing innocent smiles and exchanging nods of greeting with the regulars. Like usual, the café was a mess. Scented candles propped up guidebooks on shelves with jewelry strewn about. Packets of dried fruit and nuts sat between wool socks. In the middle of it all, the café served coffee, hot chocolate, sandwiches, and pastries. Luckily, Aunt Gertie could find anything within ten seconds, so the wacky, mixed-up system worked for her.

One reason for the traffic jam was obvious. At the table by the display of earrings, an older man lingering over coffee took up a four-seater. Dressed like an REI mannequin in a new green and blue plaid flannel shirt, new water-resistant pants, and new hiking boots, he was studying a topographic map of Mount Rainier. The tread on the man's boots was not worn at all, so I could understand his caution before setting out for a hike. New boots meant possible blisters. Noticing details like that was part of spy training, so I tried to do it all I could. I wanted to tell the man to pick up a map of easy day hikes from the ranger's station. But when I caught his eye — cold and watchful — the words stuck in my throat. Something told me he wasn't looking for advice. I tried stepping back, but the crowd held me in place.

A thought popped into my mind. It was the end of October, probably the last hike before many of the trails closed for the winter. Sure, someone might have a new vest, or even new boots. But an entirely new outfit? Early summer was typically when novice hikers would try their luck on the mountain.

Dad always said that a good secret agent was constantly on the lookout for the odd sock — something or someone that was seemingly meaningless, but out of place. This man was an odd sock.

Aunt Gertie's long purple skirt twirled as she flitted from table to table, coffee pot in hand. When she saw Stanley and me, she didn't miss a beat. She waltzed behind the counter, poured milk into to-go cups, waltzed back, handed the cups to us, and sneaked a kiss on my head. "You kids aren't planning on hiking all the way to Tim Chamberlain's warehouse, are you?" Aunt Gertie asked as she took in Stanley's outfit. "There's not enough time this morning."

"No, ma'am. That part of the path is gated off after Labor Day." Stanley pulled out a paper map to show her our route, about halfway on a popular path to the abandoned warehouse. As they spoke, the odd sock leaned in ever so slightly, as if trying to eavesdrop.

As Stanley folded up the map, Aunt Gertie bent down to plant another kiss on my head. She didn't tell me I was going to have to work at Le Petit Musée at noon to maintain my parents' cover story. She didn't need to. It was protocol. She would unlock the museum, I would hang out in the Spoon, and if anyone asked, I'd say my mom had stepped out.

"Did you have the chance to make that call?" the odd sock asked my aunt.

Aunt Gertie raised her eyebrows and motioned around the bustling café. "Not yet."

"What call?" I asked. Maybe my spy sense had picked up on something.

"Nothing to worry about." Aunt Gertie gave me a kind smile and said, "OK, Moppet. Be home before eleven-thirty."

"Moppet?" Mr. Odd Sock repeated in disbelief. "You're Moppet?"

"It's a nickname," I said, caught off guard. "Moppet" was cute when I was six years old. It's humiliating in the fifth grade. I didn't appreciate being mocked by a total stranger — especially an overdressed, eavesdropping odd sock.

"Who's that guy?" I whispered to Aunt Gertie.

"No one to worry about. He's just someone who really enjoys my coffee. Fourth cup." Aunt Gertie swooped in for another kiss. "Go on now, Moppet. Don't waste your morning here." She offered the man a refill.

"Come on, Mabel." Stanley pulled on my sleeve.

Something didn't seem right. Twice my aunt told me to not worry, but I knew from experience that adults only said that when there was, in fact, something to worry about. I hesitated. "Do you want me to help this morning?"

Aunt Gertie pointed to the door and said, "Go on your hike."

Once my aunt moved to another table, the man stared at me, holding eye contact. I felt as if I had done something wrong. Stanley yanked harder on my sleeve, but I could barely move through the thick crowd. Mr. Odd Sock smirked as if he had won some type of game. "You heard your aunt, Moppet," he said in a low voice. I strained to hear him over the noise of the café. "Get a move on now." Someone stepped in front of me, breaking our eye contact.

I ducked under a flannel-clad elbow and grabbed on to Stanley's backpack as he guided me through the hungry horde. Once outside, I chanced looking into the café. The odd sock's smirk had morphed into a full-on grin, like he had just won some contest.

In other words, I had just lost a game I didn't even know I was playing.

2

Successful spying consists of 50 percent preparation, 30 percent inspiration, 20 percent perspiration, and 10 percent action, which adds up to 110 percent because a great spy gives it her all and then some.

— Rule Number 35 from *Rules for a Successful Life as an Undercover Secret Agent*

"Stanley, have you ever seen the guy in the plaid shirt before?" I asked.

"Half the people in there are wearing plaid." Stanley drained his cup.

"Never mind." I finished my milk too. "Let's just go."

We'd walked for about five minutes, just past the outskirts of town, when Stanley stopped, pointed to a spot about halfway up a Douglas fir, and quietly took out his camera. He started snapping photos. A small bird with yellow and black feathers flew by. Stanley's face lit up. "That's a yellow-rumped warbler! Or maybe a Townsend's warbler." He checked the pictures on his screen. "Definitely not an orange-crowned warbler. Their body feathers are completely yellow."

Stanley could spot a bird that weighed less than half an

ounce hiding in some tree branches twenty feet away, but he couldn't notice the man dressed like an outdoors store mannequin smirking at me. But that was exactly what made my friendship with Stanley easy. He never asked questions about my life's oddities, like not seeing my parents for ten days, even though my mother worked next door to my house.

During our hike, I learned all about Townsend's warblers. Apparently, while they liked to munch on spiders and leafhoppers, their absolute favorite meal was stink bugs, which I'd smelled a lot of back in the summertime.

Once we reached our favorite tree grove (now with no stink bugs — thank you, warblers!), Stanley took out his tripod and lens case. Each month Stanley documented the grove, from snow-covered to spring buds, from summer's wild glory to fall's amazing colors.

Each time, he'd re-measure the exact distance from the trees and the camera's angle. Fortunately, we had a lot of notes, a sketch of where the camera should go, and a photograph taped inside his notebook. That had been a two-camera day so Stanley could photograph where his camera was located while he was taking photos of the trees and wildlife.

After Stanley was sure he had replicated the setup perfectly and started taking photos, I wandered away. Just ten feet off the paved path, voices carried through the trees and undergrowth, offering odd bits of other hikers' conversations as they passed.

Up ahead, a black-tailed deer munched on grass. I stood absolutely still for a while, fascinated. After several minutes, I felt the oddest sensation on the back of my neck — prickly and warm — like I was being watched. I breathed in, trying to ignore it, but the feeling wouldn't go away. Mount Rainier had its fair share of predators: black bears, mountain lions, coyotes, foxes, and even mountain goats (mean, smelly, and known to head-butt hikers). Slowly, I turned my head to my right. A twig snapped on my left. I whipped my head around. Through the evergreens, a flash of blue and green plaid caught my eye. It appeared that the person was quickly retreating.

The plaid kept up a steady pace and I followed. After a few minutes, the evergreens became too thick and I lost track of the blue-green flashes. I kept going for another minute, then looked up to see where the forest canopy cleared. I darted through the trees, keeping the clearing in sight, and found my way to the paved path within minutes. A group of hikers was drinking water and snapping photos of the foliage. "Did you see a man in a blue and green plaid shirt?" I asked.

"Are you lost, sweetie?" one of the women asked.

"No," I said, aware that valuable time was ticking away. "Did you see him?" I looked up and down the path, but there was no sign of Mr. Odd Sock.

"A shirt like mine?" one of the men asked. The blue and green checks on his shirt were too small. "I've seen a couple."

"Where are your parents?" the woman asked, looking concerned.

I pointed in the direction of Stanley. He was practically family, after all. "Bye," I said as I beat a hasty retreat toward our tree grove.

"Ready, Mabel?" Stanley asked as he looked up from putting his camera, lenses, and tripod away. "Where were you?"

"I was just watching a deer," I said. *Get a grip, Sunflower,* I told myself. Somehow using my code name helped calm my nerves. Maybe it had been someone else in blue and green looking at wildlife.

Stanley nodded in understanding. "You should ask your parents for a camera."

On the hike home, Stanley talked about the things he'd observed in the tree grove: a red fox out for a stroll, a golden-mantle ground squirrel, which looks like a chipmunk but doesn't have facial stripes, and a new collection of bat houses posted on trees.

We arrived in Silverton with seven minutes to spare. As per the Pear family protocol, it was time for me to hang out at the Spoon (Saturday hours were noon to four p.m.). Stanley walked me to the museum, then continued home to upload his newest photo collection. He contributed to a Mount Rainier nature blog. His posts got a few hundred visitors each month and I was usually the first to comment on them.

I heard a soft humming as I entered the museum. I bit my lip to keep from calling out. The sound came from the corner, next to the filing cabinet. I couldn't see over the display cases chock-full of silver spoons. I fought the urge to hum along to the familiar melody. Instead, using my best quiet feet, I inched closer until someone burst out in song.

"You are my sunshine, my only sunshine . . ."

"Mom!" I dashed around the display case. "You're home. How was —"

Before I could say Nauru (a tiny island country in Micronesia), she hugged me so tightly my face squished against her shoulder. I didn't mind one bit.

"While the *Nebraska* Silverware Association was disorganized," she said once she had let me go, "I persuaded the top Nebraskan to let me assist in locating the missing documents." She bent down to kiss my forehead. "Your father helped with their communication issues. Old wiring needs repairing, even in Nebraska."

No matter how many times Mom said Nebraska, I was sure she and Dad had been in Nauru. Even though they would never directly tell me where they were going, I had my ways of figuring it out.

"So, Moppet, anything exciting to report?"

"Nothing ever happens in Silverton." How could it when there are only 267 people in the entire town? We're smack in the middle of the Cascade Mountain Range, right next to Mount Rainier. Don't get me wrong — it's not like we're cut off from normal life or anything. We have satellite TV. Seattle is only two hours away by car. Plus, Silverton has its own airstrip, which makes it very convenient for my parents to fly in and out.

"That's not true. Things change every day," Mom said, pulling open the window blinds. "The leaves turned while we were gone."

"OK, the leaves changed color, we had two pop quizzes in math, it rained yesterday, I turned in my history paper, read *Fulton Sisters' Adventures* Numbers Eighty-Five and Eighty-Six, started Eighty-Seven, and Stanley and I hiked this morning. Where's Dad?"

"He's refueling the plane and filing our reports," Mom said. "Any progress on the Great Reverse Heist?"

"Oh yes. I figured out which ones are the stolen items." I bounded out of the museum, back into my house, and up the stairs to my room. While Stanley busied himself by photographing wildlife, I spent my free time hot on the heels of some very cold theft cases.

Months ago, my mom and dad let me in on one of our family secrets. I didn't think anything could've topped the whole my-parents-are-super-secret-spies thing, but I was wrong. Apparently, my mom's parents, Carl and Mabel (my namesake) Baies, hadn't been the most law-abiding citizens. In fact, it could be said (and was said, repeatedly, by the police, the FBI, and the Agency) that they were criminals.

My grandparents had used Le Petit Musée of Antique Silver Spoons as a front for selling stolen goods in the 1960s. They were a minor part of a minor criminal gang, operating in small pockets of the United States. Mom said her parents died before they were ever convicted, so that's why she and Gertie didn't know anything about it. It was only when Mom started working for the Agency that she found out because of background checks.

Get this — the stolen stuff wasn't anything really amazing like money or famous art or diamonds. Nope, it was all old American history type stuff from university collections and living museums — those places you have to go for field trips, where the poor museum guide is dressed up in old-fashioned clothing, using words like "thee" and "thou." These kinds of places were not known for their security, especially way back then. So my grandparents didn't have anything super valuable at the Spoon — just dusty old things like maps, letters, and diaries.

Mom never told her sister because she didn't want to taint Aunt Gertie's memories of their parents. So I'd been under strict orders to keep that secret from my aunt while my parents had been quietly undoing the damage my grandparents had done. The Great Reverse Heist meant that whenever they found some of the historical American memorabilia, they would extract it (extract means to remove — maybe not totally legally — in spy terms) and return the item to its rightful owner.

One of the best ways of recovering stolen property was going to auctions, which was why I'd spent the last ten days going through the *Auction-Goer's Complete Guide*, November Edition. Before they left, my parents told me that two of the items listed were stolen property. They were testing my abilities. So, besides school, eating, and sleeping, I'd been studying picture after picture of Colonial American memorabilia, using clues provided by my parents to figure out what my grandparents had stolen.

In my room, I knelt next to the head of my bed and reached under it to extract the auctioning guide. Strange. I felt nothing. I peered underneath and spotted it by the foot of my bed, about five feet away from where I had placed it before going to sleep the previous night.

An odd, prickly feeling swept up my neck. That catalog couldn't have moved itself.

I sat back on my heels and peered around my bedroom, and right away, other things caught my attention. My blue sweater was hanging on the back of my chair, instead of on the floor where it had landed earlier. One pile of my books had been straightened. Two of my history books were in my astronomy book pile. My desk drawers were all pushed in. The origami solar system model hung crooked over my dresser. And my trash bucket, which had been full the day before, was empty. I checked the window — locked. I never locked my window. There was no need to in Silverton . . . or so I thought.

Someone had been in my room.

3

Coincidences do happen, just not that often. When in doubt, check it out.

— Rule Number 36 from *Rules for a Successful Life as an Undercover Secret Agent*

I raced into the museum, calling as I went, "Mom, did you try cleaning my room? We had an agreement. Remember?" I stopped short. A visitor — an actual visitor — leaned over the display case, pointing and asking questions.

"They don't make bulldozers agile enough for that job," Mom said to me as she very discreetly put one finger up, meaning I should button my lips.

Right away, this seemed odd. Visitors in late October were not impossible, but in Silverton, tourists usually came during the summer. They'd take pictures in front of the spoon museum, buy postcards, and go hiking for a few days on Mount Rainier.

The man moved, and I got a better look at him. That blue and green plaid shirt, those new pants — creases still visible — those boots with no scuff marks and just a bit of mud. I should have known bad things come in threes. Our museum visitor was the odd sock.

Unsure what to do, but needing to do something, I walked behind a case. Going over to a tray of spoons, I put the catalog down, slipped on gloves, picked up the polishing rag, and got to work. Today's collection to be cleaned was Pennsylvania Dutch Country. On each spoon, different styles of horse and buggy were designed to fit where the handle usually goes. And if anyone happens to wonder how much tarnish gets into the lines of those horses and buggies, it's lots, let me tell you.

"Where is your jewelry display?" Mr. Odd Sock asked Mom as he tapped the glass case.

"We only have spoons here," she said, pointing to the new sign Dad had recently made of old stainless steel spoons spelling out the museum's name. Usually tourists chuckled over it. Mr. Odd Sock was unmoved by my father's handiwork.

"I'd like to buy my niece something. Maybe a spoon with her name on it," he said. "Where is your gift shop?"

"I'm terribly sorry. We don't sell spoons," Mom said. "We do have postcards. A dollar each or six for five dollars."

Mr. Odd Sock shook his head and walked away from my mother. As I rubbed off the tarnish, I thought it had to be more than a coincidence that the man was in the museum. First he'd spent the morning at my aunt's café, then he'd (maybe) hiked on a path parallel to Stanley and me, and now this.

Then again, the Star was one of two places to eat in Silverton. The path we'd used was the easiest, flattest, and best-marked route to view the mountains. Except for the glory of Mount Rainier behind us, Le Petit Musée was it for fun activities — or any activity with a roof — for fifteen miles in any direction. Coincidences do happen. Sometimes.

The front door opened, letting in the sound of giggles. "Mabel, are you here?"

"Mabel?" Another high-pitched voice called.

More giggles. "Are you here, Mabel?"

Emma G., Emma H., Grace K., and Grace L. swept into the museum, each cradling a baby pumpkin. As four-ninths of the HEGs (the two Hannahs, three Emmas, and four Graces in my class), they'd made it their mission to be super sweet to me and include me in all that they do since I had the "odd name." But I liked being the only Mabel in class. No one ever picked up my lunch box by mistake.

The Emmas and Graces were all wearing orange hairbands with orange bows. They talked over one another as they showed off their decorated baby pumpkins. They were sweet, but like candy corn, too much of them made my stomach ache.

"We knew you had to help your mom, but we didn't want you to miss the fun, so I made you one," Emma G. said as she plunked down a miniature pumpkin with a tiny green witch's hat, googly eyes, black bat wings, and brown spider legs. It was also bathed in glitter. Then Emma G. held out a couple of ghost-shaped cookies wrapped in plastic. "I saved you some of these from last night."

"The cookies look boooo-ti-ful. Thank you," I said. The pumpkin left a trail of shiny glitter on the display case. Someone was going to have to clean that up, and that someone's initials were MOP.

"Do you like it?" Emma G. asked. "I couldn't remember your favorite color."

"I said red," Grace L. interrupted.

"Blue, right?" Emma H. said.

Grace K. said nothing.

"Right now, orange is my favorite," I said to Emma G. "It's perfect."

"Yay!" Emma G. actually squealed. I'd have to remember to thank her more often. "Bring it to school on Friday, OK?" Emma G. said. "For the Halloween party."

"I will," I said, glancing quickly at Mr. Odd Sock, who was now wandering around the museum and looking at spoons, like visitors were supposed to do. Grace K.'s eyes flickered to him, which I found suspicious, so I asked the girls, "Can I see your pumpkins?" to keep them talking — and to give me more time to investigate whatever was going on.

Emma G. held up her baby pumpkin. It had the same green witch's hat and googly eyes, but also had silver cat whiskers, black yarn hair, and purple monster hands. Somehow it appeared to have even more glitter coating it. Emma H., Grace K., and Grace L. had similarly over-decorated pumpkins.

"Pretty," I said. Normally I liked to carve my Halloween pumpkins into spooky faces, but the HEGs were sweet — shiny, glittery sweet — to think of me. The glue was starting to pool off of my pumpkin and I wondered if it would be rude of me to start wiping down the display case in front of them.

"You wanna go to Mai's?" Emma G. asked. "They have baby pumpkin pies."

"You know, the little ones," Emma H. interrupted, using her hands to show how small. "Each one is just enough for one person."

Grace L. stepped in front. "And we can get caramel apple cider. With whipped cream and caramel sauce on top."

Grace K. stared at her nails.

"Sorry," I said. "I've got to polish this tray of spoons today." Not only that, but my parents had just come in from not-Nebraska and I wanted to hear about it. But I couldn't say that to the girls. Living a double life was hard.

"We'll help you, Mabel," said Emma G.

"We'll help Moppet?" asked Grace K., finally saying something.

"We will help *Mabel*," said Emma G. in such a kind way I wanted to reach across the display case to hug her. Grace K. just rolled her eyes in reply.

Mr. Odd Sock drifted our way. Grace K. glanced at him again, yet he didn't seem to notice.

Emma G. reached over to pick up a polishing rag, leaving a smear of glitter and glue on the glass case top.

"Oh no," I said. "You're too sweet to offer."

"Mabel, you can just —" Mom started to say.

I cut her off with a shake of my head, and raised one finger. I knew she probably felt bad about leaving me for so long, but I really couldn't take an afternoon of *ooh*ing and *aah*ing over mini art projects. OK, the *ooh*ing didn't bother me all that much. But having to avoid innocent questions, like, "What did you do last night?" was the problem. As much as I wanted to, I couldn't say, "While you HEGs were baking ghost cookies, I was cracking open a criminal case."

Besides not wanting to answer their questions, I wanted to stay home so I could show my parents my work. It had taken days to go through the auction catalog to identify the stolen silver-handled mirror and the stolen mother-of-pearl brush.

"I'm sorry, Mabel," Mom said, watching my face to

make sure she was getting it right. "You really need to stay here and do the work by yourself."

"Oh, all right, Mom." I dropped my shoulders and acted upset. "Sorry," I said to the HEGs.

"Next time?" Emma G. asked, all eager and hopeful.

"Sure," I said.

"Promise?"

Half expecting Emma G. to raise her little finger for a pinkie promise like we did when we were little, I said, "Yes. Promise."

"Great, we'll do Halloween together. Trick-or-treating in Bluewater, for sure," Emma G. said in triumph. "Maybe even a sleepover with a cake and eleven candles."

"Sleepover?" Mom said. A smile spread across her face. "What fun! Mabel, you girls haven't had one in ages."

No, no, no, I thought as hard as I could, but Mom didn't get the message, even as I shot eye daggers in her direction. *Don't blow my cover story. Don't say I can go.* I hadn't mentioned to my mom that I chose to not go to the sleepovers anymore because it was easier than answering questions about our home life.

"Is Mabel really allowed to go again?" Emma G. asked. "We've missed her every Friday night."

"Of course she can go," Mom said. Her pleased expression wavered when she looked at me.

"Great," Emma G. said, waving to my mom as she and the others departed, clutching their mini pumpkins and shedding glitter everywhere.

"Yeah, great," I said as I rubbed the already clean spoon. Somehow Mom had just decided that I would spend my birthday, October thirty-first, with the HEGs.

As I studied the next horse and buggy waiting to be cleaned, a shadow fell across the tray of spoons.

Mr. Odd Sock was so close I smelled this morning's coffee on his breath. I looked at him. He held my glance. Despite the desire to back away, I held my ground. Tapping the auction catalog, he said, "Good day, Moppet," winking at me as he left.

"I don't like him," I said once the front door was firmly shut.

Mom asked, "Why not?"

"Odd sock?" It came out more like a question than a statement.

"Listen to your gut." Mom nodded at me. "If he comes back, don't interact with him."

"Rule Number Three: *Trust your instincts. Your gut wants you to stay alive. Listen to it,*" I recited.

"That's right," Dad said. He had sneaked into the museum and was waiting behind me with his arms outstretched. "How about a hug for your old dad?"

While I'm too old to be picked up on a regular basis, I may have jumped into his arms and squealed in joy.

"We're closing early today," Dad said. "Now who wants to help her father make dinner?"

* * *

Dad had just prepared his special grilled cheese with tomato sandwiches when the phone rang. Mom answered. Her shoulders dropped, and she rubbed her temple in frustration. She started repeating codes back to whoever called. Then Dad got on the phone and started talking in odd phrases and number sequences. Mom grabbed two prepackaged jump bags (smallish suitcases) from the hall closet and then ran downstairs to the basement where they keep one of their hidden Cleaner stashes of fake passports, spy gear, and surveillance tools.

They were going out on a mission. Again.

"I have so many things to tell you, but now you're leaving," I said after Dad hung up. "It's so not fair."

"It's not, Sunflower," Dad said, hugging me. "But if we leave now, we should be back in forty-eight hours. Seventy-two hours at most. The job is a simple Clean."

"*Should* be. Last time was supposed to be four days, and you were gone for ten," I said, not mentioning that my birthday was just a week away. "You just got home today and you haven't even gone grocery shopping yet."

"I'll leave a list for Gertie," Mom said. "Do you think you'll be all right for a few hours until she gets off work?"

"Yes," I grumbled. "Go save the world."

4

If captured by the enemy, play along and be agreeable. Lie if you have to. You will not get in trouble.

— Rule Number 18 from *Rules for a Successful Life as an Undercover Secret Agent*

I woke up, sniffed, and, smelling nothing, I smiled. Aunt Gertie wasn't baking pity buns, which meant my parents were on their way home. I snuggled into the flannel sheets, hoping I had a few more minutes before my alarm sounded.

Today was day two of my parents' latest mission, or thirty-eight hours since they'd left me with three half-eaten grilled cheese and tomato sandwiches and a bunch of dirty dishes. Aunt Gertie and I had spent Sunday following protocol — while she worked at the Star's Tale, I spent four hours in the Spoon with no visitors, just listening to the rain. I'd gotten most of the week's homework done already.

I rolled over. Just then, my floor creaked. I tensed, keeping my eyes closed and my breathing as steady as possible. Then I heard it once more. The footsteps sounded wrong — different from Aunt Gertie's. The person hesitated too much between steps, as if trying to avoid the piles of books I'd been meaning to re-shelve. A soft *click-click-click* and a *whoosh* meant the curtains had been pulled open using the bead chain. Aunt Gertie would have draped them on the side hooks by hand.

The person stayed by the window, blocking some of the weak October sunshine filtering into my bedroom. Perhaps the gold and brown leaves of the wild apple tree had caught his or her attention. I heard soft metallic clinking, like when a woman wears a lot of bracelets on one arm. Lighter footsteps than Aunt Gertie? Jewelry? My mystery visitor was probably female.

She walked toward me, quicker this time. A familiar woodsy scent instantly brought memories of mountain hikes. Trying to keep my breath even, I listened for more movement. Without any warning, I felt a sharp poke on my forehead. I flinched.

"I know you're awake," came a girl's voice. I opened my eyes slowly. A shock of long red hair caught my attention first, and then a pair of sparkly pink rhinestone eyeglasses, which the girl pushed up to the bridge of her nose before snapping a photo of me on her purple smartphone. She pushed a few buttons, smiled, and said, "Mabel, you snore like a lumberjack. You also drool a lot."

One of my actual nightmares had come to life and was standing over me. "Give me that." I jumped out of bed and tried to grab the phone.

Victoria Baies, my least favorite cousin, who happens to be a lot taller than me, dangled the phone just out of my reach. "Who's gonna make me?"

"Me." I tripped on the bed sheets, which had snaked themselves around my legs.

"Poor Moppet. Such short little legs." In addition to being my least favorite cousin, Victoria's also my only cousin. "I wonder who else would like to see this." I tried jumping, but Victoria batted me down with her free hand. A tuft of yarn from her sweater floated by, tickling my nose. She waved the purple phone like a victory flag. "Maybe your boyfriend?"

"I don't have a boyfriend." I leaped onto my bed, just missing a grab at the purple menace as she side-stepped me.

Victoria's metallic bangles clinked and clanked as she tossed her phone from hand to hand, just out of my reach. "Come on, Mabel, you played in the woods with him during our visit in June instead of hanging out with me."

"Stanley is a classmate. We had a project, photographing trees on the mountain." I wasn't going to mention that the project was just for fun, since school was out for summer vacation. "If you remember, I invited you to hike with us, but you weren't interested."

"Your parents *made* you invite me, Moppet. Anyway, nature walks are stupid." Victoria shook her head, her shoulder length, well-behaved red hair swinging behind her. "Who else would like to see what you look like first thing in the morning with drool on your chin?"

If those photos made the rounds anywhere near Bluewater-Silverton Unified Elementary School, I'd be a laughingstock for sure. Or worse, one of the HEGs would try to cure me of my drooling and snoring.

I grabbed on to the pink and purple yarn monstrosity Victoria was wearing and pulled. Fluff from the sweater showered down on me. She swung her arm backward, knocking into my origami model of the solar system. Poor dwarf planet Pluto fluttered to the ground.

"*Mom.*" Victoria's voice sounded like a sad kitten. "Mabel has my phone and won't give it back."

"What?" I stared up at her. "I don't have your phone." Not for lack of trying, though.

Victoria tossed the phone to me just as Aunt Stella walked into my bedroom. For some stupid reason, I caught it.

Despite her bony frame, Stella managed to block the entire doorway with her attitude and elbows. "This is not a good way to start our visit, Mabel Opal." Quicker than seemed possible, she moved toward me and snatched the phone from my hand. "There you go, Vicky-girl," she said as she handed it to Victoria. Turning her attention back to me, she said, "In our family, we respect other people's property, young lady."

"I — I — I didn't take her phone," I spluttered. *Chill out, Sunflower,* I told myself.

"I saw you holding it," Stella said. "Are you calling me a liar?"

"No, ma'am." I rubbed my eyes, but the nightmare wouldn't go away. "Victoria took photos of me while I was sleeping."

"Oh, Momma. You know I would never take photos of someone sleeping." Victoria looked so innocent, I almost believed her myself.

"I know. We'll forget this happened and start over." Stella tried fluffing up her fire-engine red hair, but her efforts fell flat. "Get dressed, Mabel. Breakfast in five minutes."

Thoughts formed in my brain, and before I knew it, I'd blurted out, "Why are you in my house?"

"Get dressed." Stella smacked her lips together. "Four minutes, thirty seconds until breakfast."

"Mabel, where did your parents go in such a hurry?" Victoria asked.

"Monaco." (Monaco: small principality on the Mediterranean Sea bordered by France. Stable government. Its famed Oceanographic Museum had leafy seahorses and a collection of early twentieth century research yachts.) That was the cover story, anyway. I had been annoyed Saturday night and hadn't bothered to figure out where they were really headed. I wasn't sure how detailed the cover story was, so I simply added, "On a work trip."

"An old baroness died," Stella said to Victoria. "Jane and Fred were invited to an exclusive estate sale featuring a massive collection of fancy spoons and other silver. All Jane could talk about was acquiring some of the spoons. She kept saying it would be a big deal for their museum."

Lie, Sunflower. Lie if you have to. "Mom gets real excited about new spoons." I shook my head, trying to focus. Spoons were not top of my list. "Where is Aunt Gertie?" I asked.

"Gert is currently otherwise occupied," Stella said with obvious disdain for her sister-in-law. Little diamond and sapphire clusters flashed in Stella's earlobes.

"Mom has earrings just like those," I said.

"Does she?" Stella's voice was as sharp as her elbows.

This morning was not going according to protocol, which made me uneasy. There were only two civilians (non-Agents) who knew the truth about my parents — my aunt Gertie and me. Before I said or did the wrong thing, I needed to talk to Aunt Gertie, but I couldn't remember if she had come in last night. I had been reading *The Fulton Sisters' Adventure* and must have fallen asleep.

Choice time, Sunflower. Go along with Stella or make a fuss? While I wanted to say something like, "I think those *are* my mom's earrings," I knew the correct answer was Rule Number 8 of the original *Rules*: "Don't harass the opposition." If I hadn't figured out my parents were Cleaners, I would be making the wrong choice right now. To think, Mom freaked out big time when she found me reading *The Moscow Rules*, an old list that was typed in purple ink and smelled funny. Is it my fault she'd left her ratty old spy worksheet where I could find it?

To be fair, the worksheet was in one of her small suitcases, hidden in the basement. I did have to move lots of boxes to get to it. And I took a key from her key ring to open the suitcase. What was really interesting was hidden in the suitcase's false bottom: dozens of used passports with false names, but all with pictures of either my mother or father. So, not my fault I'd stumbled across it on a rainy day. They told me to go amuse myself, and I did. Secretly, I think they were happy I found out. I mean, living a secret life can be very stressful. Now I know.

I made up *Rules for a Successful Life as an Undercover Secret Agent* all by myself. Well, some I'd borrowed from odd sayings Dad had learned at the Agent Academy, but the *Rules*, all thirty-six of them, were mostly my creation, some based on *The Moscow Rules*. OK, the rules were like . . . 63 percent mine, but I put everything in my own words — except for a few quotations — so it's not cheating. Dad said the *Rules* were awesome and he could have used them when he first started working undercover.

"Are you going to stand around gawking in your pajamas all morning?" Stella asked. "Frank does not like to be kept waiting."

"Monaco?" Victoria was staring at the world map tacked

on the wall. "That's near Cannes, where the film festival is. All those movies stars. Oh, Momma. I wanna go to Monaco too. It isn't fair. Will they see anyone famous? Was the baroness who died famous?"

This was the most animated I had ever seen my cousin, except for when she was teasing me.

Since my parents had to give false intel when they were on a mission, it was a safe bet that they were in any one of the other 195 counties on earth, except for Monaco. I responded the only way I knew how — by avoiding any details that might give my parents away. "I don't know anything about the trip. I wasn't listening."

"It's obvious your mother hasn't paid attention to you, either," Stella said. She looked around my room, the frown lines on her forehead deepening with each pile of books and clothing she took in. "It's a wonder you can find anything in here. Four minutes."

I wasn't sure what Stella meant, but I knew I didn't like it. "I know where everything important is."

"I hope so," Stella said. "While we're here, there will be rules. You must follow them or face the consequences. Rule number one is to keep your room clean."

I snorted. My *Rules* were much better than her rules.

"Is there something funny, young lady?" Stella asked.

"No, ma'am." I glanced at the wall, about two feet away from Stella's head. The *Rules for a Successful Life as an Undercover Secret Agent* were framed and hanging right there beside her, but she'd never be able to read them. They were written in ultraviolet ink, invisible to the naked eye. Even with special sunglasses or contact lenses, she wouldn't be able to see the *Rules*. All anyone could see was a tiny yellow and black sunflower (painted by me in the first grade) surrounded by lots of blank space. The *Rules* were as safe from detection as they could be — unless someone happened to swing the beam of an ultraviolet or black light flashlight directly across the paper. But who carries one of those around?

"So Mom called *you*?" OK, maybe not the friendliest question, but I'm almost eleven years old. I could've taken care of myself for the morning if Aunt Gertie was busy. Mom hadn't seemed especially concerned about leaving me alone on Saturday night.

"You can say that." Stella shook her head again at the piles of stuff dotting my floor.

"Really?" I couldn't hide the disbelief in my voice. *Would Mom really have called them after the terrible fight she'd had with Frank during the summer?*

"Jane called yesterday, begging for us to babysit you."

"On Sunday?" I asked. So much for my parents maintaining radio silence while out on a mission. *Why hadn't they transmitted the intel directly to me if they were phoning people?* I wondered. Of course, all of my questions would have to wait until I saw Aunt Gertie. I had to keep up protocol, like a good spy. "Did they say when they'd be back?"

"The auction might last days. A week, even." Stella's grin revealed yellow-stained, crooked teeth. "Your parents couldn't bear to lose this opportunity to add to their precious spoon collection."

They must have gotten more details about the mission. A week was much longer than Dad's original promise of forty-eight hours. And something about the mission must have made Mom nervous. "Mom called you yesterday and then the three of you flew in from Alaska?"

"We're here now." Stella backed out of the doorway. "Frank really doesn't like to be kept waiting at mealtimes, so get dressed."

Even for my unusual life, this Monday morning was weird. "What exactly is Aunt Gertie doing right now?" I asked.

"Three minutes, thirty seconds." Stella turned to go. "If you're not dressed in time, you'll go to school in your pajamas without breakfast."

She hadn't answered my questions. I didn't need super spy senses to know something was wrong.

"Tick tock. Three minutes." Victoria tapped her wrist even though she wasn't wearing a watch.

Since Stella didn't seem to be joking about sending me to school in my PJs, I grabbed my day-old jeans off of the floor. Victoria wrinkled her nose in disgust. I pulled the first T-shirt I found out of my dresser. "Privacy, please," I said. No way was I going to change in front of her and her phone.

Pulling the door shut behind her, Victoria sang in a whispery voice, "Snoooore. Snooooore. I tooook viiiideeeooo of sleeeeping Moppet."

5

If you find yourself behind enemy lines and your cover holds, use this golden opportunity to observe the enemy at close range. Then escape as soon as possible.

— Rule Number 34 from *Rules for a Successful Life as an Undercover Secret Agent*

One hundred and eighty seconds — the average cooking time for a pancake to get bubbly. I had only three minutes to make sure there was nothing that could blow my parents' cover story — time for a quick check of their bedroom to see if everything was in order and to liberate the sunflower cipher. Liberate, in spy talk, means to steal. I learned that from my dad. He liked to liberate cookies from Aunt Gertie's kitchen.

Since my parents weren't allowed to *tell* me where they were, my mom had devised an indirect way of letting me know. On their bedroom dresser, she kept a bouquet of fourteen plastic sunflowers, seven in the colors of the rainbow — red, orange, yellow, green, blue, indigo, and violet — and seven in paler shades of the same colors (light red, light orange, light yellow, etc.). Red was flower one, and violet was number seven.

Light red was flower eight, and light violet was fourteen. Each flower had fourteen ray florets, the outside petals. Since there are 196 recognized countries and territories (not including the United States of America), each one corresponded to one of the 196 ray florets in the bouquet (14 x 14 = 196!). So the first petal, marked with a black dot, on the red (first) flower was Afghanistan and the fourteenth petal (going clockwise) on the light violet (fourteenth) flower was Zimbabwe. That's how I knew they were in Nauru on the previous mission. On the light orange (ninth) flower, the ninth petal was bent upward. All I had to do was match the flower and petal to the corresponding number of the country listed on the world map hanging in my room. Easy-peasy, right?

Talk about a golden opportunity to observe the enemy at close range (Rule Number 34). Frankenstella's luggage was right there, wide open on top of my parents' bed. I poked around and found a file folder full of printouts from the museum's website. Last summer, I convinced Mom that having a website for Le Petit Musée of Antique Silver Spoons would add to her cover story's authenticity. That, and it was a whole lot more fun to build a website than to polish spoons.

I didn't have enough time to read the complete dossier (another spy word, which means file folder), so I liberated a few pages from the bottom of the pile and stuffed them into my back pocket for later.

Unfortunately, the sunflower cipher didn't have a clear answer this time. Three different petals were bent upward. After quickly glancing around the room one last time, I liberated the bouquet into my bedroom. I placed it on my dresser, beside my Halloweened-out baby pumpkin, so it just looked like I was decorating.

Using the world map as a guide, I decoded the sunflower cipher. The second petal on the light red (eighth) flower corresponded to Liechtenstein, a tiny, teeny country in the middle of Europe with more registered corporations than actual people. Next was New Zealand, light orange (ninth) flower, twelfth petal, which has way more sheep than people. Last was Suriname, light blue (twelfth) flower, thirteenth petal, the smallest South American country.

This was odder than odd! If my parents were really going to all of these countries, just the flight time alone of traveling from the U.S. to Europe to Oceania to South America would be several days — way too long for a simple Clean.

Someone had to have been messing with the petals, but there was no time to think about it. Total time spent upstairs covering for my parents: one minute, twenty seconds.

I marched downstairs and into the kitchen, determined to find out exactly what was going on. The shock of seeing Frank stuffed into Dad's favorite chair stopped me. Stella was in Mom's place. Victoria had taken over my seat. And suddenly I knew how the three little bears would have felt if Goldilocks had brought her whole family.

Frankenstella were using Mom's best china, the white plates with roses and gold rims, which had to be hand-washed. On their plates were cinnamon buns — the last three buns in the house. Pity buns baked by Aunt Gertie just for me.

"Where is Aunt Gertie?" I blurted out.

"'Good morning' is the proper greeting," Stella said. "Frank, darling, I see we're going to have a lot of work teaching this one how to behave."

"Is she at the Spoon or the Star?" I asked as I glanced at the key hooks next to the back door. Four keys — my house,

Gertie's house, Spoon, and Star — were missing. Only Mom's car key hung there.

Frank grunted — at me or the food, I couldn't tell. "Sit." He pointed to the guest place at the kitchen table and I reluctantly slid into the chair.

The most nauseating stench rose up from my plate. On our very best china lay a row of tiny fish, their little mouths all frozen in silent screams. Two pieces of burnt toast completed my meal.

Sardines. For. Breakfast. They had stolen my delicious cinnamon buns — made just for me — and left me smelly fish.

"Eat." Frank scooped up his sardines and smashed their oily bodies over the buttered toast. The oil-butter mixture dripped over his hand and onto the white cream cheese frosting of the cinnamon bun. He didn't seem to notice. "Are you waiting for me to thank you for gracing us with your presence?"

Chunks of fish and toast churned in his mouth as he talked. My gag reflex jumped into overdrive, so I tore my eyes away. Victoria sat quietly. She picked at what should have been my cinnamon bun. I didn't see any dead fish or their oily residue on her plate.

Maybe I should explain more about why I wasn't exactly overjoyed to see my cousin and her parents. It all started during the first-ever Baies Family Visit, which had occurred just a few months before, during the last week of June. It had started off normal enough . . . for the first ten minutes.

Once we were alone, Victoria teased me about my hair (too curly), my height (too short), my name (too old-fashioned), and anything else she could think of. On the second day, I escaped to the mountains with Stanley. On the third day,

Mom caught Frank going through paperwork at the museum. On the fourth day, Frank had a massive meltdown, screaming that Mom had stolen his inheritance, and said we were no longer family (which was why I didn't think of them as uncle and aunt — not that I had before). On the fifth day, Frank and Stella threatened to sue my parents. That afternoon, my father kicked them out of our house. Aunt Gertie took them in, but she discovered Stella trying to enter Le Petit Musée after it was closed for the night. On the sixth day, Frank and Stella apologized to my parents, but demanded money for Frank's share of the museum or, at the very least, the return of his old red suitcase. Mom refused to pay, and we couldn't give him his missing suitcase because we didn't have it. Frank had another tantrum and Stella asked Gertie to make a judgment.

Aunt Gertie sided with Mom. She practically drove Frankenstella out of town and back to Alaska. They didn't even stick around long enough for the Fourth of July fireworks. After they left, I told my parents that I thought Frankenstella's actions were suspicious. Dad agreed, saying their behavior made his spy sense go all tingly. Therefore, I have Frankenstella's snooping and incessant demands about the old red suitcase to thank for making my parents take me into their confidence about the Great Reverse Heist. While Mom and Dad had been returning stolen American memorabilia on their own for a while, I was the one who gave their operation a cool name.

Stella ripped the outer coil from her cinnamon bun and stuffed it into her month. Smudges of white icing dotted the tip of her nose and her cheeks. After licking her lips like a satisfied cat, she said, "You're late. Next time, no food."

"No way. I got dressed in seconds." I hadn't even bothered to brush my hair, just ran my fingers through it. That's the one good thing about having short, curly hair — even if it is a "mousy" brown, as Victoria once said. It looked the same if I spent no time on it or twenty minutes carefully combing it.

Stella snatched the toast off of my plate. "Don't be rude to me, young lady."

"Sorry, but the laws of physics prove that I got dressed and down here in less than three minutes," I said. One minute, forty-three seconds to be exact.

My house is not large. Originally built by my great-great grandparents in the 1890s as a split-log cabin, my grandparents had added the second story, the basement, electricity, and indoor plumbing in the late 1960s. They'd also insulated the walls to keep snow, rain, and small critters out. I've walked from my bedroom to the kitchen countless times, timing it over and over until my internal sense could tell exactly how long it took me — all part of Dad's spy training program to teach me to be able to judge time and distance. The trip was forty seconds at a normal pace. Today, I'd sprinted downstairs in twenty-three seconds.

Stella flung the burnt toast into the garbage pail. "If I say you're late, you are late."

"Hey. I was going to eat that." But I sure wasn't going to liberate the toast now.

"I will not abide contrariness in my home." Stella wagged her bony finger in my face. "Apologize now."

"This house belongs to my parents," I said, resisting the urge to point my finger in her face. She'd bite it off, the way my morning was going. "You're the guests here."

"Right now, we are your guardians."

"Says who?" I knew for a fact that Aunt Gertie had parental rights when my parents were out of town. She always signed my school permission forms. We were not following protocol this morning, and I didn't like it. I had to find a way to get back on track.

Stella peered at me with utter contempt. "We have the right to discipline you by any means we see fit." Frank grunted in agreement.

I needed to find Aunt Gertie. She'd make everything all right again. "Uncle Frank, where is Aunt Gertie?"

"You owe my wife an apology."

I looked down at the six sardines, which seemed to stare back at me in disapproval. *What did Mom say about being captured behind enemy lines?* Survival is paramount.

I had to be nice, no matter how horrible the situation. Lying was OK if it kept you alive. Breathing out through my nose, I crossed my fingers under the table and said, "I'm sorry for being rude, Aunt Stella."

"Apology accepted." Stella smiled at me again in that freaky way.

"Oh, Momma, I'm so glad you and Daddy would never leave me like Mabel's parents did." Victoria gave me a pitying look. "I'll try to watch over my cousin. Mabel must be hurting inside something bad, knowing her parents don't really care about her."

Ugh. Victoria was doing an awful imitation of a Southern accent, yet her parents ate it up.

"You are a true little princess." Frank patted Victoria on the cheek. "Mabel is blessed to have you in her life. Now it's time for you girls to go wait for the bus."

"What?" I blurted out. Even though my stomach was

empty, I felt like I was going to be sick. "Victoria doesn't go to my school. I thought you were just here for a few days, while my parents are in Mon—"

"Don't worry," Stella interrupted. "I talked to the principal, and he arranged it so that my darling Vicky-girl has the same schedule as you."

Of course we'd have the same schedule. Bluewater-Silverton United Elementary School only had one class per grade level. I'd been stuck with the same twenty-five kids (ten girls and fifteen boys) for years.

"Cousin Mabel, we're gonna have the bestest day together." Victoria grabbed my arm. "I can't wait to meet all your friends. I'm sure I'm gonna love them," she continued in her fake Southern drawl.

Could this day get any worse? I needed help. "Uncle Frank." I clenched my fists and held my arms stiffly at my sides so I wouldn't hit Victoria. "Please tell me where Aunt Gertie is."

Frank took his time chewing the last bite of his mash of fish, bun, and toast. He wiped his mouth, missing a glob of food on his cheek, then placed the napkin on the table. Clearing his throat, he said, "Jail."

6

Never trust anyone who works hard to befriend you. Watch carefully for anyone who does special, unasked favors. Try to figure out what they might want from you.

— Rule Number 11 from *Rules for a Successful Life as an Undercover Secret Agent*

The honking of the school bus saved me from having a complete breakdown in front of Frankenstella. Before I could even think about whether Gertie could really be in jail, Victoria had yanked me out of the house, across the lawn, and into the waiting bus, carrying my book bag along with her own. Gripping my arm as tightly as possible, Victoria dragged me past the unabashed stares of the little kids, past Stanley who had saved my usual seat in the middle of the bus, past Emma G. and Emma H. in the next row and Grace K. and Grace L. in the row across — heads connected by a set of earphones as always, and into the very last seat of the nearly empty bus.

I took my backpack from Victoria. "Uh, thanks." My arm tingled when she finally released her hold on me. Stanley and

Emma G. turned around and waved. Their heads bobbed up and down as the school bus sped over potholes in the gravel road.

Aunt Gertie in jail? I couldn't believe it. I'd just seen her the day before, around 11:30, when I'd popped into the Star for lunch before my afternoon shift at the Spoon. Frank had to be lying. He had lied this summer about Le Petit Musée and about Mom stealing some old red suitcase of his. I couldn't trust Frank's word.

Bus Driver Mark sped through a yellow light, one of only two stoplights in town. Once we crossed the four-way intersection, the bus screeched to a halt to let in the rest of the Silverton kids before we began our jolting journey to Bluewater-Silverton Unified Elementary School. It was only ten miles away, but Mark drove each switchback like he was in a race car.

I usually enjoyed this part of my morning, chatting with Stanley while watching the mountain scenery. Today, all I could think of was how many family secrets I had and how many more I didn't yet know about. Mom was sure that Frank's obsession with the mysterious red suitcase was tied to their parents' criminal record. Thirty years is a long time to suddenly remember having misplaced your luggage, after all. That's why my parents had invited Frankenstella to our house for Thanksgiving — to trick them into revealing what they knew. Pretty spy-tacular, right? Since Turkey Day was a month away, my parents hadn't finalized the plan yet. Whatever that plan was, it was out the window now.

Victoria poked me in the ribs. "Now look, Cousin Mabel, I don't like you and you don't like me." Whiffs of cinnamon rolled out of Victoria's mouth.

"So you can tell the truth," I said. My head hurt from keeping up with Victoria's personality changes. "What about it?"

She took off the fluffy pink and purple sweater and shoved it into her book bag. Underneath she was wearing a pretty cool ninja-girl T-shirt. "We're stuck with each other. The only way for us to survive is to form an alliance."

"Alliance?" I repeated.

"Don't you know any big vocabulary words? Alliance means we work together."

"I know that. But who are you and what have you done with my cousin, the lovely princess Vicky-girl?"

"Don't ever call me that." Her hand balled into a fist. "What is wrong with you?" Victoria's expression had lost all its usual sass. She now looked earnest and concerned, like a kid whose puppy has run away. "Don't you see that something big is going on?"

Big? She had no idea. My parents were on a Cleaners' job, which typically involved some type of world-saving, and Aunt Gertie appeared to be in trouble.

"Pay attention, Moppet. Something really big is going on in your little world."

"Aunt Gertie is in jail." It couldn't get much worse than that in my little world. I wasn't going to think about the big world. My parents were Cleaners, the best of the Agency's spies. They could take care of themselves.

"And what else?"

Hunger made me snap. "Why do you care?"

"Because my father put her there." Victoria leaned in close to me, even though no one could hear us over the noise of the bus. "Don't you find it suspicious that your parents were invited to an exclusive estate sale *for spoons* in Europe at the same time Gertie got arrested?"

"My mom is well known in the world of collectible spoons." I couldn't very well say that whatever my parents were doing, they were definitely not spoon shopping in Monaco. The fact that my parents were gone was the least unusual thing about this situation. At least eight times since I'd learned the truth about Dad and Mom's work, they had flown somewhere to fix something. Usually no one noticed, or if they did, no one said anything. They probably assumed Dad was rewiring old phone lines on the other side of the mountain, and Mom was just keeping him company. No one ever thought to ask, *Did your parents solve that dangerous diplomatic incident that was in the news last week that suddenly went away?*

"Mabel," Victoria said, looking me straight in the eyes. "Are you sure it was a real work trip?"

"Yeah," I said, but another feeling of unease washed over me. "I am surprised that Mom called your parents, considering what happened last time."

"That's not important." Victoria studied the blur of red and gold autumn leaves outside the bus window. "Have you taken a good hard look at me and my parents?"

There was no polite way to say that I'd sort of fixated on them after the fiasco that was their last visit — especially after Dad suggested Frankenstella might be trying to restart the criminal enterprise element of the family. But to Victoria, I just shook my head in denial.

"We're nothing alike. Mom's a total control freak. She has to have every little thing done exactly her way or it's wrong. Dad always has these big, life-changing plans, but they never go anywhere. He's not a details guy," Victoria said, looking angry. "I'm different. I'm gonna be a star, and if I have to run zigzag backward up a mountain and swim through a sea of crocodiles to get there, get out of my way because those crocs won't know what hit them."

I kept myself from pointing out the fact that alligators lived in North America and crocodiles in South America, and from informing her that neither reptile was known for its mountain climbing ability. I didn't need a head bonking.

"Silverton, Washington, is the last place on Earth I want to live," Victoria continued. "Except for Nome. I am never going back there."

I wanted to turn the conversation back to Aunt Gertie, but Mom always said, "Let the source talk," so I did. "Oh?" I said, then buttoned my lips and listened.

"If I had my way, we'd be in Los Angeles right now." Victoria shook her head, her long straight hair falling gracefully over her shoulders. "I'm going to be a famous actress." She activated her phone's camera, smiled, and took a selfie. Then another. And another. Satisfied with the last result, she put her phone back in her pocket.

"Have you told your parents about your plans?" I asked, thinking that maybe they could go to Hollywood soon — like today.

Victoria merely rolled her eyes at my question. "You'd think Silverton was a magical place the way Dad talked about it all the time. For my entire life, no matter where we were living, it's been like, 'When we return to Silverton, blah, blah, blah.' I want to live in a real city, not some two-stoplight town next to a mountain."

Like it had heard its name being called, Mount Rainier

popped its volcanic head out of the clouds for a few seconds. Tourists fly in from all around the world to see this view. Victoria missed it.

"Silverton is real. We're on the map. Look at State Route 410 between Bluewater and Crystal Mountain."

"There's nothing in this pathetic town." Victoria shook her head.

"Nothing?" Did the girl not see the awesomeness that was Silverton? "Le Petit Musée of Antique Silver Spoons is written up in all the major tourist magazines." The Spoon was a source of pride for Silverton. Bluewater didn't have a museum. Sure, it had the public school buildings, the public library, the fire department, the one and only Safeway supermarket, a movie theater, and a Dairy Queen. But no museum. "We have complete freedom here. We can go anywhere, anytime, and not have to worry about any of those big city dangers on the evening news that Aunt Gertie loves to watch."

"That doesn't matter. You're going to help me get out of this place."

"Why would I?"

"It's the only way to save your aunt Gertrude." Victoria smirked. "Unless you want her to spend the rest of her life in prison. Your choice, Moppet."

"Of course I don't want Gertie to be in jail. But you're a kid, just like me. How will me helping you get her out?"

"This summer, after your mother refused to sell the spoons or hand over the red suitcase, my parents swore they'd get revenge."

"They said that to my mom's face," I said. "It's not a secret." I could still see Frank, puffed up like an angry baboon, shouting at my mom. "But they made up, remember? Mom invited you guys here for Thanksgiving." Maybe it hadn't been for the most loving and honest reasons, but I didn't mention that.

"Your mom might have forgiven Dad," Victoria said, "but my mom still wants their share of the money." Victoria glanced at my friends up front, then lowered her voice even though no one was anywhere near us. "My parents have been plotting for a while to take over the museum."

"Your parents are planning a coup d'état for the Spoon?" I asked, trying — and failing — to not laugh at the ridiculous idea.

"A coo-what?" Victoria asked.

"A coup d'état is when someone, usually in the military, overthrows a sitting government," I said, suddenly aware that most ten-year-olds didn't discuss the details of world political events with their parents over dinner. I'd have to be more careful with my vocabulary. "Don't you watch the news?" I asked, hoping to cover my mistake.

"No. I have a life," Victoria said. "Back to my parents. They think they'll live like royalty if they get control of the museum. Small-town royalty for the rest of their humdrum lives." She rolled her eyes and sighed.

Did Frankenstella's plotting have anything to do with the museum printouts I'd found in their suitcase? "Exactly how are they planning to live like royalty?" I asked.

"On money they'll make from the museum," Victoria said. "Pay attention, Moppet. My parents are going to take possession of your stupid spoon museum and live on its profits."

"Good luck starving to death," I said. "The museum only makes money during the tourist season, from June to August. And that barely covers operating costs and insurance."

I knew for a fact that the mysterious red suitcase was certainly not in the museum — nor was anything else stolen by my grandparents. I knew this to be 100 percent true because right after Frankenstella had left Silverton, Mom and I spent several long days going over every inch of Le Petit Musée. And believe you me, when a superspy like my mom decides to search a place, it gets searched in the most thorough, time-consuming way possible, with absolutely no regard for anyone's knees or cramped legs. It also gets dusted and polished because a mid-summer's cleaning was our cover story — not that anyone asked.

What we discovered was that there were no hidden nooks at the Spoon. Mom's radar gun found nothing in the walls or ceiling or under the floorboards. The 1890s building was just what it appeared to be — an old wooden house that was home to lots of old spoons.

"If the museum doesn't make money, how do you guys live?" Victoria asked.

"My father has a job too," I said. "I bet the Spoon doesn't make enough profit to pay your cell phone bill each month." At least that's the excuse my mother gave me when I asked for a smartphone like all the other fifth graders have. That, and they wanted to keep me "off the grid," meaning no one could track me using a phone's built-in GPS.

"My father says the museum is an untapped gold mine." Victoria crossed her arms as if that settled the discussion.

The museum printouts were burning a hole in my back pocket, but I couldn't take them out in front of my cousin, and I couldn't think of anything to say, so I just bit my pinkie fingernail. A bad habit, I know.

As if changing the subject, Victoria showed me her thumb. The nail had been bitten to a bloody quick.

"Aunt Gertie says she used to bite her fingernails when she was young too," I said.

"How'd she stop?"

"She started baking to keep her hands busy whenever she felt nervous or upset. She got so good, she started selling muffins and cookies at school."

"Speaking of Gertie. Do you want to get your aunt out of jail?"

"She's your aunt too."

"That's not an answer, Mabel. Yes or no?"

"I'm confused. Why did your father put his sister in jail?"

"Promise to help me and I'll tell you everything I know."

"Why should I trust you, Victoria?"

"You have to."

"You took video of me while I was sleeping."

"Insurance." She took her purple smartphone out of her pocket.

"Blackmail is more like it. Erase it, and I'll think about helping you."

"Help me, then I'll erase it." Victoria grabbed my shoulder so hard I thought she was going to pull it out of the socket.

What did the girl do up in Alaska? I wondered. *Wrestle grizzly bears for fun?*

Batting her eyelashes, Victoria sniffled. "You're my only hope." She loosened her grip. "How pathetic. I sound like Princess Leia."

"I love *Star Wars* too," I said, brightening. Maybe my cousin wasn't totally evil.

"The original trilogy is the best. Princess Leia had to beg virtual strangers for help." Victoria nodded for emphasis. "Turned out to be a close relative."

It didn't take super spy sense to know that she wanted me to ask: "So what do you want from me?"

"Help me make a video."

"Of what?" I asked.

"Me."

"Why?"

"To make me famous."

"Why do you want that?" Of course it didn't make sense to me. My parents spent their whole lives trying to blend in. I spent most of my school days trying to avoid questions about what I did on the weekend and dodging endless sleepover invitations.

"I said it earlier. I want to be an actress and live in Los Angeles," Victoria said. "It's the only place for an actress to be."

I shook my head. "I don't get it."

"You will. You wanna know a secret?"

"Sure?" I said, since saying 'not really' would probably invite some type of bruising.

"You're gonna help me become a sensation. I've got it all planned out."

Victoria was staring at me, an eager grin on her face and everything, so I asked, "How will you become a sensation?"

"By sneaking into the stupid spoon museum and recording it."

"What?" I wasn't sure I heard her right.

"It will be unique, just like me. And I'm the only one who can do it. That's the key to video stardom — you have to do something new and totally different. No one has broken into a spoon museum yet. I checked on the *Exploring Locked Places* website. I can either do it all scary — like the museum is haunted, or super silly — like 'how stupid is this place.'" Victoria barely took in a breath before continuing. "We'll shoot a couple of different reactions so I can see what works during the edits. All you have is spoons in there, right?"

"Yep." It felt good to say a totally truthful answer.

Apparently, my actual honest face didn't convince my cousin because she raised one eyebrow and said, "Really?"

"It's a museum of spoons. Old spoons, mostly silver. Nothing else. No stainless steel forks or crystal goblets or porcelain thimbles for us. Just spoons, and lots of them."

"Don't pretend. What about that FBI agent who came and totally busted Gertie for selling stolen goods?" Victoria held my gaze.

"She wasn't busted for anything." I looked down at my hands and saw that I had twisted the strap from my backpack around my fingers. "How do you know about what happened, anyway?"

She shrugged and gave me a self-satisfied smile, like her mother's. "I just do."

Victoria was right — an FBI agent and our local sheriff had come to talk to Gertie in early June, but there were no charges, no handcuffs, and no one was hauled away to jail. Later, two of my parents' co-agents also had a few words with Gertie. "The whole misunderstanding was my fault," I said.

"What did you do, Moppet?"

"You know how the Star's Tale is a little disorganized?" I asked.

She nodded.

"I was helping Aunt Gertie over Memorial Day weekend. The store had gotten crazy busy with hikers and other tourists coming through. Some lady wanted to buy a necklace, but it didn't have a tag. I looked around and found a price tag on the floor, which seemed to be the right amount. So I rang her up."

"Go on," Victoria said.

"Well, when the lady got home, she had the necklace appraised. Apparently, it had been reported stolen in 1967. It was Aunt Gertie's supplier's fault for including the necklace in the batch."

But that wasn't the whole story. What I didn't tell Victoria was that the necklace actually was one of Gertie's personal ones. I hadn't recognized it in the rush. And, as my aunt told the FBI and the Agency, it came from a collection of her mom's jewelry, which she'd had for years. She had worn many of the pieces, since it was all costume stuff — no actual diamonds or gold.

It turned out the necklace and almost everything else in the bag had been taken from a display of Virginia colonial jewelry. My mom didn't tell Aunt Gertie that her parents had been suspects in that robbery — or, at the very least, accomplices to the actual thieves. The cover story she'd given was that my grandparents had found the bag while hiking around Mount Rainier. As far as I knew, Gertie still believed that.

My aunt had been so upset by the whole ordeal, she never wanted to talk about it with me. "How do you know the FBI questioned Aunt Gertie?" I asked my cousin. The FBI agents had been very discreet when they visited Silverton.

"Gert told us when we were here in June."

"Oh." It seemed odd that Aunt Gertie would share an embarrassing secret with Frankenstella, especially since they weren't on the best of terms.

"Will you help me break into the museum?" Victoria asked again.

"Why can't we just walk in the front door?" I asked.

"It has to be at night," Victoria said, ignoring my question. "Once the *Exploring Locked Places* production team sees me in action, they'll pick my video to play. Then it's goodbye, sucky Silverton. L.A. is calling my name." Victoria tapped on her purple phone. "I can't waste my time talking to you. Mabel, are you in or not?"

We both chewed our nails and liked *Star Wars* . . . it was hardly the basis for an alliance. "I don't know," I said.

"If I leave, my parents will leave with me. Think about it." Victoria paused, then took out her phone and swiped her index finger across the screen, playing the video from this morning. In it, my eyes were shut, my mouth was open, and I sounded like a cross between a grunting pig and a chainsaw. "But not for too long."

She took out half of the now squished cinnamon bun and handed it to me.

7

Anticipate surprises. No one — not even a supergenius — knows all the facts.

— Rule Number 29 from *Rules for a Successful Life as an Undercover Secret Agent*

Our twenty minutes of silent reading time first thing in the morning was my favorite part of the school day. But just thirty seconds after I sat down, my peace and quiet was interrupted. A note landed on my desk from Emma G.

The HEGs were curious. It wasn't every day a new student arrived in our class. It wasn't even every year. In fact, Grace K. was still sometimes called the new girl and she'd moved to Silverton during fourth grade. For a new girl, she was lucky, since she already had one of the three pre-approved names.

A long time ago, in third grade, the two Hannahs decided to form a club based solely on the first initials of their first names. They called themselves the H-Girls — really original. Right away, the Emmas just had to join, and the Graces would not take no for an answer, promising to be good little minions. Sometime that afternoon, the H-Girls morphed into the HEGs, and the Es and Gs were stumbling all over each other to be next in line after Queen Bee Hannah and Princess Bee Hannah decided something was cool.

In the world of cliques and mean girls, we'd all lucked out. Our Queen Bee Hannah was a benevolent dictator. She wanted everyone to be happy and full of school spirit. Princess Bee Hannah, while not as kind, enforced the "be nice" policy with an iron fist. They even allowed/forced me to join despite my name, but they refused to change the name of the club. I really couldn't blame them, since HEGM sounded at best like a type of igneous rock, and at worst like a cross between a bad cough and a hiccup.

Queen Bee Hannah usually decided what our daily fun would be: wearing matching hair ribbons, helping the kindergarten class finger paint during our recess time, or, my personal non-favorite, deciding the theme of this week's sleepover while dissecting the events of last week's sleepover.

At the last sleepover I ever hosted, my parents had departed on a mission during the middle of the night. It was the first weekend of October of fourth grade. At 2:14 a.m., a Black Hawk helicopter swooped down on my front lawn to extract (pick up) my parents. To cover for them, I told my friends that the Mount Rainier park rangers had a telephone wire emergency. I was afraid my parents' covers would be blown if one of the HEGs mentioned the event to someone else. It was just too risky, so after that, I stopped inviting the HEGs to my home. Since the host of each sleepover rotated through the group, I pulled out of the sleepover circuit. It was safer that way.

The HEGs were glancing at Victoria and me, waiting for a reply, so I scribbled the truth: *visiting cousin*. The quickly-made origami tea cup disappeared off my desk corner, expertly handled by the network of girls.

The next note was written in unfamiliar handwriting: *From where?*

Victoria leaned in to read it, but when I shoved it closer to her, she tossed her hair like she didn't care. She had to know that all the gossip would be about her as the new girl. Being the topic of conversation was what she wanted, right?

I folded the paper square into a crane and wrote, "Alaska," across its wings.

I studied the world map hanging on the wall. Nome was far, far away. It was located on the west coast of central Alaska, the part of the state that was closest to Russia. I twirled a curl behind my left ear as I did the math. Stella claimed that Mom had called her yesterday to ask them to stay with me. While possible — depending on flight schedules — it would have been difficult for Frankenstella to fly to Seattle and drive to Silverton in less than one day. That wasn't even counting buying tickets and packing. So while it wasn't impossible, it was really improbable.

I nearly jumped out of my seat when Ms. Drysdale shouted, "Mabel! I haven't seen you turn a page in five minutes."

I looked up quickly, startled, and then looked back at my book. Didn't she have some quizzes to grade or something? The HEGs were passing so many notes the classroom resembled a blizzard, but did any of them get into trouble?

Left alone after that, I spent most of morning reading time wondering if I should trust Victoria — while being sure to turn the page every couple of minutes. The spy rules clearly stated that I should not trust her.

I glanced at Victoria. She tapped the screen of her smartphone. The video of me sleeping with my mouth opened wide played silently.

I waved my hand and called out, "Ms. Drysdale?"

"What is it, Mabel?"

"Can I introduce my cousin, Vicky, to the class? She's from Alaska."

"That's a lovely idea." Ms. Drysdale beamed her approval. "Vicky, come on up with your cousin. We could all use a break before writing time."

"Sit, Moppet." Victoria glared at me. "I can do it myself," she said to the teacher in her sweetest voice as she strode to the front of the room. "Hello," she began with a wide smile. "I'm so happy to meet all of you."

"Vicky, are you really from Alaska?" Emma H. asked, waving her hand in the air.

"We went to Alaska on a cruise last summer," Grace L. said, "and saw a chunk of ice drop off a glacier and smash into the water."

"Did you take the helicopter tour?" Queen Bee Hannah asked. "That's the only way to see Alaska."

"Hannah's right," Princess Bee Hannah agreed. "The only way. Do you travel by helicopter in Alaska, Vicky?"

"No," Victoria said. She waited a beat, soaking up their disappointment. "Please call me Victoria, and we travel by sled dog."

Then came a universal response from the class: "Cool!"

Within a minute, Victoria had the entire class on the edges of their seats as she described a wild ride in the Alaskan wilderness. Snow flying, dogs running, wolves howling. I had no idea if it was true, but — and I hated to admit this — her storytelling was fascinating. Maybe she could make it as an actress, after all.

I tuned out the rest of her introduction and grabbed her phone to delete the video of me snoring and drooling. I also erased the photo of me in bed. One problem solved.

Now on to problem two: Mom and Dad were gone again, and it seemed unlikely that they would've asked Frankenstella for help. According to the *Rules*, though, I should assume nothing. I would have to wait until this evening when their handler, Roy, called to check up on me. His job was to relay messages between my parents and me when they were in the field.

Number three: Frankenstella were planning some type of museum takeover. It would be bad if they found the spare key. Who knows what mischief they could cause in there?

Note to self: Find and hide the spare museum key.

Problem number four was a big one: Aunt Gertie was in jail. Why would Frank put his sister in jail? He'd have to accuse her of something bad and he'd need to have proof. I hoped she was nearby in the county jail, which was three holding cells in the Silverton sheriff's office, just down the street from the museum and the Star's Tale. After school, I decided, I'd go see her.

Frankenstella living in my house was problem number five. Even their own daughter thought they were up to no good.

I had liberated two pages from Frankenstella's luggage — one with a photograph and the other with lots of handwritten numbers and many cross outs. They rustled as I took them out. Victoria glanced my way, but didn't stop talking about winter days with very little sunlight.

I instantly recognized the photo as the New Orleans Silver Spoon Historical Collection. I'd just polished that set last week — seventy-five spoons in all. The spoons came from various events, including Mardi Gras Balls (some as old as 1908), the 1984 World's Fair, and the Pope's visit in 1987. Some of the plainer-looking soup spoons had the initials JL engraved in fancy script. Mom said they were rumored to have belonged to the pirate Jean Lafitte. The New Orleans collection was valued at $7,000, which I knew because all the spoon information is typed up on little cards next to each exhibit.

On closer examination of the second page, I realized it was a mess of dollar amounts, ranging from $5,000 to $25,000. All the amounts had lines drawn through them except for $14,500. That number was circled in red ink. *Are these two pages connected?* I wondered. Victoria glared at me from the front of the class, so I refolded the paper.

I reflected on all five of the major problems I was facing. The only one I couldn't do a thing about was talking to Mom and Dad. If I could just think of a plan to bust Aunt Gertie out of jail, she'd help me retake my house. Easy-peasy, right?

Victoria, who had finally finished delighting my classmates with her cute stories about snow and wildlife, poked me with a pen under the table.

"What?" I mouthed.

"The HEGs seem nice," she wrote in my notebook. "Why don't you go to the sleepovers?"

"Because," I whispered, not wanting to lose my train of thought. I rubbed my temples in an attempt to get my brain working. My mom always did it when she was pondering a problem. *Just think of Aunt Gertie, Sunflower!* I told myself. She was in jail, and she needed me.

Suddenly a crackled, distant voice filled the room. "Mabel Pear, report to the principal's office." It was the voice of Ms. Jones, the office secretary, coming in over the loudspeaker. "Bring your books and all belongings."

Just great, I thought.

8

Never blow the cover of a fellow agent. Deny all knowledge of their work. Deny all evidence. Deny, deny, deny.

— Rule Number 5 from *Rules for a Successful Life as an Undercover Secret Agent*

Principal Baker was on the telephone when I walked into his office. He stopped running his hand through his short brown hair long enough to gesture for me to sit down in one of the chairs in front of his desk. As a principal, he's not so bad. He knows all the kids' names, not just the troublemakers, and sometimes he teaches classes when teachers are sick.

Mr. Baker didn't say much, just a few "hmms" and "uh-huhs" to whoever was on the phone. He alternated toying with his wire-rimmed glasses and rubbing his eyes. Now and then, he jotted a word or two down.

I retied the bright-pink skull laces on my favorite pair of black Converse All Star high-tops — a gift from Aunt Gertie for helping out at the Star's Tale all summer — as I waited for him to finish the call.

After what seemed like an hour, Mr. Baker finally hung

up the phone and turned to me. Mr. Baker was usually jovial, but today he was serious. "Mabel," he said. My stomach flipped, wondering what this could be about. "How are you holding up?"

That was a strange question. What was he getting at? "Um, I'm OK."

"Mabel, where are your parents?"

"Why?" I asked, skeptical.

Mr. Baker sat up all straight and serious. "You know my wife, Prue, is the Silverton Sheriff."

"Yes." Of course I knew. In a town as small as Silverton, it's impossible *not* to know.

"She informed me they have a federal warrant to hold Gertrude Baies for dealing in stolen goods."

"That's crazy!" The words exploded out of me before I could think. "I'm the one who made the mistake, selling that necklace. Anyway, the police and the FBI said Gertie wasn't at fault. And that was months ago."

"The indictment does not concern the Star's Tale. It's for the Spoon. The federal warrant claims that Gert has been using the museum as a front for smuggling rare artifacts in and out of the country."

"What?" I knew for a fact there was nothing but spoons in the museum. "That can't be true. How can Aunt Gertie be in jail for that? Why?" *What lies had Frank told?* I wondered.

"Mabel, those are all good questions. But first we need to contact your parents. Gert isn't doing too well."

An awful feeling swept over me. My aunt wasn't young, and I began to wonder if she was being treated OK in prison. "What's wrong?"

"I don't know." Principal Baker shook his head. "When Prue told her that Frank and his wife would take care of you, she muttered a lot of nonsense. She insisted I tell you to have . . ." He stopped to look at his notes, then continued, "to have farfalle for dinner."

"What's farfalle?" I asked. My dear aunt. She was locked up, but still she was worried about what I was eating.

The principal shrugged. "Maybe it's a family recipe. You can ask your uncle tonight."

"How did you know Frank and Stella are in town?" I asked.

"I talked with Mrs. Baies a few weeks ago about enrolling her daughter here."

My jaw dropped. Weeks ago? That couldn't be possible. The Great Reverse Heist was supposed to involve Frankenstella visiting for a week at Thanksgiving time. That's all.

Mr. Baker searched his desk drawer and brought out a file folder. Opening it, he pointed to a paper titled "Application for Enrollment." Below, in Stella's handwriting, was Victoria's name and information. "They used your parents' address, so I figured you knew."

He looked at me, questioning. Rats. If I admitted I didn't know, it was sure to lead to questions about my parents being away. *Lie*, I thought. *That's what the* Rules *advise.* "I thought they weren't coming until Thanksgiving."

"Your aunt Stella didn't have a firm date, either. I guess they sold their house in Alaska quicker than expected."

House? During the summer, Victoria had said they rented an apartment.

But I couldn't focus on that now. There were too many lies floating around. What I needed was the truth about what was going on, and that started with getting Aunt Gertie out of jail. "I can prove Gertie is innocent. She never goes inside the Spoon. The museum belongs to my mom and dad."

"Not exactly." A familiar-looking older man wearing a dark blue suit entered the room. He nodded at Principal Baker, then turned to me. "Legally, Le Petit Musée of Antique Silver Spoons belongs to Jane Baies Pear, Fred Pear, Gertrude Baies, and you, Mabel Opal Pear."

Mr. Odd Sock! He wasn't just a novice hiker, overdressed in his brand new gear. I knew there was something off about him.

"I asked you to wait outside, Inspector Montgomery." Principal Baker stood up. "Under Washington State law, you are not allowed to question a minor unless a guardian is present."

The words "inspector" and "question" sent tremors down my spine. Maybe it was a good thing I hadn't had much breakfast. The half cinnamon roll was threatening to reappear soon.

"Don't worry, Miss Pear, you're not being held responsible." Inspector Montgomery leaned against Mr. Baker's desk, blocking the principal from my view. "No judge would charge an almost-eleven-year-old minor with being the mastermind of an international antiques smuggling ring."

How did the inspector know my birthday was coming up? He must've seen my shocked face, because he pulled out a small notebook from his coat pocket and said, "October thirty-first. Then you will be a regular eleven-year-old minor." He waited for me to digest the fact that he knew more about me than just my embarrassing nickname. "Your parents, on the other hand, are named in the indictment as ringleaders."

"That's impossible."

"I'm sure it's all a big misunderstanding." Principal Baker walked around his desk so he could sit in the chair next to me. "But we'll need your parents' assistance to figure it out."

I nodded, grateful for his support.

"When your parents went on their last spoon-buying trip, where did they go, exactly?" Montgomery asked.

Deny. Deny. Deny, I told myself. *Do not blow their cover.* "I don't remember."

"To a convention?" he continued. "Did they meet with a private seller? Did they leave the country?"

As far as I knew, no one knew about their most recent trip — the "Nebraska" one. I played it safe. "An antiques convention, I think." I let my voice rise up, making my statement into a question, as if I didn't remember or care.

Montgomery asked, "Where was the last place your father flew his plane?"

"To fix the telephone lines at a ranger station on Mount Rainier." A semi-honest answer. "On October tenth."

The inspector tapped his pen against the notebook. "You're positive?"

"We had an early season snowstorm on October eighth," Principal Baker said. "Then unseasonably warm winds melted it the next day, snapping lines all over the area. The roads were clear by the tenth."

The inspector nodded at Mr. Baker, then turned to me. "Mabel, this is very serious. Where are your parents right now?"

"Monaco," I said, sticking to the cover story. "At an estate sale."

"Your aunt, Ms. Gertrude Baies, also claimed that," Montgomery read from the little flip notebook. "But there's a record of them leaving Sea-Tac Airport and catching an international flight to Vietnam. After that, the trail goes cold."

Of course it did. They were highly trained international spies. "They told me Monaco," I repeated. "A rich old lady had lots of silver spoons."

Principal Baker looked at me. "I believe you," he said.

"This isn't school. It doesn't matter what your principal thinks." Montgomery pulled out a piece of blue paper. "All that matters is what is written right here."

I grabbed it. "Which agency do you work for?"

"Washington State Border Patrol. I'm the head of the Anti-Smuggling Task Force."

That explained a lot. He was domestic. He probably didn't even know the Agency existed. Even his boss might not know. My parents usually worked outside of the United States as Cleaners, so their names probably didn't pop up as anything special. "Aunt Gertie always knows what to do. Let's go see her."

"No," Montgomery said.

"Why not?" I asked.

"It would be imprudent for you to have contact with the accused at this time."

"Because?"

"Young lady, this situation is serious. Gertrude Baies is an accused criminal." Montgomery peered at me, his nostrils flaring. "You may not contact her in any manner until I deem it appropriate."

"You can't do that." I turned to the principal. "Can he?"

Principal Baker didn't answer. Instead, he glared at Montgomery. "Inspector, you're scaring Mabel. This interview is over."

"Children today are too coddled," Montgomery said in a flat voice, looking straight at me. "I will not sugarcoat the truth. This situation is a big deal." He narrowed his eyes. "Your parents have gotten themselves into a world of trouble. But you can help."

I was getting the uncomfortable feeling that this was more than a big misunderstanding. "I need to go home."

"Why?" Montgomery's pen was poised over his notebook.

I ignored him and turned to Principal Baker. "I need to go home now."

In a special hiding spot in my room, inside of an old book, I had a cell phone to use for emergencies. Only one number could be dialed on it: Roy, my parents' handler at the Agency. He called most nights when my parents were on a mission, at 7:02 exactly, just to check up on me. Come to think of it, he hadn't called the previous night.

I didn't know what Roy looked like, but I always imagined him bald and heavy-set, wearing a gravy-stained tie, sitting at a desk, and saying in his deep voice, "Yes, Sunflower. All is well." Roy was awesome at helping with subjects like math, science, and spelling. Some nights he'd quiz me repeatedly until I got all twenty of my spelling words correct. He'd listen to my book reports and give suggestions to make them better. He also knew a lot of American history and could recite at least three major events that happened in any given year.

I'd never had the need to call him before. Until now.

"I'll drive you." Montgomery flipped his little notebook closed and started for the door.

"No," Principal Baker said.

"Excuse me?" Montgomery straightened his blue tie. "This situation does not concern you, Principal Baker."

"Mabel is one of my students. It is during school hours. I will not let her leave with a stranger, no matter how shiny his badge. I'm driving her in my car."

"Fine." Montgomery glared at the principal. "I'll come with you."

"Impossible." A smile crossed Principal Baker's face. "I drive a Smart Car. Two seats. But you're welcome to run behind us."

"I will follow. Take the girl straight home." Montgomery's nostrils flared again. "Don't try anything funny or I'll arrest you too."

9

Always have an escape plan. Always.

— Rule Number 12 from *Rules for a Successful Life as an Undercover Secret Agent*

Principal Baker glanced over his shoulder as we drove along State Route 410 toward my house. "Montgomery doesn't seem to be the trusting sort."

"Government agents aren't supposed to be," I said.

Principal Baker stared intently at the road ahead, as if he hadn't traveled it thousands of times. "Very insightful, Mabel."

Uh-oh! A normal fifth grader would not know about the usual habits of agents, secret or otherwise. To hide my mistake, I started babbling. "I woke up this morning to find my parents gone, Aunt Gertie in jail, and virtual strangers living in my h—"

"Victoria and her parents are your family."

"Extended family, and I only met them for the first time in June." State Route 410 had become Silverton's Main Street without my noticing.

"That's right." Principal Baker nodded as if remembering the events of the summer. Frank's epic temper tantrum had been the talk of Gloria's Mini-Mart for weeks. There are no secrets in small towns. Well, almost none. "That wasn't Frank's first dust-up," he said, turning into the driveway. He put the car in park but didn't immediately unbuckle his seat belt. My mom's old green Subaru was parked next to the house, but my dad's new car — a red Subaru — wasn't in sight. Everything seemed normal. "I'm sure your parents have told you about what Frank did to Gert and your mom years ago."

"No. No one has told me a thing," I said.

Principal Baker tapped his fingers on the steering wheel. I wanted to ask questions, but Mom's advice sounded in my head for the second time this morning — *Let the source talk* — so I sat quietly.

"I probably shouldn't be the one to tell you this," Mr. Baker said, "but Frank absolutely refused to help Gert raise your mom after your grandparents died in the car crash. Emptied the bank account and left one day without saying a word to anyone. Gert came to school the next day, red-eyed from crying, clutching little Jane in her arms. She couldn't believe her brother's betrayal, especially so soon after the deaths of their parents."

This was a new part to my mom's story. "I didn't know the details," I said quietly.

"We all watched Jane and helped Gert as much as we could."

"You used to babysit my mom?" My home and school worlds were suddenly crashing together, and I didn't like it one bit.

"When Gert was baking cookies and cakes to sell, I'd sit and play with Jane." He chuckled. "Your mom was very quick, even when she was just learning to walk."

"That's so weird," I said. "Why has no one told me about this before?"

"Your mom probably doesn't remember any of that time. She hadn't started school yet, and Gert doesn't like to talk about those sad years," Principal Baker said. "I'm surprised your parents agreed to let them stay with you after everything Frank said and did."

"*You're* surprised?" I snorted. "I'm the one who has to live with them."

"I want you to know, Mabel, that you can come to me for help, no matter what."

Rule Number 11 popped into my mind: *Never trust anyone who works hard to befriend you. Watch carefully for anyone who does special, unasked favors. Try to figure out what they might want from you.*

"Why are you being so nice?" I asked, more bluntly than I should have.

"As I said, Gert and I were friends in high school."

"So?"

"Close friends."

Ugh. "Did you date my aunt?" I asked. Rule Number 11 didn't cover the romantic lives of adults.

Principal Baker sighed and looked out his side window. "We went steady for two years."

"Eww." I never even thought of the principal outside of school, let alone dating my aunt. My curiosity got the better of me. "What happened?"

"Gert decided to focus her energy on raising Jane and

keeping the Spoon in the family." He ran his fingers through his short hair. "When I came back from the University of Washington with my teaching degree, Prue came with me."

"Well, thanks for sharing," I said, a bit sarcastically.

"Mabel, what I mean is, Gert and I will always be friends. She trusts me."

"Good to know." Was Principal Baker saying what I thought he was saying?

"She knows I would never betray a confidence." He opened his car door and got out.

I did the same, wondering if that meant he knew my parents' secret. I couldn't ask him directly, of course, because asking him would betray the secret. This spy stuff was confusing. No wonder Mom liked working with old spoons in her spare time.

From the driveway, my house looked the same as always — forest-green front door set into the rustic split-log exterior. Each summer, we'd apply a coat of water seal on the old logs and Dad would say, "They don't build houses like this anymore." With a smile, Mom would always counter, "Probably a reason for that."

Just before we walked in the front door, I whispered, "If I can get to my room without Frankenstella stopping me, I might be able to get some answers."

For once, an adult didn't question my actions. Mr. Baker said, "I'll run interference on the infamous Frank and Stella Baies."

As I reached for the knob, the door opened.

"You're in trouble." Stella didn't waste any breath greeting me. "How your parents manage you is a mystery."

I wanted to protest that nobody "managed" me, but I was on a mission to call Roy and I couldn't let anything interfere. Stella had only opened the door about two feet, just wide enough for me to squeeze through sideways, as long as I ducked my head to avoid her bony elbow. She started to close it behind me, but Principal Baker stepped into the house with his right foot, preventing the door from being shut. I hoped he was wearing steel-toed shoes.

"I'm Ted Baker, the principal of Bluewater-Silverton Unified Elementary School." He leaned into the door with his right shoulder, opening it more.

"Just how much trouble are you in, Mabel?" Stella asked me.

"Oh, she's not in trouble at all, Mrs. Baies." Principal Baker extended his hand to my aunt, but she gave him an icy glare.

"I know who you are." Stella held the door firmly, as if she was deciding whether to slam it against him.

"Is Frank here?"

"No."

"We talked on the phone a few weeks ago about your daughter, Victoria," Principal Baker said. Now both his feet were inside the house. "I'm also very good friends with your sister-in-law, Jane, and her husband, Fred."

Good friends? He'd just admitted to dating Aunt Gertie years and years ago, but he hadn't said a word about my parents. Well, besides the whole babysitting thing. *Maybe Mr. Baker is trying to use his principal powers to protect me,* I thought.

Stella relaxed her hold on the door and stepped into the living room. "If Moppet is not in trouble, why are you bringing her home from school at eleven in the morning?" She remained standing, even though there were two sofas and a chair less than six inches from her . . . and five feet away from their rightful places.

Suddenly I realized that nothing was where it had been this morning. The bookshelves were empty. Piles of books dotted the floor. Framed family photos were missing from the walls. Two pieces of red pottery caught my eye, shards from the little bowl I'd made for my mother in first grade. I picked them up, pricking my finger in the process. I couldn't find the rest of it or my dad's matching blue bowl. "What did you do to my house?"

"Don't raise your voice to me, young lady."

"Principal Baker, look." I pointed around the room, too many messes to count.

He squeezed my shoulder. "Mabel, polite manners are one of a young lady's greatest assets."

Oh yeah. *Try to be pleasant to the enemy* (Rule Number 10). *Focus, Sunflower.* I nodded.

Stella turned her back to me. "Thank you for your concerns. I'll handle Mabel Opal from here." She still didn't sit.

"Can we talk privately? Without Mabel?" Principal Baker sat on the nearest sofa, acting as though my house was not in total disarray. "It's a delicate matter."

I flew up the stairs before my aunt could object.

10

If your contact doesn't make contact at the agreed upon time, assume the worst. Go immediately to Plan B. Or Plan C. Or whatever is the next plan. Just go.

— Rule Number 20 from *Rules for a Successful Life as an Undercover Secret Agent*

When I pushed open the door to my bedroom, I was relieved to find that it seemed untouched. After closing the door, I checked the sunflower cipher to see if I had somehow missed Vietnam. Nope, the eleventh petal on the fourteenth flower (light violet) was straight with no creases. Rats! Where were my parents?

I walked to the other side of the room and stood in front of the tall, skinny bookshelf. Skimming my fingers along the spines of the *Harry Potter* series, Madeleine L'Engle's *Time Quintet*, *The Fulton Sisters' Adventures* series, and Mom's ancient Nancy Drew mysteries, I came across *An Abridged History of the United States*. The pages of the old high school textbook stuck together. Gently, I opened the back cover to reveal a hiding spot. Inside the carved out pages was a super thin silver cell phone.

Unlike a regular cell phone, this one had no display or memory, so the secret number could not be discovered. My fingers shook as I dialed Roy. It rang four times. I hung up, as I was supposed to, then dialed again. I let it ring three times, hung up again, then rang twice and hung up one last time, per protocol. I dialed it the last time, praying that Roy would pick up on the first ring.

"Tweedledee." Roy's familiar voice sounded in my ear.

"Tweedledum," I answered.

"You're not supposed to call this number, Sunflower," Roy said. "Except for when the Uhms are —"

"But they are," I interrupted.

"No." Roy didn't say anything for what seemed like an eternity. "They returned to home base Saturday, midmorning, filed reports, and are currently off-duty."

"They left again."

"I'll double-check. Sometimes headquarters forgets that the peons in the field need current intel in order to do our jobs." The *click-click* of typing filled the silence. "Sunflower, are you sure they didn't just step out for a little while?"

"Where would they go?"

"Maybe they went for a drive and got held up in traffic?"

The image of my parents being held up by one of Silverton's two stoplights infuriated me. Did the Agency think I'd panic if I was left alone for five minutes? I sucked in a big gulp of air so I wouldn't scream in frustration. "They've been gone since Saturday, when they got a call during dinner. They left on a new mission."

"According to their status updates, the Uhms are not on duty at the current time." Roy's normally calm, deep voice was strained. "That's why I didn't call you last night."

I felt as if I had been punched in the stomach. "The Uhms left forty-two hours ago. Supposedly on a flight to Vietnam."

"That's impossible."

Could one of the bent petals on the sunflower cipher represent my parents' actual destination? "Would New Zealand, Suriname, or Liechtenstein be possibilities? Definitely not Monaco, right?"

"Wait. What are you talking about, Sunflower?" Roy was speaking faster than I've ever heard him. "How would you know where they went, if they'd gone somewhere?"

I couldn't tell Roy about the sunflower cipher. It was against the Agency's rules, and I didn't want to get my parents in trouble. "I'm just guessing," I lied.

"Never mind. Hang on." I heard Roy talking to someone. The only words I could make out were "unusual" and "potential problem." He cleared his throat with a loud cough. "Sunflower, it's probably just a glitch, but have Starfish call her handler." Starfish was Aunt Gertie's code name.

"Can't."

"Why not?"

"She's in jail."

"Back up, Sunflower." I heard other people breathing on our phone line. "Did you just say Starfish is in jail and your Uhms are out on . . . you know?" Roy's voice was higher pitched than usual.

This was bad. Really, really bad. Now the only potentially normal thing about this day — my parents being gone on a mission — was definitely a huge problem. "You don't know where they are?"

"I didn't say that," Roy said.

"Yeah. You did."

"Hang on." Roy muted the phone for what seemed like forever. The murmur of voices from downstairs came through the heating vent. Roy came back on the line. "Why is Starfish in jail?"

I repeated what Principal Baker and Inspector Montgomery told me.

"Are you alone?" Roy asked.

"No." Frankenstella and Victoria didn't have code names but I knew to not use their real names. "Remember our unpleasant summer visitors?"

"The ones who were interested in the museum?"

"Exactly," I whispered. "The female searched our living room for something. Everything is on the floor in a huge mess. And there's an anti-smuggling inspector. He was checking out the museum on Saturday. He says the Uhms and Starfish are smugglers."

"Sir," Roy said, sounding a little bit away from the phone, "the living room has been ransacked."

"What?" An unknown woman's voice screamed into my ear. "Do not. I repeat, *do not* tell them anything."

"I know."

"Have they gone into the museum?" Roy asked.

Gertie was locked up, my house was being torn apart, and my food eaten, and all the Agency cared about was some old spoons? "I don't think so."

"*Do not* let them enter the museum," the angry woman said.

"Why not?" I asked. "There's nothing in there."

Silence was the only reply. I'd been cut off.

I went through the whole dial, ring, and hang-up rigmarole again, practically shouting "Tweedledum" over Roy's "Tweedledee."

"Roy, what is going on?"

"I will call you tomorrow at our scheduled time with an update."

"What update?" I asked. "You haven't told me one thing yet."

"Sunflower," the woman interrupted. She didn't sound angry now. "I know you feel anxious, agitated, and quite possibly disconcerted. Those are appropriate emotions to have at this time. But there is no need to become overwrought. This situation is just a puzzle waiting to be solved. Don't upset yourself."

"Upset?" I was glad this wasn't a video call. The blood rushed to my cheeks, betraying my temper. "I'm freaking *out*. My Uhms got sent somewhere, but you don't know anything about it. The border patrol guy, who Mom agreed is an odd sock, thinks the Uhms are —"

"Your parents are fine," Roy interrupted.

"Fine? If you don't even know where they are, how do you know they're *fine*?"

"Instinct," Roy said. "Your parents are the best Cleaners. I trust in them and in their abilities. Just like they trust in you."

Roy's soothing voice made me feel better. Maybe even he didn't know the details of the operation because it was super-super-super top secret.

"Your job, Sunflower, is to go about your day in a regular manner," the woman said. "And remain calm. Panicking leads to disaster."

"I'm not the one screaming at a girl whose Uhms have been lost. By you."

"I apologize for my earlier outburst," the woman said. "You may rest assured that we will investigate the situation and enumerate the probabilities until we have exhausted all channels."

Apparently, my parents forgot to mention that the *Rules* would need a spy-to-normal-person translation guide. "English, please."

"Leave this to the professionals," she said. "Roy will contact you at the usual time tomorrow. And remember, no one is to enter the museum until proper clearance has been granted."

"Hang in there, Sunflower," Roy said before he hung up on me. Again.

11

Try to be pleasant to the enemy. Don't be rude. Use polite manners.

— Rule Number 10 from *Rules for a Successful Life as an Undercover Secret Agent*

I performed the crazy phone routine three more times, but Roy never picked up. I was on my own, like a real secret agent behind enemy lines. I knew that spies had to cover their tracks to remain undetected, so the first thing I did was return the cell phone to its hiding spot.

We spies also have to be prepared for anything, so I rummaged around in my sock drawer until I found my super-secret pocketknife. OK, it was a regular pocketknife, except for the fact that Dad had burned my initials, MOP, into one of the wooden sides. The other side had a big "A" for Agent. But even a regular pocketknife could come in handy for some spy activities, such as picking locks.

By now, Stella's bellows could be heard all over Silverton. I went downstairs to investigate, which I immediately recognized was a big mistake. My newest least favorite person had joined the party. Perched on our hideous coffee-stained brown and beige flower print sofa, Montgomery smirked.

If any of the so-called grown-ups were dismayed by the state of the house, they sure hid it well. Mom, on the other hand, would've been furious if she'd seen it in this state. Suddenly I had a horrible thought: what if it hadn't been Mom who'd moved the auction catalog and took out the trash in my room the other day? I tried to remember what had been in my wastepaper basket. Math homework that I'd messed up and had to redo, copies of the spelling words I missed on the pretest, and some doodles. I think I had torn up the list of possible Great Reverse Heist items from the auction catalog and put it in the kitchen wastebasket.

"I need a copy of this guardianship decree for Mabel's school records," Principal Baker said, interrupting my thoughts. He glanced at something in his hands. "The process moved rather fast, don't you think?"

Stella snatched the paper out of Principal Baker's hand. "It's really not any of your business." She stood next to the open front door, her message clear.

"My students are my business, Mrs. Baies." Principal Baker walked outside. "Mabel, let's go. School's a-waiting."

"No." Stella shook her floppy red mane. "You'll have to excuse Moppet for the rest of today. Family issues."

"Mabel has a big history test coming up." Principal Baker winked at me. "I'll have your cousin bring your homework to you. I *trust* you to do it all."

Great. I couldn't even get a free pass today. I managed to wave goodbye before Stella slammed the door in his face.

I bit my bottom lip. It was the only way to keep from blabbering before I had a chance to think through the situation. I had to be polite, according to the *Rules*. "Aunt Stella." My smile was so large and fake it hurt my cheeks. "What can I do to help you?"

Stella wagged her finger in my face, a too-common occurrence today. "Do what the good inspector tells you."

"Sit." Montgomery pointed to the sofa facing him.

I pasted on another super-wide grin and took a seat. "I'm sitting. Anything else?"

"I'll ask the questions," he said. "You provide the answers."

"I'm sorry, I don't mean to be rude," I said in the sweetest voice I could muster. "But didn't Principal Baker say it was illegal to question me without my parents present?"

Montgomery flipped open his little notebook and held the tip of his pen just above the surface of the page. "Your uncle and aunt are your legal guardians now, according to the State of Washington."

"What?" I twirled a curl behind my left ear.

Stella shoved the piece of paper at me and grinned that freaky smirk of hers. "Hot off the presses."

"A guardian is an adult who has legal power over another person. Like a parent. The guardian makes decisions in the best interest of the minor. In this case, you," Montgomery said. "It comes from the word 'guard.' To protect."

"I'm not stupid." Now I sounded like the angry woman on the phone. Shouldn't someone have asked me if I wanted Frankenstella as my guardians? "What I want to know is how did that happen?" This seemed like an important question since they sure weren't acting in my best interest.

"Your parents are international fugitives, and your aunt Gertrude is behind bars." Montgomery clicked his pen.

"You're fortunate Mr. and Mrs. Baies agreed to be responsible for you. Otherwise, you'd be a ward of the state."

Fortunate? I'd much rather take my chances with total strangers. Or a maybe a rabid raccoon or a hibernating black bear.

Keep cool, Sunflower. "Lucky. Sure. Today is my lucky day," I said. "If I had any more luck, a big black hole would pop up in the living room, suck me in, and crush me until my eyeballs exploded and my bones turned to gelatinous goo."

"That is a disgusting image, child." Montgomery frowned at my outburst.

"When you're done, Mabel, clean up in here." Stella turned to Montgomery. "She's all yours, Al."

Al? They know each other?

Victoria was right. My parents and Aunt Gertie had been set up. I was living behind enemy lines. This situation wasn't going to resolve itself. *Time to go into super spy mode, Sunflower.*

I was going to have to use the *Rules* for real. When my parents went into hostile situations, they relied on each other. I needed backup — help from someone I trusted. Victoria had insider information, but I couldn't completely trust her. Frank and Stella were the source of my problems, after all.

Montgomery looked like he was itching to arrest someone — namely me. I'd bet my measly savings account Frankenstella had fed him a whole pack of lies about my family. Would he believe me if I told him my suspicions?

Get your head in the game, Sunflower. I met the inspector's eyes and held his gaze. I wasn't the three-time class champion of the annual Bluewater-Silverton Unified School District Staring Contest for nothing.

"Mabel, you're a smart girl," he finally said. "This can be easy or hard." He cracked the knuckles on his left hand. "Your choice." Then he cracked his right-hand knuckles. "Choose wisely."

I wanted to say that Montgomery had been misled, that Gertie and my parents were innocent and had been framed by Frankenstella. But I remembered Rule Number 22: *He who talks first loses*. Besides, I had no proof. Only my instincts.

Montgomery's eyes swept over me, as if trying to memorize my every feature. I tried to do the same, but his clothing was boring: black shoes, blue suit, white shirt, blue tie. Even his face was bland: medium-sized nose, brown eyes, brown hair cut short, no scars or birthmarks. He appeared older than my parents, maybe even older than Aunt Gertie and Principal Baker. He looked like a typical television detective — totally forgettable.

"Well, Mabel Opal Pear?"

He talked first. A point for Sunflower! "I'm not sure what you mean."

Shaking his head, Montgomery imitated me in a squeaky, high-pitched voice. "I'm not sure what you mean." He smirked, just like at the Star's Tale. "Think of my questions as a point system."

"For prizes?"

"As in, if you don't do it right, I'll point it out to you." He double-clicked his pen. "Where are your parents?"

"I have no idea." At least I could answer the first question honestly.

"Before the October trip, when was the last time they went out of town?"

Be helpful, but vague. "It must have been a couple of months ago."

"Summertime?" he asked.

"Sure. That sounds right."

"And where did they go?"

I squinted as if I was thinking deeply. "To an antique silverware convention, just like I said in Principal Baker's office."

"Where?"

"Somewhere in the south. Mom complained about the heat. Arkansas, I think." I bit my lip, pretending to be lost in thought. "Or was it Alabama?"

"The southern United States." He wrote something down and then tapped his notebook. "Have your parents ever been to . . ." Montgomery raised his left eyebrow. "Anau?"

I scrunched up my face to cover my shock. How on earth did he know they had gone to Turkmenistan (fourteenth petal, light indigo or thirteenth sunflower)? *Play it cool, Sunflower.* "Uh. A new what?"

"Anau, Turkmenistan." Montgomery twisted his lips to better pronounce the city's Persian name. "Next to Iran and Afghanistan."

Deny. Deny. Deny. "Aren't those countries, like, far away?" I asked, knowing full well that my parents had been there to clean up some huge diplomatic mess just a few months ago. "Like on another continent or something?"

"Have you seen this?" He handed me a photograph.

And there it was — the old-fashioned red suitcase. This had to be the one Frank would not stop going on about during his explosive June visit. This was the picture of the thing, along with Frank's outrageous reaction, that had made my father's spy sense tingle.

"Well, have you?" Montgomery leaned toward me.

"Nope." Another honest answer. Then I asked, "What does that have to do with Turkey?" Turkey, thirteenth or light indigo sunflower, thirteenth petal.

"Turkmenistan." He cracked his knuckles again. "I'm asking the questions, remember?"

"Yes, I remember." But meanwhile, I was wondering: *How had someone who worked for the Washington State Border Patrol gotten intel on my parents?*

"How many gold-handled spoons does the museum have?"

Talk about changing the topic. "A hundred or so." Factual information, available to all on our awesome website. Most were gold-plated. The ones with solid gold handles were kept in a locked case. Only Mom could polish them because too much pressure would bend the gold, which I'd learned the hard way.

"Any have the initials TJ on them?"

My head hurt. His questioning made no sense. Was this how Mom and Dad got enemy agents to talk — by dazing and perplexing them? "Not a clue."

"So, it's possible."

"Look, Inspector, some of the spoons are used. People put their initials on them. Legend has it that even a pirate like Jean Lafitte found the time to get his soup spoon engraved."

"Think, Miss Pear. Any gold spoons with TJ on them?"

"I. Don't. Know." My tone was a lot sharper than I meant for it to be. "What does TJ stand for, anyway?" I thought of my favorite store in Seattle. Trader Joe's? No. That wasn't right. "I can't think of anyone with the initials of TJ. I mean if it was JTK, that could have been James Tiberius Kirk, one of my dad's favorite TV characters."

By this time, the inspector was shooting me annoyed looks, but I couldn't stop babbling. This was the first interrogation I'd experienced, so who could blame me for being a bit nervous? "That can't be right, either. I don't remember them using gold spoons in the future on the starship *Enterprise*. Because if they did, that is one spoon my parents would definitely buy."

"I'm going to ask you one more time, Miss Pear." He tapped the picture of the red suitcase. "Have you ever seen this?"

Again, an honest answer. "No."

"If it was in the museum, would you have had the opportunity to see it?"

"I would have noticed an old piece of luggage lying around." Mom was tidy. And we had searched every square and round corner of the place with a radar gun that penetrated the wooden walls, ceiling, and floor.

"For your sake, you'd better be telling the truth."

Or what? I wanted to ask, but I swallowed the question before it popped out on its own. For all I knew, Stella would ask him to haul me off to jail.

TJ . . . I kept repeating the letters in my mind, trying to figure out what they could stand for.

Just then, an unfamiliar ring sounded. Montgomery took a cell phone out of the inside pocket of his jacket. "This better not be another excuse, Madison." He wasn't happy with the caller named Madison, but that might've just been his normal sour disposition. "Seriously? You and Jackson should be able to figure out if he found the key." He closed his eyes and scratched his head. "Now? OK." He hung up.

"Thomas Jefferson," I blurted out.

"What did you say?" Montgomery's neck muscles tensed, making it look as if he was dry swallowing a big pill and having problems getting it down.

"TJ. Thomas Jefferson, the president. He would have used gold spoons. People did that back then — kept their wealth in silver and gold. Right?"

Montgomery rose up on his tiptoes. He leaned even closer to me. "You've seen the spoons?"

"No." If we had gold spoons that belonged to an actual president, those would be in their own display case, front and center. They'd be locked up, but on display for all the visitors to see. Spoons like those would give serious credence to the museum. "What other famous person has the initials TJ?"

"I couldn't think of anyone else either."

"Jefferson didn't have a middle name," I added. "So the TJ fits."

"Good reasoning on your part, Miss Pear." Montgomery's eyes darted around the room. For a second, I wanted to confide in him, tell him that Frank and Stella were interested in the red suitcase too. But I couldn't. Because when Stella called the inspector Al, it made me feel uncomfortable, like when a bug crawls over your skin. I guess that's what Dad says is the tingly spy sense.

Montgomery snapped his flipbook closed. "One more thing, Miss Pear. What were you doing in your room?"

Think, Sunflower. Deny. "I tried calling Aunt Gertie's house, just in case she'd been let out of jail." I stared at the brown carpet, afraid that Montgomery would see I was lying. I needed to deflect his attention, so I asked, "Why were you at the Star and the Spoon on Saturday?"

"A good agent always makes sure he has the right person in sight."

I couldn't argue with that. "Inspector, what's inside the red suitcase?"

"No more questions, Moppet."

12

Act natural. Be consistent in your cover story. Simple, true statements work best. Don't get fancy.

— Rule Number 7 from *Rules for a Successful Life as an Undercover Secret Agent*

It took me more than three hours to get the living room back to normal, minus two handmade, lopsided bowls. I discovered the rest of the red bowl crushed under a pile of my parents' home and garden books. The blue shards I found under a stack of cookbooks left no hope for my father's bowl, either. I'd made those for my parents' Christmas presents several years ago.

What type of person destroys a kid's art projects? The type that stuffs her face with my leftovers (pepperoni and red pepper pizza from Mai's) while I cleaned up her mess — that's who. Still, I doubted that Stella would have ripped apart this room just to be malicious. She must have been searching for something specific. But even if she thought Mom had Frank's suitcase somewhere, it wouldn't have been squeezed in between books.

Stella popped into the living room every ten minutes to screech that I wasn't cleaning fast enough. When I suggested she help me since, you know, she made the mess, Stella used "driving" words — words Mom says I'm not allowed to use until I'm at least sixteen, have my driver's license, and can buy my own car.

Since then, Stella left me alone to think. Unfortunately, my brain doesn't work on an empty stomach. There was nothing in the *Rules* about what to do when the enemy was camped out in your own kitchen.

My plan from this morning — bust Aunt Gertie out of jail and get rid of Frankenstella — seemed stupid now that my parents were probably missing. Roy said he trusted my parents' instincts and that my parents trusted me. Was Roy trying to send me a message about trusting my instincts too?

I took out the museum printouts. The circled "$14,500" stood out on the page. A terrible idea hit me. Frankenstella were planning on selling spoons. That's what Frank meant by calling the museum a gold mine. He should have called it a silver mine. This time, I noticed "10130" written next to it. I couldn't figure out what that number meant. Maybe it was a secret code. *Suddenly everyone thinks they're a secret agent,* I thought.

Stella was on the phone in the kitchen as I re-shelved the last book, *The Definitive Northern Italian Cookbook*. Knowing she wouldn't come out to growl for a few minutes, I tortured myself by flipping through the pictures of gnocchi, tortellini, and farfalle.

Farfalle — the Italian name for bow tie pasta! Suddenly it dawned on me — Aunt Gertie's handler's name was Ms. Bow

Tie. *Oh!* My aunt was trying to tell me to contact her Agency handler.

All I needed now was Ms. Bow Tie's phone number, Aunt Gertie's password, and her spy phone. But how was I going to talk with Gertie when she was in jail? Before I could think of a good plan, my least favorite cousin walked in through the front door, smiling like she'd won a million dollars. "Mabel, you missed so much today."

"What happened?"

"Nothing." Victoria rolled her eyes. "You are gullible." She grabbed my wrist, pulling me close to her, and whispered directly into my ear, "Are they here?"

"Your mother is in the kitchen," I answered in the same low voice. "Your father's been gone all day. And I'm hungry."

"She didn't let you eat." It was a statement. "Go to your room. I'll be there in a few."

I sighed, sick and tired of being bossed around in my own home.

"Mo-o-om!" Victoria's wail grated my nerves, so I beat a hasty retreat upstairs.

In my room, I stared out the window, wondering where on earth my parents might be. Gusty winds blew scattered clouds across the deep blue sky. The leaves of the apple tree glimmered in the late afternoon sun. I tripled-checked the sunflower cipher for clues but came up with the same random smattering of bent petals, which meant nothing since it could be any one of those places — or none of them.

Victoria walked in with two glasses of milk and two bags of chips, one bag tucked under each arm. I took a milk and a bag from her. She pulled a peach out of her pocket and gave it to me with her free hand. Then she sat on the floor, nibbling her fingernails. "Are you ready now?"

"For what?" I asked through a bite of peach.

Victoria rolled her eyes again, but at least she smiled this time. "To help me, silly." She popped open her chips and crunched one.

"I have a few problems of my own right now."

"Helping me helps you."

"How?" I asked.

"Once the producers of *Exploring Locked Places* see my entry, they'll know I'm a natural star. Last year's winner got an endorsement deal for shampoo and styling gel, and her own web series."

"Oh," I said, trying to sound impressed. "I didn't know." Of course, I hadn't heard of *Exploring Locked Places,* either, so that was probably why.

"And if Mom and Dad think there's more money to be made in Hollywood, we'll be out of here like that." Victoria snapped her fingers.

The whole scheme seemed so far-fetched that I was sure Victoria had better odds of being struck by lightning while Hula-Hooping and singing the national anthem at a Seahawks game. "What if your video doesn't get picked?"

"Why are you so negative?"

"I'm not. It's called worst-case scenario planning."

"Sounds more like planning to lose. You wouldn't recognize big dreams if they slapped you with a wet rag, would you, Mabel?"

It wasn't true, but I didn't have the luxury of arguing with Victoria. I had real problems to deal with.

"So are you going to help me?" Victoria asked.

"I'll think about it," I said, stalling.

"Is that the pumpkin the girls made for you?" she asked, pointing to my glittery pumpkin.

"Obviously."

"It's cute. One of the Hannahs said I could make one with them this weekend."

"You're making plans for the weekend?" I said, hating the squeak of my voice.

"Yeah. Why? Is that a problem for you?"

If Victoria was still here this weekend, it would mean my parents weren't, and that meant that they'd be missing my birthday. I shrugged like it didn't matter, but I don't think I fooled her.

"Face it, Moppet. You're stuck with us." She smirked. "Unless you want to help me with my dream." She rummaged around in her backpack until she pulled out a big beige envelope with my name printed on it. "Ms. Drysdale said to give you this."

"Thanks." I guess Principal Baker was serious about making sure I didn't miss any homework assignments.

"Are you failing your classes?"

"No," I snapped. Not that it was any of her business.

"You sure? She seemed real concerned that you do your history homework, but she only gave the class ten pages of reading for a quiz tomorrow."

"Teachers. Who can figure them out?" I found it weird that Ms. Drysdale and Mr. Baker had both fixated on history of all subjects. I'd made perfect scores on all the tests and assignments so far.

Ding! Ding! Suddenly my spy sense kicked in. What if they

were trying to tell me something? I had to get rid of Victoria quickly.

"Would you like to borrow a book?" I asked. "I have the new *Fulton Sisters' Adventure*."

"Number Eighty-Seven? It's so awesome when April and Samantha find out the waitress is a ninja who —"

"No. Stop with the spoilers." I covered my ears. "Do you want to watch television?"

"Do you guys have cable?" Victoria opened the door to the hallway.

"Dad installed satellite dishes. We get a couple hundred channels."

"Excellent. I have some serious catching up to do on my favorite shows." A smile spread across her face. "Coming, Moppet?"

"Nope." I tried to appear sad. "Gotta get my homework done." I waited until I couldn't hear Victoria's footsteps, and then I tore open the envelope. There, under the history assignment, was a note from Mr. Baker:

Mabel -

I talked with Gert.

Farfalle is a type of pasta shaped like bow ties. She really wants you to have some for dinner.

Do you have a carbohydrate deficiency?

Seriously, I think the idea of being in jail is too difficult for her. Is there any way you can contact your parents?

- Mr. B

Well, that helpful note came too late. Something hit my bedroom window before I could despair. I pushed it open and was rewarded with a pinecone to the face.

"Sorry, Mabel." Stanley stood at the base of the apple tree. "What happened to you today?"

"Long story. Please, whatever you do, don't knock on the back door or the front door. Or go near them."

"OK," Stanley said. I liked that he took my word for it and didn't ask any questions.

A flash of inspiration hit me. "Hey, do you want to go for a walk?" I called down to Stanley. "But we can't be seen." Dad would've called this a covert operation — spy talk for a secret job. It usually involves breaking the law for the greater good.

"Sure." He said it like we sneaked out of our houses all the time. "Where to?"

"Jail."

"OK." If Stanley was surprised, he didn't show it. "I have to be home before nine."

"Give me thirty minutes," I said.

Stanley nodded, plopped down on the ground, pulled out a sketchbook, and started drawing.

"No whistling," I added, before he could start. "And stay away from the windows."

My very first covert ops mission, and I was going to break *in to* jail. I bet Montgomery never expected that.

13

If all else fails, beg like a puppy, making big eyes. But don't whimper. No one likes a whiner.

— Rule Number 28 from *Rules for a Successful Life as an Undercover Secret Agent*

Part one of the spy mission involved me going downstairs and standing really close to Stella. Whenever she moved, I followed, asking any question that popped into my mind.

"What is life like in Alaska?" I asked as she rummaged through the refrigerator.

"Cold," Stella said. "Leave me alone."

"How do you calculate cube root?" I asked as she took a bite of Aunt Gertie's leftover baked mac and cheese.

"I don't know," she answered with her mouth full.

"How deep is the Pacific Ocean?"

"Mabel, how would I know?" Stella searched the freezer.

"How did you meet Uncle Frank?" I asked as she ate a spoonful of Mom's homemade strawberry ice cream. "Come to think of it, where is Uncle Frank today?"

Stella tried to walk away, but I stuck close. "Mabel, stop bothering me."

"Your eyebrows are brown. Is your hair naturally red?"

"I'm warning you." She flung the empty ice cream container into the sink. "Stop with the stupid questions."

"Here's a smart question: How many stars are in the Milky Way, Aunt Stella?"

"Your contrarian attitude is giving me a headache."

"Where did you get that pearl necklace? It looks just like the one my mother has." I started counting the freckles on her arm. "One, two, three, four. Oh, are there really thousands of words for 'snow' in Native Alaskan languages? Five freckles. Six. Sev—"

"That's it. Go to your room." She slapped my hand away. "You may not step foot downstairs for the rest of the evening. No dinner. No television. Go."

Mission successful! I tried to act upset by slouching my shoulders and hanging my head as I plodded up the stairs. I planned on obeying Stella's orders. She never mentioned that I couldn't shimmy down the old apple tree outside my bedroom window, hang out with Stanley Brick, and visit the town jail.

Stanley gave me two thumbs up as I grabbed a sturdy-looking branch and swung my body toward the tree trunk. Once I had firm footing on a lower branch, I climbed down the branches until I could jump onto solid ground. I made it with only a few scratches.

Stanley smiled. "Smooth." Two freshly eaten apple cores lay at his feet. His sketch pad was opened to a half-done drawing of a tree grove. He pulled out a stack of photos from his backpack and handed them to me.

I'd been so annoyed with my parents leaving on Saturday, I'd forgotten to check out Stanley's blog posting of October's pictures. I had always been commenter number one each month. Luckily, he also printed out the photos for his sketches.

I shared a couple of granola bars I'd managed to snag from the kitchen before I was banished. Then I plucked a low-hanging fruit for myself. Sweet and tart. Stanley and I moved out of sight range of my house, past the Spoon, and stopped behind the Star. We munched on the bars and apples as I flipped through his photos. I kept glancing about, but no one was around. *Of course not,* I thought. *Everyone is in jail. Or out of the country. Or eating my food* (lasagna and garlic bread — I could tell by the aroma) *in my house while watching my television.*

The photos were what I expected — trees, leaves, bushes — all crisp and clear in amazing detail. "What's that?" I asked. One of the trees had a black box on it.

"A bat house," Stanley said. "Did you know bats are the only mammals able to fly?"

"I do now," I said, handing the photos back to him. We started walking; the fallen red and orange maple leaves squished under our feet. The sun set quickly, and the chilly, damp air felt like Halloween. Four more days until my birthday.

One of the nice things about hanging out with Stanley was that he didn't ask a lot of nosy questions. Sure, he'd spend hours explaining why guano (bat poop) was valuable for farming, but not once had he ever questioned where my parents were. I think he was just glad to have a hot dinner and didn't care if it was my mom, my dad, or my aunt making it.

"Mabel." Stanley lightly touched my arm, stopping me. "Are we going to wander the back side of Main Street forever?"

"How do I explain this?" I asked, twisting a curl behind my left ear. "I need a huge favor."

"Sure." He brushed his hair out of his face.

"You don't know what it is yet."

"Aunt Gertie was arrested, so I thought you'd want to talk to her."

I opened my mouth, but nothing came out.

"I overheard your cousin telling the HEGs about it at lunchtime," Stanley said.

"What exactly did Victoria say?"

"That your aunt stole valuables from the museum and tried to sell them. The FBI arrested her."

"No." I felt my face get hot with anger. "It's not true. She didn't steal anything. The FBI is not involved. It's the Washington State Border Patrol."

"OK." Stanley pushed his glasses up his nose. "Do you want to go talk to her?"

"Yes. I need your help, but I can't tell you anything and you can't repeat anything you overhear."

"OK."

"I mean it, Stanley. Swear."

"Mabel, who am I going to tell?"

"I don't know. I just need to believe that I can trust you."

His eyes darted from corner to corner, like they did when he was making a difficult decision or trying to remember an obscure vocabulary word. "OK. I swear."

"Thanks. Now, help me break into jail."

Stanley had his thinking face on: mouth open, eyes shut, and eyebrows wiggling. "The cell windows have bars."

"What's your point, Stanley?" Did he think we could yank them out?

"No glass, just shutters. You can talk to your aunt from outside."

"Good point! Let's go." I grabbed Stanley's sleeve and pulled him after me.

We darted across the street and sneaked into the alleyway that ran behind Main Street. The all-brick Silverton Town Jail was a National Historic Landmark, which doubled as a tourist information center and sold backcountry hiking and camping permits. Luckily, there were no tourists around at this time of day to give us away.

Light spilled out of one tiny window, about the size of a loaf of bread. Unfortunately, it was about eight feet off the ground.

I stood on my tiptoes below it and whispered, "Aunt Gertie. Hello?" She didn't answer, so I tried again a bit louder. "Aunt Gertie." She still didn't reply. "How can I get her attention?" I asked Stanley. "I don't want to scream."

"Wait a second," he said as he fished around in his pockets. He pulled out two pens, a pad of sticky notes, a small rubber ball, three sticks of gum, a couple of paper clips, and a pinecone. "Use this," he said, handing the pinecone to me.

I flung it through the bars on my first attempt.

"What on Earth?" came my aunt's familiar voice. I heard her shuffle toward the window.

"Aunt Gertie," I whispered again. "I'm outside."

"Mabel, is that you?"

"I need information." I squeezed my eyes shut and tried to think. *Speak in code, Sunflower.* "How do you make farfalle?"

Stanley looked at me like I had lost my mind and said, "Eight to ten minutes in boiling water."

I couldn't hear Aunt Gertie's response.

"Shush, Stanley," I whispered. "You swore you wouldn't say a word."

I heard another voice from inside the jail. Sheriff Baker must've been checking in on Gertie, but she spoke too quietly for me to understand the words.

Aunt Gertie spoke again, but this time not to me. "Oh, just talking to myself, Prue. I'm fine." She paused. "Have a nice dinner at Mai's." I could hear something being dragged along the floor. "Mabel."

"Yes, I'm here."

"Come closer and I'll give you the secret family recipe."

"How can I get up there?" I whispered to Stanley.

He pointed at a metal garbage can at the end of the alley. Together we carried and placed it under the window. With Stanley's hand for support, I climbed on top of it. Standing on my tiptoes, I grabbed hold of the wide metal bars, pulled myself up, and peered inside my aunt's jail cell. "Ready."

"Mabel," Stanley whispered.

"Shush, Stanley. Aunt Gertie hasn't said one word yet."

"Mabel." Stanley tugged on the leg of my jeans. "We gotta go."

"What are you kids doing sneaking around back here?"

I turned toward the voice. A blinding light flashed in my eyes.

"Step away from the window and come here," the voice demanded.

I froze, clutching the bars. Stanley didn't. He walked toward the voice.

"Mabel Pear, is that you?" Footsteps approached and the flashlight beam still blinded me. When the person came close enough, she lowered the flashlight, revealing her face. Sheriff Baker looked at me and sighed. "Get down." She flashed her light on Stanley. "And who is this?"

"Sheriff, this is my friend Stanley Brick," I said. "Stanley, this is Sheriff Baker."

"Nice to meet you, Sheriff," Stanley said as he held out his hand.

"So you're the Brick kid Mabel is always hiking with." The sheriff shook his hand and said, "You're not going to make a habit of hanging out behind the jail, are you?"

"No, ma'am." Stanley raised one eyebrow and looked at me.

"Please don't be mad at us," I pleaded, begging like a puppy. "I just want to talk to my aunt for a few minutes."

"You could've just come in the front door, you know," Sheriff Baker said as she ushered us down the dark alleyway and into the Silverton Town Sheriff's Office and Jail. Only one row of hall lights was on, casting spooky shadows among the Halloween decorations. The sheriff grabbed her wide-brimmed hat off the desk. "Stanley, you look like you could use a piece of Mai's pie."

He nodded so fast his black-rimmed glasses slid down his nose. "Yes, ma'am."

"Tell your aunt I'll be back with her supper in about fifteen minutes." Sheriff Baker winked at me. Turning to Stanley, she said, "I'm partial to Mai's cherry pie. What's your favorite?"

The creaking hinges drowned out Stanley's reply as they exited.

My sneakers squeaked on the marble floor as I walked

down the hall toward the holding cells. Shivers ran down my spine. I'd never been back here.

The first two cells were dark, but the third one had a lamp in it, spilling light. My aunt was standing on the cot, curly gray hair frizzed out by the evening's humidity. She wore her favorite long purple skirt, lime green socks, electric blue sandals, and an orange and pink tasseled shawl.

I caught my breath for what seemed the first time all day. "When I woke this morning, Victoria was in my room taking video of me sleeping."

"That sounds almost worse than waking up in jail," Aunt Gertie said as she stepped down and walked toward the bars.

"Frankenstella ate all of my cinnamon buns." I knew it was a petty complaint, but I couldn't help myself. "Why are they even here?"

"I know your mother wants things to be different with him, but I wish she hadn't called them when I wasn't available." Aunt Gertie clenched her fists. "Frank is an opportunist pig. I'll strangle him myself when I'm out of here."

"When will that be?"

"Soon, I hope. Montgomery thinks your parents' travel schedule is suspicious. And he's right."

"Mom and Dad are smugglers?"

"No, Mabel," Aunt Gertie said. "Their globe-trotting is odd. Strange destinations on a moment's notice. Montgomery is wrong about why Jane and Fred travel. He's made an honest mistake."

"If it's their traveling that's the problem, why are you in jail?"

"It's that necklace from the Memorial Day sale. Even though it wasn't real gold, it's rather valuable."

"How's that?" I asked, not sure how much Aunt Gertie knew about the necklace's origin.

"Well for one thing, it's pinchbeck."

My look of utter confusion encouraged her to keep talking.

"It's counterfeit. The necklace was made to look like gold, but it's really copper and zinc."

"Valuable how, again?"

"The necklace was made in the 1700s."

"Old. OK. That gives it worth, I guess."

My aunt bit her lip in thought. "It's not unreasonable that the inspector wants to make sure I'm not hiding anything else." She shrugged. "It's what I would do if the situation were reversed."

My aunt and I looked at each other. "So this situation is all my fault," I said. My aunt — my favorite aunt — who provided me endless love and cinnamon buns, was locked up. "If I hadn't sold your necklace . . . if I had taken two minutes to ask, instead of picking that tag up from the floor. If —"

"Don't blame yourself, Moppet," Aunt Gertie interrupted. "The necklace was never mine, apparently."

I did blame myself, but I didn't have much time to talk and I had other important questions to ask before the sheriff returned. "Do we have any of Thomas Jefferson's spoons?"

"No. That would be nice, though. People would want to see them. We could probably even charge more than a dollar for admission."

I wasn't so sure about that. It seemed to me that the general public wasn't too interested in spoons. "Could the suitcase that Frank talked about be in the house?"

"There is no suitcase. We never traveled anywhere.

We were too poor. The first time I went to Seattle was the summer after I graduated from high school."

"Maybe it belonged to your parents?" I asked. "Or a friend who came to visit?"

"Moppet, honey, I was sixteen when my parents died. Frank took off weeks later. I remember so much. Too much." Aunt Gertie shook her head. Her frown lines made her look even older than she was. "Child, I swear, if anyone ever mentions that thing to me again, I might just . . . I don't know what. Scream, maybe." She sighed. "I guess my having that bag of costume jewelry didn't help matters. If Momma had known it was stolen, I'm sure she would have left it and kept on walking. But she was poor and the necklaces were pretty." She sighed, long and deep. "Who would have guessed that old stuff would cause so much trouble?"

I could. No police anywhere looked kindly upon the possession of stolen properly — especially when there was intent to sell. However, I'd promised my parents that I wouldn't tell Aunt Gertie about her parents' crimes. And even her being locked up wasn't reason enough to break that promise.

"Cheer up, Mabel. Once the Agency steps in, I'll be freed. Until then, we deny everything." Gertie tapped the bars. "I'm supposed to be in solitary confinement. Prue and Ted must think I've gone insane, telling you to eat farfalle, which is —"

"Bow tie pasta," I interrupted my aunt. "I need your handler's phone number and your password."

"And my cell phone," Aunt Gertie said. "It's in my house."

"I'm busting you out of jail." Imagine my surprise when I touched her cell door and it flew open. "Let's go." I felt elated. Finally something had gone my way.

"I can't." Aunt Gertie slid the door back into place.

I reopened the cell door. "You can. It's not locked." Sometimes I seriously wonder how any grown-up can get through the day. "We can go home."

"Sorry." She slid the door into place. "I meant to say that I will not."

A huff escaped before I could control myself. "Are you telling me you could've walked out of here at any time, but you *chose* to stay in jail?"

"Mabel, this is a complicated situation."

"Speak slowly, and maybe my little brain can understand if you use small words."

Aunt Gertie shot me the don't-be-rude glare. "Prue left the door unlocked so that I can use the restroom whenever I need to. I gave her my word that I would be here until this situation is resolved and I'm no longer under suspicion."

"Did you make a pinkie promise with the sheriff too?"

"I won't betray her trust."

"Who cares about Sheriff Baker? I need you."

"And I am right here."

"How am I going to get rid of Frankenstella without your help?"

"Calm down and think about this for a minute, Mabel. If I leave this jail cell, where is the first place Sheriff Baker would search for me?"

My best-laid plans crumbled like a sand castle at high tide. Obviously the sheriff would search my house, the Star's Tale, and the Spoon for my aunt. "What am I gonna do?" I sounded just like Victoria whining to her mother.

"Well, if you can't call Ms. Bow Tie, you should call your special person and ask for assistance."

"He hung up on me. My parents are missing and no one cares."

"No." She shook her head. "It must have been a glitch. Your parents are too valuable to the Agency." Aunt Gertie reached through the bars to pat my shoulder. "If it makes you feel any better, this is not the first time they've gone off the radar."

I could feel the heat from the red splotches as they grew on my cheeks and neck. "Why would I feel better knowing my parents have been lost before?"

"Not lost, exactly. It's just that some missions are so secret, the Agency doesn't share the information even internally."

"Doesn't matter." I crossed my arms in frustration. "They aren't doing a thing about it."

"Don't be ridiculous, Mabel. I've no doubt they are working double time to make sure your parents are safe." Aunt Gertie paced about in her cell for a few minutes, a sign she was thinking hard. She opened her cell door.

I leaped into her arms. "Thank you for escaping from jail for me."

"Mabel, don't be so dramatic. I'm just getting paper and a pencil." Aunt Gertie walked over to the sheriff's desk, grabbed a notebook and pencil, and jotted down a series of numbers. "Memorize this." She handed the slip of paper to me and returned to her cell. "Then destroy it."

I repeated the phone number to myself until I felt sure I had it. I tore the paper into tiny shreds, dropping half into the garbage can and half into the recycling bin, as per the emergency disposal protocol. "Key, please."

Aunt Gertie patted her pockets but came up empty. She shook her head in annoyance. "I must have left them in the

Star when Montgomery insisted that I go with him," she said. "Use the spare key under the back doormat."

"Where's your phone hidden?"

"It's in the spine of *Breads of Europe* by Anne Eleanor Johnson, on my bedroom bookshelf. Let it ring twice. Hang up. Call again. When Ms. Bow Tie answers, the password is 'meatballs.'"

"Victoria believes her parents are behind this." I motioned to the jail cell. "I think she's right. And . . ." I paused for dramatic effect. "I bet Montgomery is in cahoots with Frankenstella."

"Cahoots? You've been reading too many old-fashioned spy novels." Aunt Gertie pulled her long gray hair into a ponytail.

"But Montgomery said —"

"Mabel." Aunt Gertie lifted her hand to cut me off. "No more silly spy stuff. But whatever you do, don't let my rat fink brother into the museum. Ever."

"Are you really afraid he's going to sell all the silver spoons?"

"I know your mother has let you play spy around the house writing those silly rules," Aunt Gertie said, ignoring my question. "I don't mean to be harsh, child, but this situation isn't make-believe." The squeaking of the front door stopped her from saying anything else. Footsteps echoed in the empty hallway. "Promise me you'll just go to school and stay out of trouble."

"Dinnertime for Silverton's favorite inmate!" The mouth-watering smell nearly knocked me off my feet. Sheriff Baker walked in and handed the food container to my aunt. "Mabel, I'm driving Stanley home. Can I give you a lift?"

"I'll walk," I said. Her message was clear: visiting time was over.

14

Any operation can be terminated at any point. If something feels wrong, stop. Remove yourself from the situation.

— Rule Number 9 from *Rules for a Successful Life as an Undercover Secret Agent*

Built like the old Mount Rainier cabins of logs and stone, Gertie's house looked like it had always been there. But while my house and the museum were both built in the 1890s, my aunt had designed and constructed her house just five years ago. Before that, she'd lived with us. The Star's Tale took up the entire bottom floor, and Gertie lived upstairs.

I tried both the front and back doors of the Star's Tale, but the knobs wouldn't turn. I looked under the back doormat — no key.

As I was putting the mat back in place, a *squish* sounded nearby. It was like a footstep on wet leaves, and I panicked, darting around to the side of the house. I knew it could have been a coyote, raccoon, or even a deer this time of year, but I didn't want to take any chances. I paused, pressing my back against the side of the building. Then came another squish.

I walked up two steps of the outside staircase, then hesitated, listening for any sound louder than the beating of my heart. Ten seconds passed. Hearing nothing, I tiptoed to the top stair.

Squish, squish. Now it was clear: someone — or something — was walking right below me, loud and careless. I hoped it was a black bear, hunting for one last snack before hibernation.

I stood very still on the little landing outside Gertie's door and attempted to shrink into the shadows. I tried the door — locked. My panicked breathing left fog on the glass pane.

Down below, around the corner of the house, someone shook the shop's front doorknob with enough force to rattle its glass panes. "Do you think she knows anything?" Frank's gruff voice gave him away.

"Not sure." Stella's voice had lost its edge. "Sometimes I think she's cleverer than she looks, but then she goes and does something stupid."

Were they talking about me? I willed Frankenstella to not look up.

"The Baies women — rocket scientists, all of them." Frank guffawed as he walked around the outside of the café.

"Because the Baies men are so brilliant?" Stella snorted. "All your schemes combined have gotten us nothing. The Baies women may not be geniuses, but they own this museum, the silver, and the map. You have nothing."

The map? I thought. *What map?*

"Hush up, Stella." Frank's voice grew fainter. "Go see if any of the windows are unlocked on the other side."

As soon as the sound of squishing wet leaves grew softer, I tried jiggling the door handle again. Nope. I stared at the dark windows. I knew I had to get that cell phone, by any means necessary. I was sure Gertie wouldn't call Sheriff Baker on me for breaking and entering, so I slipped my arm into my hoodie sleeve, bunching up the cloth around my fist. With as much strength as I could muster, I punched the glass pane in the front door. Nothing happened.

Come on Sunflower, you can do this.

I stepped sideways, twisted my torso, pulled my elbow back, and swung. *Crack.* The glass splintered. I stopped, waiting to see if Frankenstella would come rushing toward the noise.

When they didn't, I pushed against the growing lines until the glass fell inside. I carefully snaked my arm through the window, unlatched the door, and then opened it, stepping over the shards of glass. I snagged a banana from the fruit bowl sitting on the kitchen counter and gobbled it as I inched my way down the hall and into Gertie's bedroom.

I peered through a crack in the curtains, and seeing nothing suspicious in our joint backyards, parted the curtains to let in the moonlight. Stella cackled, but it sounded far away. I skimmed the bookshelf until I found *Breads of Europe* and pulled the phone out of its spine. The phone was just like mine with no screen.

I dialed the number, and as soon as it rang twice, I hung up, then redialed. After ten or so rings, I tried again, sure that I had the right number, but no one answered. Did Ms. Bow Tie somehow know that whoever was calling wasn't Aunt Gertie?

Frank's gruff voice was too low to make out his words. I went to stand by the window to eavesdrop.

"If we want to get in, we'll need Mabel Opal's help." Stella sounded as if she was right below the bedroom window.

I shoved the cell phone into my jeans pocket.

"You mean Moppet?" Frank asked.

Stella chuckled. "What a terrible thing to call a child."

"I don't care what she's called," he said, "as long as she opens the museum for us."

Uh oh! Time to go, Sunflower! I dashed down the dark hallway and out the front door, only slowing down to close it. Then I rushed down the staircase. After checking to make sure that Frankenstella were not nearby, I raced in front of the Star and the Spoon. My lungs were on fire as I ran up the front steps of my house. Sixty-eight seconds in total, beating my old record of seventy seconds flat from Aunt Gertie's to my house.

Praying that no one had locked the door, I took a deep breath and tried the handle. Success. I darted into the front hall, my breath coming quick and shallow. The entire house was dark. Frankenstella were chattering as they approached the back door. I had to make it up the stairs, then I'd be home free.

I sprinted across the floor toward the staircase, but just ten feet from the first step, my foot hit something and I wobbled. The something moved, sweeping my leg out from under me. *Splat* — down on my face I fell.

Doors flung open, lights switched on, and suddenly I knew what that something was that I had tripped on. Victoria was lying on the floor, inches from where I'd landed.

"What are you doing downstairs, Mabel?" Stella shrieked.

"I — I — I . . ." I couldn't think of a plausible lie.

"Relax, Mom." Victoria rolled over to face her parents. "She's helping me with my homework."

"On the floor?" Frank asked, disbelief written all over his pudgy face. "In the dark?"

"I told you guys at dinner." Victoria went straight to whine mode. "The science teacher wanted us to try to use our senses feeling around in a dark room. Remember?"

"Yes. Yes, I remember. Of course." Frank shot a glance at his wife. "I didn't think you were doing that tonight."

"You guys never listen to me." Victoria's pout could've been adorable — on a three-year-old. She stood up and crossed her arms. "It's my first day at a new school, and I want to get everything right. To make you proud."

"Well, of course we're proud of you." Stella patted Victoria's head like a puppy. "Did you get everything finished?"

"Nooooo." Victoria grabbed my arm and pulled me up, rougher than necessary. "Mabel and I have to quiz each other on vocabulary words now." She started climbing the stairs. I followed, since I was mightily attached to my arm.

"I want to talk to Mabel first," Stella said.

"*Da-a-ad.*" Victoria let loose. "I have homework and Mabel has to show me how the teacher likes it."

Frank put his hand on Stella's shoulder and gave her the briefest shake of the head. "It can wait until tomorrow morning. Good night, girls."

15

Keep your friends close and your enemies closer. Invite your archenemies over for tea and cookies. It will confuse them.

— Rule Number 27 from *Rules for a Successful Life as an Undercover Secret Agent*

Once inside my room, I did a quick visual check — sunflower cipher, *Rules*, world map, *Abridged History* textbook — all in their proper places. Rubbing my arm, I thought about Rule Number 11 for the second time today: *Watch carefully for anyone who does special, unasked favors. Try to figure out what they might want from you.* "Thanks for covering for me," I said. "What were you doing on the floor in the dark?"

"You owe me," Victoria said, not answering my question. "Where were you?"

Deny. Deny. Deny. "I needed some air. I've been locked up in the house all day."

"You don't fool me, Cousin Mabel."

"I don't?" I placed my hand over my jeans pocket to hide the bump of Aunt Gertie's cell phone.

Victoria smirked. "I know what you were doing."

Did Victoria follow me? I wondered. *Could she have overheard me talking to Aunt Gertie?*

"The mud on the cuffs of your jeans says it all."

I followed her glance down to my ankles and asked, "My pants can talk?"

Victoria rolled her eyes.

"It's damp outside," I said. Hunger was definitely messing with my ability to come up with snappy replies.

Victoria smirked. "You were looking at the spoon museum, weren't you?"

"I walked past it."

"I knew it! You were there to see if we could break in, like I asked you to."

"You're right." Relief flooded me. Victoria didn't know I had broken into Aunt Gertie's home or visited her in jail. "I guess I shouldn't try to hide anything from you, Victoria."

"You really are a terrible liar." She plopped down on my bed.

"Please get off my bed. The air mattress is yours."

She rolled her eyes again. "Do you have the key to the museum?"

Oh no. I'd forgotten to find and hide the spare key. I felt comforted knowing that since Frankenstella were checking for unlatched windows, they surely didn't have it. "Nope." I knew I had to get that spare key first thing tomorrow. I also had to hide the New Orleans Silver Spoon Historical Collection so that Frank didn't sell it off.

"We should go back," Victoria said. "Now. Let's do it."

I rummaged through the top dresser drawer, pulling out a fresh pair of pajamas. "Your parents would catch us tonight."

"Are you afraid of getting caught?"

Yes. Yes, I was. But not by Frankenstella. The angry Agency women had sounded terrifying on the phone. I didn't want to have to explain why I had gone against the strict orders I'd been given. I wasn't going to share my reasoning with Victoria, so I simply said, "Don't you need flashlights and stuff for lighting to record?"

"Yeah. Good point, Moppet." Victoria looked at my baby pumpkin and then chuckled to herself.

"What?" I asked.

"Just thinking about something the HEGs said today at lunch."

"What's that?"

"You're a ghoul."

My blood froze in my veins. "A what?" I managed to croak.

"You were born on October thirty-first." Victoria waved her fingers in the air. "Halloween. Ghost. Ghoul. Get it?"

"Yeah." I exhaled. Ghoul was also a spy term for an agent who dealt with undercover names, obituaries, and cemeteries. Not a pleasant job.

"So are you going to have a party?"

"Probably not," I said.

"Gosh, Moppet. You act like a birthday party would be torture. What is with you?" Victoria frowned at me. "Why does everyone call you Moppet, anyway?" she asked.

"Mop was my nickname when I was four years old." I twirled a curl around my finger. "Mabel Opal Pear. M-O-P. Mop became Moppet. Get it?"

"Mabel's a weird name, no offense."

"It's our granny's name. And her granny's name." We have lots of silver jewelry with the name Mabel engraved on it. How many family pieces have Victoria engraved on them? None.

"Why did your parents name you after a musical instrument?"

My head ached from fatigue. "What are you talking about?"

"Oboe's your middle name." Victoria started making bellowing sounds.

"O-P-A-L. My birthstone." My dad says that I'm just like an opal, milky white on the surface with flashes of green, but hidden inside are fiery reds waiting to explode like molten lava. I'm still not sure if that's a compliment or if he's trying to be funny.

I could see Victoria thinking of insults concerning my last name. Instead of waiting for the next put-down, I went on the attack. "Now do you have anything clever to say about Pear?"

"You don't have to be so mean." Victoria huffed, as if I'd hurt her feelings. "I was just trying to get to know you better." She sniffled.

I suppressed a groan. I really wanted to call Aunt Gertie's handler again so that someone in the Agency would do something, not ignore me like Roy and the angry woman. There was no way I could call in front of Victoria, so I said, "I'm getting ready for bed."

"Good thinking, Moppet."

I walked down the hallway to the bathroom. Once inside, I dialed Ms. Bow Tie's number, going through the standard ritual of calling, letting it ring, and hanging up. I was waiting for Ms. Bow Tie to pick up when I realized that the light from the hallway that was shining under the door was being blocked by two feet.

I pushed the cell phone deep into my pocket. Quietly, I walked to the door and flung it open.

Victoria was unfazed. "You forgot these," she said, handing me my black-and-red Hello Kitty pajamas. "What are you doing in there?"

"Using the bathroom." I wanted to slam the door in her smirking face, but I knew all it would take was one wail for Stella to come to her defense.

"Typically one uses water in the bathroom," Victoria said as she leaned against the doorjamb.

Ms. Bow Tie would have to wait another day.

16

Don't stand out. Follow the crowd. Never call attention to yourself. Shop, eat, and act like the locals.

— Rule Number 6 from *Rules for a Successful Life as an Undercover Secret Agent*

Mom's favorite blueberry and walnut coffee cake sat on the super fancy cake plate we used only at holiday time. It overshadowed a platter of scrambled eggs and bacon. Stella must have found the deep freezer.

The table was set with more of the best holiday china, crystal glasses, and fancy silverware. I grabbed a healthy serving of food and started to eat. I didn't know when Frankenstella were going to start something with me, and I needed nourishment.

"Mabel," Frank said through a bite of eggs. "Where's the museum key?"

Oh no! With all the craziness yesterday evening, searching for the spare key had slipped my mind again. I chewed the bite of egg until there was nothing left in my mouth. I couldn't think of anything to say but the truth. "I don't know."

Frank peered at me. As he crunched a piece of bacon

between his teeth, he shared a meaningful glance with his wife. "How many keys are there?"

I squinted as if I was thinking hard about the question. "One." My face didn't flush at all. I was getting much better at lying. "And it should be there." I pointed to the empty hooks next to the one with Mom's car key. Frank didn't need to know that Aunt Gertie had a key too, probably somewhere inside the Star, or that there was a section of loose floorboards I could squeeze under to get inside. "Why?"

"The museum is a business." Frank pointed his fork at me. "It has to be open so that customers can come in."

His buyer must be coming soon, I thought. "Don't you mean *visitors*, Uncle Frank?"

"Of course he does." Stella shot a loaded glance at her husband. Blue oval-cut sapphires sparkled on her earlobes. Mom had a pair just like those.

"Don't worry about it," I said. "This late in the season, we almost never get visitors."

"Business concerns are for us adults to worry about," Stella said.

Like they would have a clue about anything in the museum if an actual visitor came. Right now, we were using real silverware to eat eggs. The sulfur dioxide in the yolk oxidizes the silver, making silver sulfide, otherwise known as tarnish. My fork was already discoloring to an ugly gray. I foresaw hours of polishing in my not-too-distant future.

"In the off-season, viewing hours are by appointment only," I quoted the sign from the museum's front door.

"Your mother said someone important was coming this week," Stella said. "She stressed that when she called to ask us for help."

Yeah, right. I shoveled more eggs into my mouth, trying to keep the look of disbelief off my face. While it was true that sometimes Le Petit Musée of Antique Silver Spoons got visits from real-life experts, those meetings were planned months in advance and were clearly marked on the calendar. Today, Tuesday, October twenty-eighth, was as blank as the rest of the week.

Oh! Suddenly, while looking at the calendar, it was like a light bulb switched on. The number "10130" written on the liberated printouts wasn't a secret code. It was a date: 10/30. Frankenstella were planning to sell the New Orleans collection on Thursday, October thirtieth.

To cover my shock, I asked, "Who's coming?"

"I don't remember offhand," Stella said. "Is there any other place the key could be, Mabel dear?"

I nearly choked when I heard "Mabel dear." Swigging a drink of water to hide my reaction, I shook my head. "It's always there or with Mom." I stabbed a chunk of coffee cake.

"By any chance, do you know the code or password?" Stella asked.

The coffee cake in my mouth turned into dry sponge. I coughed it up, spraying both Victoria's plate and my own with crumbs.

Victoria thudded me on my back. "Something go down the wrong way, *Mabel dear*?"

I could feel a bruise starting to form on my mid-back. "Yeah, a walnut must have gotten stuck in my throat."

"Your aunt asked you a question," Frank said. "About the code and password."

Had they found my secret phone in the old history textbook? How could I get out of this? Aunt Gertie's phone was still burning a hole in my front pocket, next to my pocketknife. If I told them my password and they used the phone, the operation would be in trouble. Worse yet, what if Frankenstella found out about the Agency, or about my parents' jobs?

Rule Number 24 stated: *If you panic, stop whatever you're doing. Breathe. Ask "Huh?" Or eat something as a diversion*. Eating hadn't worked well for me at all.

Stella put another piece of the coffee cake on my plate and poured more water into my glass. "Do you know the security code for the museum's alarm system?"

"The Spoon doesn't have an alarm system."

"What, then, is the flashing panel with a keypad, next to the back door?" Frank asked.

"I don't know." That sounded unconvincing, even to me. But I was relieved they were asking stupid questions about the museum, not the Agency.

Frank grunted. "It has red and green lights and says PNW Security."

"It's only on the back door?" I asked, trying to stall.

"Alarms are connected to all points of entry." Stella tried to smile at me. The effect reminded me of a computer-generated dog grinning. All wrong. "I was under the impression that you helped your mother in the museum quite a lot."

I nodded.

"That's a big responsibility."

"It's my weekend job."

"Doesn't your mother trust you?" Stella asked.

"Of course she does."

"Do you know either the security code to turn off the alarm or the password if it accidentally gets set off?"

I shook my head no. Something was terribly wrong. The museum key was missing. I couldn't remember the last time I saw it hanging on the hook. And someone had put a security alarm on the museum between Sunday night and this morning without me noticing? Who could do that?

There was only one group I could think of that specialized in covert ops and was connected to Le Petit Musée — the Agency! It would be a piece of cake for highly trained Cleaners to roll into Silverton, wire the Spoon up, and depart, all without leaving a trace.

Relief flooded through me. The Agency had taken action when I called yesterday. The only question was why. The museum was a cover story for my parents, sure. But the Agency had no reason to care about some old spoon museum. Unless there was something else in there. . . .

17

Change up your routine so that the enemy has a harder time tracking you. They will follow you, but make them work for it. Don't ever rush. Unless you have a bus to catch. Then run.

— Rule Number 8 from *Rules for a Successful Life as an Undercover Secret Agent*

The honking of the school bus saved me from answering any more of Frankenstella's nerve-wracking questions. Victoria's iron grasp threatened to cut off blood flow in my right arm. If this kept up, I'd be totally black and blue by Halloween. Add some green skin paint and there's a costume: zombie.

"Come on, Mabel. We don't want to be late," Victoria said as she pulled me out of the front door and across the lawn to the waiting bus. Victoria didn't release me as she hopped on board, so I was forced to climb up the bus stairs with my face pressed against her backpack.

The Emmas sat in their usual seat with the Graces across from them. Their four faces were scrunched in puzzlement as we got onto the bus. There was nothing I could say to explain the situation, so I just said, "Hi," as I walked by all causal, like I was used to being dragged around by my cousin.

Stanley sat in the third-to-last seat of the bus. His brown wavy hair touched the tops of his ears. He scooted over toward the window as we approached. "Hi, Mabel." He held a book in his lap.

"Hey." I glanced at his book, ignoring the fact that Victoria's fingers were still clamped around my arm. Sketches of manga superheroes filled the pages. "Did you draw those?"

"Yeah, last night." He held it up to show me.

I sat down next to him, aware that Victoria was breathing fire on my head. "They're really good." I wanted to ask if Sheriff Baker had said anything when she drove him home. Instead, I traced one with my fingertip. "I like the way her cape is flowing in the wind."

"I brought some more photos from the tree grove," Stanley said. "You should take a look at them."

Victoria snorted. "We don't have time for this today." She yanked me up and pulled me into the last seat in the aisle opposite Stanley.

"Victoria," I whispered. "I was talking with Stanley about his art." And I was getting ready to pump him for intel, but I didn't tell her that.

"You can't talk to him today."

"Why not?" I tried standing up. Victoria yanked me down. Hard. *Well,* I thought, *if she pulls my arm out, that will make my zombie costume extra realistic.*

Victoria took out her purple smartphone, pointed it at my chin, and clicked a picture. "You have a zit."

"What?" I touched my face. There was a tiny bump about

half an inch below my mouth. I hadn't even noticed it this morning.

Victoria zoomed in on the little red bump on my chin so that it took up half of her phone screen. "It will fill up with pus and look like a hot-air balloon, then pop off your face and zoom around making farting noises until it deflates and dies."

Stanley wouldn't care about that. We were best friends. *For goodness' sake,* I thought. *The boy still burps the alphabet for fun.*

"You totally freaked out there," she said.

"How did I freak out?" I asked, confused.

"At breakfast, just a few minutes ago. It's like you'd never heard of a security alarm before."

"I've heard of them." I knew the Agency wanted my parents to have one, but they'd refused. An alarm system would have drawn too much attention in a town like Silverton. Plus, who would service it? Silverton's too small to even have its own fire department.

Why hadn't the Cleaners contacted me before installing it? Still, it was a relief to know they were around. I was anxious to tell Aunt Gertie the good news. With the Agency in town, she'd be freed in no time. Part of me imagined the undercover agents had wired the museum, then marched straight down the street to the sheriff's office. In fact, Aunt Gertie was probably getting out of jail right this minute.

There was no way I could sit through a day of school, waiting to find out what fake excuse the Agency had used to free my aunt. The bus pulled up to its last stop in Silverton. An escape plan presented itself.

Victoria started to remove yet another horrific fluffy sweater she was wearing. While her arms and head were entwined in the bright yellow monstrosity, I dashed down the aisle, flashing an apologetic smile at Stanley and the Emmas. I pushed aside the younger kids who were scrambling to get seats, and I hopped off the bus. Before Bus Driver Mark could say a thing, I'd sprinted across the street and down the road.

I don't think I breathed until I reached the sheriff's office. The squeaky door was a welcome sound to my pounding heart. I burst through the second set of doors. "Aunt Gertie?"

"We're back here," Sheriff Baker answered.

I raced into the jail section. The two of them were drinking coffee and playing cards at the sheriff's desk. Discarded food containers from Mai's Diner were in the trash. Aunt Gertie's cell door was open. Had the Cleaners already asked for her release?

"Have you talked with them?" I asked Aunt Gertie.

"Your parents?" Sheriff Baker asked before my aunt could speak.

"No, not them. I mean the people who . . ." — I tried to think of a different word, but failed miserably — "clean the museum. They came yesterday." I couldn't talk too freely in front of the sheriff. "They did a nice job. Of cleaning. Don't you think, Aunt Gertie?"

"Mabel, I was here all night long." Aunt Gertie got up to hug me. "What are you talking about?"

Did she want a neon sign with fireworks going off around it? "Didn't the *cleaning* crew contact you?" I tried again, emphasizing the word "clean."

Aunt Gertie's bewildered face told me that she knew even less than I did.

"Jane has maid service for the Spoon?" Sheriff Baker asked.

"Yes. Yes, she does." I tried to think of a way to get my message across without blowing my parents' cover.

"That's new," the sheriff said as she reached for a pencil. "Gert, that's exactly the type of thing you should have told me about when I asked you if there was anything different going on with the Spoon. What is the name of this cleaning company, Mabel?"

"I don't remember. They only come randomly, and you wouldn't have heard of them, anyway. They're from out of town." *Stop babbling, Sunflower,* I thought. "But that's not important. This morning there's a security alarm on the museum," I blurted out.

Aunt Gertie had a shocked look on her face for a moment, but she recovered quickly. "Did you have pasta last night?" She paused, allowing me to make the connection. *Bow Tie.*

Sheriff Baker rolled her eyes. *Maybe I should fake a carbohydrate deficiency,* I thought.

"The water wouldn't boil," I said. "The museum key that normally hangs on the hook by our back door has been missing for a few days. You sent the *cleaning* crew to get it. Right?"

"No." Aunt Gertie turned to Sheriff Baker. "Prue, have you been able to reach Fred or Jane?"

The sheriff shook her head. "Neither of them has returned my phone calls."

"You called my mom and dad?"

Sheriff Baker nodded. "Ted gave me the numbers from the school's emergency contact list. Both went straight to voicemail."

"Oh, Mabel," Aunt Gertie said. "Have you talked with Principal Baker lately?"

What a weird question, I thought. "Yesterday," I answered.

"Isn't Ted's office so nice and sunny? Lots of flowers."

"Umm . . . sure."

"It's nicely decorated, too." Aunt Gertie winked at me when Sheriff Baker wasn't looking. "I noticed lots of good, helpful art on the walls when I visited in July."

Had jail cracked my aunt's mind? For one thing, the school had been closed in July. Second, one of Principal Baker's office walls was covered in student artwork. In fact, one of my drawings from first grade, a sunflower — *Oh!* I thought. *She must have hidden something there.* I nodded. *Message received.*

"When exactly were you arrested?" I asked.

"Inspector Montgomery returned to the Star's Tale on Sunday afternoon," Aunt Gertie said. "He and two state troopers questioned me for hours, then he formally arrested me."

"When the inspector showed up here with your aunt at six," Sheriff Baker said, "I thought it was some type of joke. It took him a while to convince me. Finally I called the state judge who'd signed the warrant. He wasn't pleased with being questioned by a small-town sheriff."

"Sunday was a regular day," I said, not mentioning that I'd sat in the Spoon for four hours by myself with no visitors. Then I'd walked the twenty steps or so to my house, ate leftovers by myself, and fell asleep reading, waiting for Aunt Gertie to arrive.

"Jane and Fred might not even know Gert is in the pokey." Sheriff Baker continued to fiddle with the playing cards.

"I wonder how Frankenstella arranged it all." I twisted a curl.

"I still don't see why Frank would or could orchestrate Gertie's arrest," Sheriff Baker said.

How can adults be so naive? I wondered. "Frank swore revenge in front of the whole town," I said. "Remember?"

"A grown man having a hissy fit, throwing plastic spoons everywhere in the mini-mart, is a sight no one in Silverton will soon forget," Sheriff Baker said. "Even so, I don't see how Frank could manipulate the state troopers into arresting your aunt and indicting your parents as the ringleaders of an international smuggling operation."

"Because Frankenstella are in cahoots —"

"Mabel." Aunt Gertie cut me off and gently tugged on one of my curls. "Don't interrupt the sheriff."

"This situation makes no sense." Sheriff Baker gathered the playing cards, tapped them lightly on the table, and put the deck in her desk drawer. She took out a notepad and pencil. "Mabel, have a seat, catch your breath, and think. Have you seen the alarm yourself?"

I shook my head.

"Well, that will be the second item on my agenda for today."

"What's number one?" came a deep voice. Montgomery stood in the doorway. I hadn't heard the front door squeak. Two state troopers stood behind him, blocking us all in.

"Good morning, Inspector." Sheriff Baker rose to greet him and shake his hand. Then she turned to the state troopers. "Trooper Raleigh," she said as she shook one trooper's hand, then turned to the other one. "Trooper Carson. To what do we owe the pleasure of your company on this lovely autumn day?"

How funny that both their last names are also state capitals, I thought. But with the surname Pear, who was I to mock their forefathers?

Wait a minute . . . I thought. *Montgomery is the state capital of Alabama.* Stella had called the inspector Al. Al . . . Alabama? There were no coincidences, only hard-to-trace links. That's what Mom always said.

"It's a good thing I'm here," Montgomery said. He pointed to Aunt Gertie. "Criminals should be behind bars."

"*Accused,*" Sheriff Baker corrected him. "Gertie is innocent until proven otherwise."

Montgomery handed Sheriff Baker a folded piece of paper.

She opened it up, and her lips grew tight as she read. "This is ridiculous. Gertrude Baies is the exact opposite of a flight risk," the sheriff said. "We all know she didn't steal that jewelry. She was too young when the original crime was reported."

"I'm the one who sold the necklace," I said. "Arrest me."

"While your family might be breaking child labor laws, that's not my domain," Montgomery said.

"Gertrude can stay here," the sheriff said. "At taxpayers' expense."

"Judge Pierre does not agree." Montgomery's eyes swept over the open jail cell. "I wonder what he'd think of you socializing with an *accused* criminal."

"Gertrude owns a home, has a business, and is involved with the community," Sheriff Baker said. "And she has strong family ties."

"Two of whom have already fled overseas." Montgomery motioned to the troopers. "Cuff her."

18

Most people believe what they want to believe, despite overwhelming evidence to the contrary. Don't be most people.

— Rule Number 14 from *Rules for a Successful Life as an Undercover Secret Agent*

"Why didn't you stop them?" I asked the sheriff. I felt tears well up, but I blinked them back.

"Montgomery had a judge's order," Sheriff Baker said. "I'm a lawman."

"Law*woman*," I muttered.

"I've sworn to uphold the law." I guess the sheriff saw my quivering bottom lip, because she quickly added, "And I firmly believe in your aunt's innocence. Can you tell me anything about why your parents left the country?"

Sure. *If* I wanted to betray them and the Agency, which I did not. "No."

"I didn't think so. You're just like your aunt." Sheriff Baker said as she grabbed a huge key ring from her desk. "That's a compliment, you know."

She handed me the transfer order. Gertie was being moved from Silverton's jail to state custody in Yakima, three hours and a couple of mountains away — all because of a lousy necklace and my parents' weird travel schedules. It was totally unfair.

"My parents didn't leave because they feared being arrested."

"Where are they?" she asked. "Don't say Monaco. We both know that's not true."

I closed my mouth. Stretching the truth wouldn't work this time.

"I've known your family since I married Ted and moved here to become sheriff. Gert was the first person to welcome me to Silverton. She's a good friend." Sheriff Baker looked at me with concern. "Mabel, if there is something I can do to help resolve this situation, would you tell me?"

"First, we should check out the alarm on the Spoon."

"Agreed."

Sheriff Baker was listening, really listening, to me. It had been weeks since anyone cared what I thought. I was tired of Victoria dragging me around and of Frankenstella trying to get intel out of me. Taking a minute to prioritize my thoughts, I said, "Then you should see if there is a criminal gang using state capitals as aliases."

"Mabel, be serious." Sheriff Baker shook her head.

"Montgomery, capital of Alabama; Raleigh, capital of North Carolina; Carson City, capital of Nevada. You don't think it's a strange coincidence?"

"No, Miss Pear, I do not. I think I'll wait until Miss Little Rock or Mr. Baton Rouge appears on the inspector's team before I start worrying about that. I do, however, have a sudden desire to bake a pear tart." The sheriff's mouth twitched upward.

"If you won't look into the state capital names, we should at least go to Yakima and get Aunt Gertie out."

"We can't do that." Sheriff Baker shook her head. "How about I take you to school after we inspect the museum? And then I'll call my contacts in the state troopers?"

What to do, Sunflower? The sheriff was taking some of my suggestions seriously, and she wasn't pressing me too hard about my parents. This seemed like the obvious place to compromise. "You'll call me at school if you learn anything?" I asked.

"Bluewater-Silverton Elementary is first on my speed dial," she said with a smile.

"Help! We need help!" a familiar voice called from the front room.

Sheriff Baker shot through the double doors in a flash. I followed, taking my time.

On the visitor's side of the information desk, Frank and Stella stood, his flabby arm around her bony shoulders. Her face was red and splotchy and she seemed sad — a look I'd never seen on her before. "Our niece is missing," Stella cried out. "Help us, please."

"I'm here," I said, wondering if it was too late to get myself arrested. Playing cards and eating take-out didn't look like that bad of a deal.

"Oh, thank the Lord." Stella rushed around the desk and enveloped me in a suffocating hug. "We were so worried when you disappeared." I pulled back as far as I could, which wasn't that far. For such skinny arms, they were all muscle.

On her left pinkie, a star ruby twinkled at me. *No way!* Stella was wearing my mom's engagement ring. Mom couldn't wear it on assignments because it was unique and, therefore, instantly recognizable.

Frank shook the sheriff's hand vigorously. "I don't know how you found her so quickly, but thank you." He turned to me. "Don't ever scare us again like that, Mabel Opal."

What was going on? How did they know I'd gotten off the bus? *Of course!* I thought. *Their little princess Vicky-girl must have ratted me out.* I tried to speak, but Stella hugged me again, her bony arms threatening to cut off my air supply.

"We know you're upset about Gertrude and your parents, but skipping school only hurts you." Stella patted a tissue to her dry cheek. "I just didn't know what we'd do if you had run away."

I stole a glance at the sheriff, but her face was unreadable. "I am going to escort Mabel to school now," she said.

"We can take her from here." Frankenstella each grabbed on to one of my black-and-blue arms and pulled. I now knew where Victoria got her brute strength. *Is it possible to die from bruising?* I wondered as they dragged me out the front door.

"Sheriff, are you going to . . ." I couldn't say what I wanted in front of Frankenstella. "Do the things we just talked about?"

"You do what you're supposed to," she said with a slight nod of her head. "And I'll do my job."

19

Everyone overlooks the quiet ones. Gather your ordinariness like an invisibility cloak and make some serious mischief.

— Rule Number 30 from *Rules for a Successful Life as an Undercover Secret Agent*

Frankenstella drove me to school and dropped me off without so much as an excuse note or a wave goodbye. In front of the L-shaped, three-story, two-toned gray school building was the entire Bluewater-Silverton Fire Department — three large ladder trucks and one small emergency vehicle. The fire chief had a stopwatch in one hand and a clipboard in another. He was laughing with Principal Baker, so I was pretty sure this was a drill.

Ms. Drysdale waved to me from our designated emergency meeting spot. "Mabel, where have you been?" She checked my name on her clipboard.

I shrugged, not wanting to explain myself. Thankfully, Ben threw a soccer ball at Doug's head just a moment later, demanding her attention. I walked past everyone to my place at the front of the line. Being the shortest was the worst.

"Mabel, you OK?" Emma G. asked. "Why'd you run off the bus?"

"Didn't you hear us calling you to come back?" Emma H. asked.

"Are you sad about your aunt?" Grace K. asked.

"My dad says the real crime is not having your aunt's gluten-free blueberry scones in the morning," Emma Z. said. "He says no one who bakes like Ms. Gertrude Baies could be a criminal."

"It's OK to cry," Grace T. said, putting a gentle hand on my shoulder. "I cried all day when my cat died."

Victoria stood at the back of the line, chatting with the Hannahs.

"Is something else wrong, Mabel?" Grace L. chimed in. "Did you get motion sick? On car trips, my little brother has to sit next to a window, otherwise he just pukes everywhere."

"I'm OK," I said. "I just forgot something at home." *Like how to get Aunt Gertie out of prison while keeping my parents' secret about the Great Reverse Heist under wraps. And, oh yeah, not telling anyone my parents are Cleaners off on a mission, which will probably help everyone on Earth, but no one can know about it.* "No big deal."

"When you're feeling sad about your aunt, you can tell us," Emma G. said. "My grandma always says if you share your troubles with your friends, your friendship will grow stronger and your troubles will grow smaller."

"Thanks, Emma," I said, knowing I could never share my troubles. I gave her the best smile I could. "But like I said, I just forgot something."

Stanley stared at me, his eyebrows wiggling like mad, but his lips pressed tightly together as if it was taking a lot of self-control to keep his thoughts to himself. This wasn't the time or place to talk.

"Hey, Moppet," Grace K. said. "Is your spoon museum still open?"

"Not today," I said.

"Tomorrow?" Grace K. asked.

"I don't know. Why?"

"My parents thought that my uncle would like to visit it. He used to live in Silverton a long time ago. He's into history and old stuff. Could you let us in?" she asked. "Soon?"

"I don't know," I said. "It's sort of a bad time."

Queen Bee Hannah was examining Victoria's bracelets with loud *oohs* and *ahhs* when she started clapping her hands. "I have the best theme for the next sleepover. Listen up, everyone."

"We already have a theme," Emma G. said. "Halloween and Mabel's birthday. And she really needs a party right now." She turned to me, her smile bright. "Right? You promised you'd come."

The two Hannahs, the two other Emmas, and the four Graces all stopped talking and stared at me.

Blood rushed to my cheeks. The weight of their stares increased. No one said a word. "Yeah, I did," I said. I scrambled to think of an excuse — apparently, no one cared that my aunt was in jail. "But that was before Victoria came. It would be rude of me to leave her." *Even if an evening of goofing off does sound fun,* I thought.

"Oh, silly Mabel," Queen Bee Hannah laughed. "Of course Victoria is coming to the sleepover. Her bracelets are the theme's inspiration. You're coming, right?" she said, turning to my cousin.

"Why not?" Victoria said in a careless tone, but she didn't fool me. She stood a little straighter, and her eyes sparkled. "What do you have in mind?"

"Well," Princess Bee Hannah said. "First, we'll trick-or-treat in Bluewater. Fortunately, this week's host, Grace T., lives three blocks from Marmot Lane."

"Every house on Marmot Lane gives full-sized candy bars," Grace T. said. "And last year, there were two haunted houses. And my parents will let us walk there by ourselves. And —"

"And," Princess Bee Hannah said the word with such emphasis, Grace T. stopped talking at once. "We'll get to celebrate Mabel's birthday with her."

"This will be so great." Emma G. hugged me, jumping up and down.

It would be great . . . if I knew where my parents were, I thought.

"My mom will make your costumes tonight," Princess Bee Hannah said to Victoria and me.

"Our costumes?" Victoria asked.

Princess Bee Hannah eyed Victoria and me, marking something down on a notepad, probably our heights. "This year's theme is a surprise, known only to me and Hannah."

"We always dress as a group," Emma G. said. "It's going to be great. Aren't you excited, Mabel?"

"Yeah, excitement," I mumbled. "That's what I need now. More excitement in my life."

Just then, the fire chief blew his whistle, signaling the end of the fire drill.

"Good job," Mr. Baker said over a megaphone. "You've earned an extra ten-minute recess, starting now."

All craziness broke loose. Ben and Doug's roughhousing entrapped more of the boys, plus a few soccer balls. As the HEGs continued discussing the upcoming sleepover, Stanley headed to the side yard where the little kids played.

Emma G. was distracted, so I took the opportunity to follow Stanley. He stopped once we were around the corner and out of sight from the big kids' yard. Stanley leaned against the wall, looking straight ahead. "I wanted to show you my photos," he said.

"Later, maybe?" I said. The trees could wait. "I have to get into Principal Baker's office when he's not there."

"Too bad you missed this morning's fire drills," Stanley said. "During the first one, three first graders went out the wrong door and were waiting on the baseball fields. You would have had at least twenty minutes uninterrupted."

"I can't wait a month for the next drill." I slouched against the cold wall. *Buck up, Sunflower. You're on a mission.*

"I know," Stanley said. I could tell he'd started thinking because his eyebrows were wiggling a mile a minute. "We do it at two for maximum payoff."

"Do what at two?"

"Another fire drill would give you another chance to get into Mr. Baker's office. I overhead the fire chief say he and the rest of the crew are doing avalanche rescue training on Mount Rainier at one this afternoon. By two o'clock, they should be high up on a glacier, way out of cell phone range."

"Aren't they supposed to leave someone at the fire station?"

"Yeah, but the guy who usually covers is out on vacation, so they're rerouting all the calls to Enumclaw."

"That's thirty minutes away," I said. "If there's no traffic."

"Exactly. They'll only come if it's a real emergency." Stanley nodded. "The chief was thanking Principal Baker for being flexible. Our monthly fire drill was scheduled for this afternoon, but the principal changed it as a favor to the chief."

"So, maybe they'll double-check before sending a truck and ladder out?" I couldn't believe I was going to break the law again. "You know, Stanley, it's illegal to pull the fire alarm without cause."

"I know." Stanley paused. His eyes darted around. "It's Tuesday. PE is in the afternoon today. There's an alarm near the gym water fountain that's out of everyone's sight. If someone were to pull it, no one would see."

My cheeks flushed just thinking about it. "We'll get in big trouble."

Stanley shook his head. "Only if we get caught."

* * *

A school day has never lasted so long. Ms. Drysdale taught American history as if it were the most fascinating subject on Earth. Today I just couldn't care that William Taft was the first president to have a car at the White House, or the first president to play golf, or the first president to throw out a baseball on Opening Day. His picture reminded me of Frank, only happier looking, better dressed, and with an impressive handlebar mustache.

At lunchtime, Victoria sat at the head of the table with Queen Bee Hannah and Princess Bee Hannah. The other HEGs clustered around her, paying homage to the new princess. She passed out her bracelets, letting everyone try them on, as if the bracelets in Washington were subpar to the ones from Alaska. Emma G. sat next to me, going on and on about how much fun my birthday was going to be. I tried to sound interested, but it was hard to care about what color hair ribbon we should wear to mark my eleventh birthday when my parents were missing.

In PE, we played kickball. I had just struck out and was sitting on the sidelines when I looked at the clock. 1:58. Stanley stepped into the path of an oncoming ball and he was already jogging toward the water fountain when Coach Wilson yelled, "Out!"

My mouth grew dry and my palms sweaty and my stomach heaved itself into my throat. *It's go time, Sunflower!*

Stanley bent over the water fountain, his right hand on the button. From my side of the gym, it looked like he was just getting a drink of water. *Come on, Stanley,* I thought. *Pull the alarm, already.* His body tilted toward the left a few inches. The screeching of the fire alarm caught everyone by surprise. Well, everyone except Stanley and me.

I took advantage of the confusion and ran out of the gym toward the main hallway. Kids poured out of their classes and headed for the exits, looking thrilled. Teachers looked exasperated. Following Stanley's advice, I ducked into our pre-arranged meeting spot: the downstairs boys' restroom.

The restroom's heavy wooden door was propped open, probably to let in fresh air. I huddled in the last stall until Stanley showed up a couple minutes later.

In the hallway, Ms. Jones, the office secretary, was rushing everyone out of the building. Principal Baker followed, saying, "It was still on the schedule. Who was supposed to cancel it?"

I counted to ten silently, then motioned for Stanley to follow me. His job was to stand guard outside Principal Baker's office. We had come up with a signal. If Stanley was spotted, he would break out in a coughing fit. We sneaked down the hallway, looking left and right. The screeching of the fire alarm echoed through the empty building. The door to the administrative offices was ajar.

Stanley sat on the bench outside. He smiled and gave me two thumbs up. I pushed the door open slightly, just enough to squeeze through. When I got through, though, the door to the principal's office was shut. My heart sank. Taking a deep breath to steady myself, I walked over to it and tried the knob. It turned. I was in.

Wasting no time, I went directly to my painting of the sunflower, which hung on the lower left side of the wall. It had three thumbtacks holding it up. The others only had one.

That's because they weren't as heavy.

I lifted the paper and found a medium-sized Ziploc bag taped to the back of my sunflower painting. I carefully removed the tape and opened the bag to find several papers inside. I unfolded them. First was a sketch of a room. It was empty of all furniture, but I felt I had seen this place before. It looked big with a low ceiling. Second was a blueprint — the type architects use for buildings. The third had seemingly random sets of letters and numbers. There were several more pages, which I flicked through quickly, until suddenly, the shrieking alarm stopped.

The hair on the back of my neck rose. I turned and looked out the window to the playground. Victoria stood on the other side of the open window. Her purple smartphone was aimed at me. "What do you have there, Moppet?" she asked.

"Nothing." I replaced the sunflower painting and refolded the papers to fit into their plastic bag.

"That doesn't look like nothing to me." She placed one hand on an ear. "Hear that?"

"No," I said.

"Mrs. Drysdale is calling for us to line up." She smirked. "Time to go now. Better hurry with that *nothing*."

I shoved the bag down my shirt and dashed out of Mr. Baker's office, out of the main office, and into the hallway. Voices came from around the corner.

Then Stanley cleared his throat. Was that his idea of a coughing fit?

I started limping and sniffling. *The best defense is a good offense,* Dad said every Sunday during football season. "Hey," I called out in the weakest voice I could manage while still projecting it down the hallway. "Help. It hurts." I crossed my fingers and hoped Stanley remembered his part.

Principal Baker appeared around the corner, with Stanley following.

"See," Stanley said, scowling at the principal. "I told you Mabel was hurt. I was just trying to be a good citizen like you said we should all be at last Friday's assembly."

"OK, I'm sorry I doubted you." Mr. Baker shook his head. "You kids know you have to evacuate the building when the fire alarm sounds."

"I'm sorry." I dry sobbed, as if I was trying hard to keep the pain in. "It's just — my leg." I took a big, sharp breath in. "It hurts so much I couldn't." Another gasp. "And Stanley was the only one who waited for me."

By this time, students and teachers were re-entering the school.

"The alarm was manually activated," Ms. Jones said to the principal as she ushered children down the hallway. "This was not a computer generated drill."

"I don't suppose either of you know anything about this fire alarm." Principal Baker glared at Stanley and me.

I moaned and made big puppy eyes, grabbing my leg for dramatic effect.

Principal Baker ran his hands through his short hair, shrugged, and said to Stanley, "Get her some ice from the nurse and return to wherever you're supposed to be."

Stanley got one of the freezer packs from the nurse's office and gave it to me as we returned to the gym for the last five minutes of class. I limped to keep up my cover story.

"Did you get what you needed?" Stanley asked in a low voice.

"Got something," I whispered. I wasn't sure what I had.

"Mabel." Suddenly Victoria's arm was around my shoulders. I almost jumped out of my skin. The plastic bag stuck to the sweat of my stomach. "Let me help you to the girls' locker room."

"I'm fine. Thanks."

"Oh, I think you *need* my help." She glared at Stanley until he drifted into the boys' locker room. Victoria made sure no one was near us. "I'll keep your secret, but you owe me."

I said nothing.

She tossed her perfectly straight, super glossy red hair over her shoulder. "We break into the museum tonight and your boyfriend is not invited to our party."

20

Be in control. Act. Be the one who chooses the time and place for action. Only retaliate if absolutely necessary. Know the difference between reacting and responding.

— Rule Number 15 from *Rules for a Successful Life as an Undercover Secret Agent*

Victoria sat next to me on the bus, allowing no one, especially Stanley, to come near. I couldn't wait to get home so I could examine my stolen — liberated, I mean — documents in private. At that moment, in all honesty, I just wanted to peel the plastic baggie off of my sweaty stomach.

Of course, as soon as I walked through my front door, I wished I had stayed on the bus. Frankenstella were waiting for me.

"Get everything on the list," Stella said, holding a piece of paper and a wad of crumpled-up dollar bills. I'd bet my last cinnamon bun (if I ever had another cinnamon bun, that is) the money had come from Dad's "driving words" cookie jar, which had more than fifty-three dollars last time we counted. "Is that clear?" she asked.

I almost answered "yes" until I realized that Stella was trying to give the money and list to Victoria. I had to elbow my cousin, who was staring at her phone.

"Where am I supposed to go?" Victoria whined.

"The mini-mart is on the next block," Frank said. He pointed to a seat at the kitchen table. "Mabel, sit." Victoria walked out the front door without a second glance.

Though I really wanted to ignore Frank's order, I figured that Rule Number 18 should guide my actions in this situation: *If captured by the enemy, play along and be agreeable. Lie if you have to. You will not get in trouble.* I was determined to be nice and would lie to protect my parents' secrets.

Frank lowered himself into a chair across from me. "Mabel, do you know where the museum key is?"

"No." If my prediction was correct, the New Orleans spoon collection buyer would be coming in two days — on Thursday, October thirtieth. *They must be getting worried,* I thought.

"Moppet," Stella asked, "do you remember the alarm code or password?" She was standing next to Frank.

"Nope." I stared at my aunt's ears. She was now wearing Mom's pearl and garnet drop earrings and a garnet pendant. For a thief, Stella had really good taste.

"Do you know how to contact PNW Security?" Frank asked.

"No."

"You must remember the alarm code and find the missing key today," Frank said. He clenched his hands. "Or you will be very, very, very sorry." He thudded the table with each "very" in case I missed his threatening tone.

I laid my hands flat on the table and met his eyes. "I don't know anything about an alarm." I paused. I was pretty sure my common sense was yelling at me to stop and think about what I was going to say. I ignored it. Sometimes you have to say the truth, no matter the consequences. "But I do know who's been stealing my mother's jewelry."

"How dare you!" Stella slapped the table. I guess no one liked the poor table today.

"The key is the first issue here." Frank laid his hands flat on the table, just inches from mine. "What do you know about the key?"

"They're used for opening locks."

"Don't be a smart aleck, Mabel," Stella said. "The security alarm wasn't there in June. When did your parents install it?"

"I don't know," I replied. Of course, they hadn't installed it, but I could hardly tell Frankenstella that, could I?

"When's your birthday?" Frank asked.

"Throwing me a party?"

"Using the wrong code is too risky," Stella said to Frank before she stared at me, raw hatred distorting her face. "He warned us."

Who? Who warned you? I wanted to ask.

"Look, Frank, if we can get in there soon, we can cut *him* out and keep everything for ourselves."

"It's his buyer — er, friend — who is interested," Frank said. "And he hasn't told us his friend's name."

Buyer? I thought. *I knew it.*

"We can make other *friends*," Stella said. "*Friends* will come to us. What's important now is that the code has to be correct the first time." Her freaky smile returned. "And I know just how to jog poor little Moppet's memory."

Victoria, bless her bratty self, waltzed in the back door and said, "There is nothing I'd eat at that mini-mart."

Frank and Stella glanced at each other.

"Moppet, you have one hour to find *everything*," Stella said, looking around the kitchen. "How can you stand to live in such filth? Clean up this kitchen." Shaking her head in dismay, she stormed out, fussing at "Vicky-girl" to hurry up if she wanted food. A minute later, Frankenstella and their offspring — who, I was pretty sure, had just saved me some unpleasantness — drove off in my mom's car.

How did they expect me to find a key, find a code, and clean the kitchen in one hour?

The only important question on my mind was *what was in the liberated documents?* I peeled the baggie off my stomach, determined to find out.

A soft *thunk* at the back door startled me. I eased it open and was relieved to find Stanley, pinecone in hand, standing in my backyard. I wanted to hug him so badly, but I didn't because I knew he wouldn't like it.

"I saw Frankenstella leave. How much time do we have?"

"An hour, but it may be best if you went home. I don't want to get you in trouble."

"Trouble is just another word for adventure." Stanley brushed his wavy hair off of his face and smiled. "My dad used to say he learned the most when he figured out how to get out of trouble. Also he had the most fun."

I was pretty sure Stanley's mom didn't share that view. "Getting caught is not fun."

"No one saw today, Mabel. Don't worry so much."

I didn't bother to correct him and tell him about all

the many things there were to worry about. The less Stanley knew about Victoria and my family, the better for all of us.

"You might need this if you get into some sort of jam when I'm not around to help," Stanley said, shuffling his feet as he took out his favorite pocketknife.

"Um," I said. *Get a grip, Sunflower.* "Thanks, Stanley. That's really thoughtful of you. But I have one." I took out my pocketknife, and its wooden sides gleamed in the light.

"Oh, that is a good one." Stanley started fiddling with my knife's blades and gadgets. "What's this skeleton key for?" He opened up his knife, but there wasn't a key on it.

"A tiny lock," I guessed. "I need to examine the documents and make a game plan."

"And clean the kitchen. I've never seen your house like this before." Stanley glanced at the pile of teetering dishes. "Tell you what. I'll wipe down the counters and table, sweep the floor, and then dry for you if you wash those."

"Thank you," I said. "That's really kind of you, Stanley."

He shrugged off my thanks and started whistling as we worked. So, while I might have been cleaning the kitchen like Stella ordered me to, it didn't feel that way. I was cleaning my house with help from a friend. I powered through the dishes in less than ten minutes.

On the newly cleaned kitchen table, I spread out the papers Aunt Gertie had hidden in Principal Baker's office: the sketch of the big, empty room with a low ceiling, the blueprint, the paper with letters and numbers, another drawing — definitely inside the Spoon — and others. What did these items have to do with the museum or my parents? I pointed to what looked like swirls of various shades of green inside rectangles. In one of the rectangles, there were two orange dots. "This is a topographic map, right?"

"With no markings. That makes it useless. How strange," Stanley said. "The U.S. Geographical Survey mapped every inch of the continental United States. If we only knew which quadrangle it represents, the locations marked by the dots would be easy to find."

Stella had said something about the Baies women having the silver, the museum, and a map. *Could this be the map she was talking about?* I wondered. "How can we use it when there aren't any names or landmarks on it?"

"It's obviously a heavily forested area," Stanley said, his eyebrows wiggling in thought.

"The darker the green, the denser the trees," I guessed.

"I can compare it to a master map I have at home."

Of course he has a "master map," I thought. Stanley carefully recorded every hike we did. While I couldn't tell him any family secrets, I knew I could trust him. Feeling calmer, I gave the map to Stanley for safekeeping.

The blueprint was of my house. Maybe those 1960s hippie contractors Dad complained about so often did know what they were doing. A blueprint is just a type of map detailing the construction of a house. Why Aunt Gertie felt the need to hide it, or a drawing of the Spoon's interior, was beyond me. I twirled a curl behind my left ear as I paced around the kitchen.

"Mabel." Stanley pointed to a tiny trail of dirt, running from the sink to me. It came from the cuff of my jeans.

"Ugh. You'd better go, Stanley." I couldn't remember the last time I'd washed my jeans. "I have laundry to do, and Frankenstella will be back here soon."

"See you tomorrow," Stanley said as he grabbed a bag of chips from our pantry so he wouldn't starve on the way home, then hustled out the back door. I carefully hid the liberated documents in the living room. Stella had ransacked it the very first day she arrived, so I figured the papers would be safe in *The Definitive Northern Italian Cookbook*. I changed into a pair of old pink sweatpants. After I gathered my dirty clothes from the bathroom hamper, I headed into the basement feeling like Cinderella.

A blast of cold air greeted me. The sole source of light — a bare light bulb that dangled from the ceiling — cast a lonely shadow on the washer and dryer.

I loaded up the washing machine, remembering to remove Aunt Gertie's phone from my jeans pocket. Since I had nothing better to do, I dialed Ms. Bow Tie's number. I let it ring ten or twenty times, but no one picked up. It never went to voicemail. *How would voicemail sound for a top secret agency?* I wondered. *Something like, "Hello. Please leave a message and then forget all about it."* It would've been better than the endless ringing, at least.

As I waited for someone to answer the phone, I glanced around the basement. My cast-off dollhouse and discarded science experiments were piled in a corner on top of a blue tarp. Stacks of large Tupperware boxes covered the back wall. An old chair leaned against the side wall. The basement felt damp and chilly, but that wasn't what caused the hair on my neck to stand up. I had that weird feeling — the one I get when someone is watching.

I hung up the phone and examined the room. No other living creatures except for spiders were there with me. There was something odd about the basement — it was tidy.

For a second, I imagined the basement totally empty. It was big and the ceiling was low, just like in the drawing. Suddenly it hit me: this was the room! This was the drawing that was so important Aunt Gertie had hid it at Bluewater-Silverton Unified Elementary School, after Frankenstella's disastrous visit in June. *What could be in here?* I wondered.

The Cleaners equipment — of course! Somewhere in the piles of boxes were emergency supplies.

Each container was marked with its contents: Christmas decorations, Halloween, swim & summer, Valentine's Day, Easter, Thanksgiving, and camping. Everything looked normal, except I couldn't remember my parents ever putting up decorations for Valentine's Day. They'd never even given each other cards or flowers.

I moved the containers until I had the Valentine's Day box open. To my surprise, the top layer was actually a bunch of valentines. All of the little lace hearts and red-foil creations I had made for my parents over the years were stored in it. Even a red and pink finger painting of a heart that I'd made in kindergarten was here, with "Love, MOP" smeared proudly on the side.

However, that layer wasn't deep at all. Underneath were three portable lanterns, a pack of batteries, a flashlight, four bottles of water, two emergency freeze-dried food packets, a key (*another key!*) taped to the side, a blue blanket, and — surprise, surprise — a slim, silver cell phone. In all honesty, I'd been hoping for something more helpful, like an instruction manual entitled, *So the Cleaners Are Out of Town and the Enemy Has Taken Over Your House.*

I tugged at the blanket, but it was stuck inside the container. I dug my fingers into it and found that it was wedged around something hard. I put batteries into one of the lanterns to take a closer look. Peeling back the blue blanket, I saw red.

I tipped the plastic container onto its side and wiggled the red thing out, along with the blue blanket that was still partially wrapped around it. I realized at once what it was.

The red suitcase. The one from the photograph that Montgomery had showed me. The one Frank badgered everyone about. The one that sent my father's tingly spy sense into overdrive. The one thing that made my parents decide to train me for the Great Reverse Heist.

My parents had found it. Obviously. They found it, hid it, and didn't tell me. I couldn't believe it. My rat fink parents had just left me here with it, along with Frankenstella and everyone else who wanted to get their grubby hands on it.

Whatever the red suitcase really was — whatever was inside of it — Montgomery wanted it. Frankenstella wanted it. And now I had it. A numerical combination lock was built into its top. I tried random numbers but nothing worked.

The *Rules* hadn't prepared me for this. Actually Rule Number 21 sort of had: *Assume every agent is a double agent. Could Mom and Dad be double agents?* I wondered. But I refused to believe my parents were the bad guys, no matter what Montgomery said.

If only someone from the Agency would help me, I thought. I tried using Gertie's phone and dialed Ms. Bow Tie once more for old time's sake. Nada.

I picked up the shiny silver cell phone I'd just found in the box and dialed the same phone number. Nothing happened. Desperate, I tried Roy's number. It rang twice before rumbling sounds, like traffic, filled my ear.

"Hello," I whispered, since that seemed to be the right way to talk on a spy phone. "Can you hear me?"

I heard breathing.

"Do you know who I am?" I asked.

I thought I heard an "mmmm."

I couldn't start talking about the Agency because I wasn't one hundred percent sure that this was a secure line, so I just asked, "Can you help me?"

No reply. Then the sound of breathing dropped off. I had been disconnected.

I dialed several more times, but it just rang and rang and rang.

What kind of Agency couldn't answer their phones? No wonder they'd lost my parents.

21

Always have a Plan B. And a Plan C. A Plan D would be good too.

— Rule Number 16 from *Rules for a Successful Life as an Undercover Secret Agent*

What was the point of having these cell phones if no one from the Agency answered them? I imagined Roy, Angry Woman, Ms. Bow Tie, and Unknown Breathing Person sitting around an office table at the Agency, staring at the ringing phones, saying, "I got the last emergency. Your turn," while eating take-out Chinese food.

After I put both phones in my pocket, I moved the laundry into the dryer. Looking through some of the other boxes, I couldn't figure out a use for our inflatable Rudolph or life jackets. Then I went back to the original Valentine's box and picked up the key — smaller than a normal door key — and slipped it into my sock. After hiding a bottle of water and a food packet behind the washer, I put the rest away just as I'd found it. I returned to the kitchen, which was cleaner than it had been since Sunday.

There was still no sign of Frankenstella. I hadn't yet had a chance to examine the new alarm system on Le Petit Musée of Antique Silver Spoons, and this seemed as good an opportunity as any.

As I opened the back door, I heard an angry male voice.

I popped my head out. The man, facing away from me, stood on the museum's back porch next door — Inspector Montgomery. He was supposed to be on his way to Yakima with Aunt Gertie.

He said, "The roadblock is holding."

I leaned against the back door, holding my breath.

"Look harder. PNW Security has to exist somewhere." Montgomery said each word very carefully, just like my teacher did when she was about to hold the whole class in from recess for misbehaving. "It's either our shell, one of our competitors', or theirs."

Shell? As in a fake company?

"No sign of the red case yet, Jackson," Montgomery said.

Wrong, I thought. But I wasn't going to point that out to the inspector.

Montgomery's footsteps reverberated on the back porch. "Not a lot of crime here. Town's pretty much the same as it was thirty years ago. The sheriff is a rule follower, but she's not stupid." Montgomery kept talking as he walked closer to the Star's Tale and out of my hearing range.

I wanted to sneak after Montgomery, but the familiar whine of my mom's car meant that Frankenstella had returned. I grabbed the broom and pretended I was still sweeping the kitchen floor. The car doors slammed, and a moment later Frankenstella thudded into the house.

"Remember anything yet?" Stella asked, barreling into the kitchen.

"No, ma'am." I stood straight and didn't fidget. "My mother never told me the alarm code."

Stella eyed my legs, and asked, "How did you get so filthy?"

I looked down at my pink sweatpants, now brown and grubby. "I was doing laundry." To cut off further questioning, I returned to the basement and waited until the dryer buzzed.

As I was making my way into the kitchen with the clothes basket, Stella pursed her lips. "Take a shower before dinner."

"And hurry up," Frank snapped as he dumped deli food onto serving plates.

"Five minutes," Stella added.

Is five minutes the only time interval the woman knows?

The aroma of rotisserie chicken caused my stomach to growl as I stomped out of the room and leapt up the stairs.

Oh, joy. When I turned the corner at the top of the staircase, I could see that Victoria was already reclining on my bed. Her air mattress lay on the other side of the room. She had my glittery pumpkin next to her on my bedspread. I quickly looked around my room. The invisible *Rules*, the world map, the origami solar system, the fourteen plastic sunflowers — everything was in its proper place, except for the pumpkin. I picked it up and returned it to its rightful place on my dresser, next to the sunflowers.

"Ready yet?" Victoria was furiously typing away on a tiny laptop.

"No." Was everyone in the Frankenstella family impatient all the time? "I have to shower first."

"Obviously." She cast a disdainful glance in my direction. "Why won't my web page load?"

"The mountain," I said.

"What does that chunk of rock have to do with the Internet?"

I skipped the lecture that Mount Rainier was actually considered one of the world's most dangerous volcanoes, and at more than fourteen thousand feet high, it was way bigger than a chunk. "Some days it casts a weather shadow, and the Internet can't get through," I told her. A half-accurate answer, but I had five minutes to shower and I wasn't going to waste any more of it. Besides, what would I say? In reality, my parents had high-tech shielding around the house that allowed cell phones to work, but screened all Internet traffic through a super-secret encoded transmission thingy. I obviously couldn't tell Victoria that.

"I need to show you what we're going to do." Victoria tried a different web address.

"What do you mean?"

"The audition for the show. All the rules are on their site." She tried reloading the page, but nothing happened. "Silverton sucks."

"Four minutes." Stella's voice bellowed up from the first floor. She could count backward, I'll give her that.

"Later." I grabbed some warm clothes from the laundry basket and ran into the bathroom.

22

Just be around a lot. The enemy will get so used to seeing you, they'll no longer notice you.

— Rule Number 2 from *Rules for a Successful Life as an Undercover Secret Agent*

The dinner table conversation reminded me of dialogue from a bad sitcom. Frankenstella asked "Vicky-girl" about her day. She chatted cheerfully about all the supernice girls in class. I refrained from talking since I was busy stuffing my mouth. I never thought cold roasted chicken, congealing mashed potatoes, and soggy mixed veggies could taste so good.

Just as I was wondering why I had been allowed to eat at the table like a regular person, the doorbell rang. Stella's smile looked practiced as she said, "Vicky-girl, why don't you see who's visiting us at dinnertime?"

Victoria exchanged a glance with her father that I could not decipher. He motioned with his hand for her to hurry up and answer the door.

I kept shoveling chicken into my mouth, focusing on eating as much as possible while I was allowed a spot at the table.

A memory struck me and I was ashamed. A few days ago, I got annoyed by Aunt Gertie's homemade cinnamon buns. What I wouldn't give to have her free and here with me now.

When Victoria returned from the front door with a too-bright smile on her face, she was accompanied by Principal Baker.

"Mr. Baker, what a pleasant surprise," Stella's voice was smooth and warm, yet her words rushed together. "We weren't expecting company." She grabbed a plate and silverware, which were sitting on the kitchen counter next to the Safeway deli containers. "We have more than enough to go around. Please join us."

Was this the same Stella Baies who had kicked the principal out of the house yesterday, slamming the door in his face?

I stopped eating, thought about pointing out her inconsistencies, thought again about how that would not work out well for me, and resumed eating.

"I didn't mean to interrupt your dinner." Principal Baker blushed beet red. "I just wanted to check on Mabel's leg."

Oh, stupid me. I forgot my cover story. *Get a hold of yourself, Sunflower.* "It's fine."

Frank stopped eating. "What happened to Mabel's leg?"

"She hurt it during the fire drill," Victoria said. "She must have tripped over her own short legs trying to get away."

"During PE, actually." I glared at my cousin.

"You're healthy now." Stella sipped from her diet cola.

"Must have just been a strained muscle," I said. "The ice pack worked wonders."

"You seem awfully concerned about her." Frank frowned at Principal Baker. "I don't remember my elementary school principal ever making house calls. Much less two of them in as many days."

"That would have been Mrs. Klebba, if I remember correctly." Principal Baker stared right back at my uncle. "You probably spent enough time in her office that she didn't need to." After a beat, he turned his gaze to me. "Mabel, everything else OK?"

"She's upset about Gertrude's arrest," Stella answered before I could say anything. "I know I was being too softhearted, letting her stay home yesterday. I hope that wasn't a problem for you."

Let me stay home. Ha! I didn't know who was a better liar — Frank, Stella, or Victoria. But everyone was staring at me, so I meekly nodded.

Principal Baker left soon after, since it was obvious I wasn't going to say anything incriminating. Stella whisked my plate of food away as soon as he was out the door. No cold, factory-made apple pie with non-dairy whipped topping for me. Frankenstella sent Victoria and me to my room. I wondered what "Vicky-girl" had done to provoke her parents, but I had the feeling she wouldn't share even if I asked.

"Family fun time is over," Victoria said, plopping onto my bed and opening her laptop. "At least Principal Baker's visit scored us an almost complete meal."

"How did they know he was coming?" I asked.

"My parents hear things. Sometimes they even listen. Sometimes." Victoria clicked the back button on the Internet browser until she found a cached website. "Read this."

Two guys in their mid-twenties were in what looked like a cave. They had headlamps strapped to their foreheads and were standing in front of a yellow and black no trespassing sign with their thumbs up and stupid grins plastered on their grimy faces.

The website, exploringlockedplaces.com, said, "We don't recommend going where you don't belong, especially if you're under eighteen. However, if you do find yourself on the wrong side of a locked door, record your adventure, send it to us, and we might just make you famous. If you dare!"

"That's breaking and entering," I said. "They're encouraging kids to break the law. For entertainment. And the worst part is that the kids are supplying the evidence to be used against them."

"A kid might get community service," Victoria said. "No big deal."

"The punishment doesn't matter. It's still illegal."

Victoria tapped her purple phone. "How illegal?"

"I don't know," I said. "Illegal means it's against the law. That pretty much sums it up."

A self-satisfied grin, so much like her mother's, spread across Victoria's face. "Like pulling a fire alarm and stealing something from the principal's office? That type of illegal?" She waved her phone, keeping it far from my grasp.

I'd have to find a way to erase yet another video from that evil device. I knew when I was beat. Or I at least knew to follow Rule Number 27: *Keep your friends close and your enemies closer. Invite your archenemies over for tea and cookies. It will confuse them.*

Victoria and I may not be baking buddies, but I could at least go to her tea party. "What do you want from me?" I asked.

"It's three days till the thirty-first."

"I'm well aware of the countdown to Halloween."

"That's the deadline to submit my adventure." Victoria tapped her wrist with its nonexistent watch. "Since I'm obviously going to have to download and edit the video at school, far away from Mount Rainier's shadow, we'll need a few days to make sure we've got it right."

I twirled a curl behind my left ear. "What do I have to do?" I tried to keep my voice light and friendly, but my spy sense — and my common sense — were practically yelling at me to stop and think. I was going to ignore them again.

"We break in," Victoria said. "You film me the entire time so I get the credit and you don't have to show your scaredy-cat face."

Small favor, but I'd take it. "And how will this convince your parents to move out of town?"

"Once *Exploring Locked Places* chooses my video, I'll be famous."

I still thought she had a better chance of being struck by lightning while Hula-Hooping at a Seahawks' game, but I kept that to myself.

"And then we're off to Los Angeles," Victoria said, pointing to California on the world map.

"Sounds good to me."

"Plus, it will really tick off my parents if I get into the museum before they do." Victoria's eyes shone with excitement. "They will go ballistic."

They weren't the only ones. I was pretty sure that angry woman from the Agency would have more than a few choice words for me.

"And we — you and me, Cousin Mabel — will be the ones who outsmarted them." Victoria kneeled on the floor and gathered her long red hair into a ponytail, just like Aunt Gertie often did. "It will be so much fun. Think of their reactions."

I shivered. I didn't have to imagine — I knew. So much yelling. "What if we get caught?"

"You and your boyfriend didn't get caught today."

"Stanley is not my boyfriend."

"Whatever." Victoria smirked. "What do you think will happen if I tell my parents that it was you and your boy, who is not a friend, who set off the fire alarm today and stole papers from the principal's office?"

The blood drained from my head. I didn't care about myself, but Stanley shouldn't have to pay for my choices. His mother, who was really strict, would not laugh it off as an adventure. Just for starters, he'd lose his camera and not be allowed to go on hikes for months. Plus, if Frankenstella knew about the papers, I wouldn't be safe. "That's blackmail."

"I like to think of it as persuasion," Victoria said. She pointed to the website on the computer and then back to the purple menace. "This time I uploaded the video to my cloud account, so erasing it from my phone won't help you."

"Why can't you get famous in a normal way, like taking some singing or acting lessons and then going on YouTube?"

"Look, I don't care why you were in the principal's office." Victoria sighed dramatically as she plucked an invisible piece of lint from her jeans. "Or what you stole. But I think other people, like Principal Baker and my parents, might feel differently."

I rolled my eyes.

Victoria took a flashlight out of her backpack. "You are so lucky, Mabel, and you don't even see it."

My parents were missing. My aunt was in jail. I had

broken the law — maybe twice. "You must have a different definition for luck in Alaska."

"Oh, come on. You are lucky. Every one of those girls at school asked me why you didn't want to be friends with them anymore. They wondered what *they* had done to *you*. They're worried about you. Don't you like them?"

"Of course I like them."

"They're practically begging you to hang out with them, go to sleepovers, have fun together," Victoria said, her finger waving in my face. "And you won't. You act like it's a terrible thing that they want to celebrate your birthday."

She was right, but not for the reason she or the HEGs thought. The problem was that I couldn't share my troubles. I couldn't sleep over at their houses because I couldn't risk having them come to mine when my parents might have to leave at a moment's notice. Still, I hadn't handled myself well with them at all. "You don't know what you're talking about," I said. Flimsy, I know, but *deny, deny, deny* was the closest rule I could think of.

"Whatever. It's your stupid life," Victoria said. "Are you in or not?"

Rule Number 19 stated: *If you're working with a co-agent, never look for him/her. Never acknowledge the other agent unless it is appropriate to do so. When leaving an operation, never look back.* I had to protect Stanley. But doing so would violate direct orders from the angry Agency woman. There was another reason for going into the Spoon, though. I needed to hide the New Orleans Silver Spoon Historical Collection from Frankenstella.

If my parents found out I'd entered the principal's office to retrieve sensitive documents, they would be . . . well, I wasn't exactly sure how they'd feel. Maybe they'd be proud of me for figuring out Gertie's clue and for liberating the map. Or perhaps they'd be furious with me for breaking the law. Either way, I knew they'd listen to my reasons. Stanley's mom would not listen to him, and it wasn't like he could give her a good reason why he pulled the fire alarm anyway. She'd be angry, and he would take his punishment, but that wasn't fair.

"Videotaping my adventure will be so much fun," Victoria continued. "And so easy." She got up, walked across the room, and shut the lights off. Then she clicked on the flashlight and waved it around the room. "Even a small town girl like you can do it."

My stomach dropped as I noticed purple dots glowing on the floor.

"What are those?" Victoria asked.

Think, Sunflower. "Chemicals from a science project," I lied.

Victoria continued waving the black light flashlight around. If that ultraviolet beam hit my Sunflower watercolor, the *Rules for a Successful Life as an Undercover Secret Agent* would be exposed. "This is boring," she said. "I'm going to show my parents some videos."

"Wait." I weighed my choices. *Follow the angry woman's orders? Or protect Stanley while hiding the New Orleans collection?* It was a no-brainer according to Rule Number 25: *Never leave a fellow agent behind. You're in this together. Go team Secret Agent!* I snapped the lights on. The choice was easy. "I'm in."

23

Everyone else could be the enemy. Or they could be working for the enemy. Or they could be under the influence of the enemy. Or they could just not like you.

— Rule Number 4 from *Rules for a Successful Life as an Undercover Secret Agent*

We practiced in my room, Victoria holding the flashlight under her chin so that her face was properly lit while I filmed on her cell phone. She must have done her signature gasp and shocked expression ten times until she said it looked real enough on camera. "This isn't your first time making this type of thing?" I asked.

"Nope." Victoria grinned. "I told you. I know what I'm doing."

"You broke into museums in Nome?"

"There's only one museum in Nome, with exhibits about the gold rush and how Siberian huskies were bred as sled dogs," she said. "I gotta say, it was a lot more interesting than spoons."

I thought about mentioning how we *might* have the soup spoon of the pirate Jean Lafitte, but Victoria was right.

Huskies were more interesting than spoons. "So where did you illegally enter?"

"Someplace even more boring than your spoon museum, if you can believe it — school." She shook her head and her ponytail swung from side to side. "That stupid school never proved a thing. Mom was sure I was the poor victim, bullied into it by those terrible middle-school boys and girls."

"What happened?"

"It was August — summer was almost over. My friends and I were just hanging out in the apartment building. Mom and Dad were busy doing whatever it is they do," Victoria said. "I don't remember who showed us the *Exploring Locked Places* website, but I knew if I got picked that it could be my way out of Nome."

"So?"

"We got a reply the next day. But the *Exploring Locked Places* guys said hiding until night in a school bathroom was boring. Everyone does it. And destroying the desks and books was actually criminal, so they would never air the clip. Mom didn't want me to start the school year with the rumors that I was a juvenile delinquent."

Start the school year? A sinking sensation grabbed hold of me. "When did you guys leave Alaska?"

"Whenever Mom said." Victoria looked down quickly and tapped her smartphone. There it was, a video of me removing the sunflower picture from Principal Baker's wall. The fire alarm shrieked in the background. She clicked it off. "Now, back to our plan for this evening. Can you get us into the museum without setting off the alarm?"

All I could think of was how this might be a trap. What

if Victoria was a double agent, pretending to befriend me in order to help her parents get into the museum?

A muffled *ring-ring* interrupted my thoughts.

Victoria raised one eyebrow in question. "Where's that ringing coming from?"

The clock read 7:02.

I pounced on my alarm clock and acted as if I was fumbling with the buttons. "I must have messed up the a.m. and p.m. switches," I lied, returning her quizzical raised eyebrow with one of my own. I guess that genetic quirk was something else we had in common. The ringing stopped. But I knew that it would start again soon, and my lie about the alarm clock would not hold up if Victoria stayed in the room.

"Make sure your parents are busy. I know how to get into the Spoon. We'll sneak out in ten minutes."

"You're sure you can get us in without setting off the alarm?"

"Yes."

"You have the key?"

"No."

"You know the code?" Victoria looked impressed.

"No. No. Just go."

"Nine minutes, Moppet," she said, walking out of the room. "Don't be late."

As soon as I heard her feet on the steps, I yanked *An Abridged History of the United States* off the shelf and opened it to the hiding spot. The shrill ringer pierced the air. Since I had to wait the usual number of rings, I held the phone under my pillow to muffle the sound. When the phone had gone through the normal cycle of *ring-ring*, silence, *ring-ring*, I opened it. "Tweedledee."

"Tweedledum," Roy's deep voice answered. "Sunflower, we've got good news and bad news."

"How bad?" I whispered into the phone.

"Your Uhms are not in Vietnam."

I breathed in slowly. "Where are they?"

"Good news. Paraguay."

"Impossible." The sunflower cipher was all wrong. Either Mom misled me or something had happened to them.

"We know." Roy's voice was calm, probably due to years of training. "However, a set of their passports has been tracked there."

"So, the Agency did, in fact, lose them?"

"No." Roy cleared his throat. "We just weren't informed of their movements beforehand."

"You're searching for them?"

"Of course, Sunflower." Roy whispered something I couldn't make out. "The Agency is on full alert. Once there is a positive, in-country sighting, we are positioned to take appropriate action."

I didn't like the way that sounded. "By action, what do you mean?"

"Don't worry, Sunflower. Allow the professionals to do their jobs."

Sure, but where the heck were the professionals when I was being blackmailed in my own home?

"Sunflower, whatever happens, do not let your uncle or aunt into the museum."

"Sooner or later, I'll have to open it for visitors." Keeping the Spoon operating on its normal hours was protocol. An idea hit me. "Unless you want to share with me exactly why I should not?"

"No can do." Roy's shaky voice betrayed his anxiety. I had never heard him nervous before. "This is a direct order from the highest link in the command chain. You must obey."

"Roy," I pleaded. "Things are not good here. I have to do something. Starfish has been moved to a jail three hours away. I am alone."

"I know, Sunflower." Roy lowered his voice. "I'm trying to convince the higher-ups to send you backup."

"Like the Cleaners that put the alarm on the museum?"

"No agents have been assigned to Silverton."

"Who is PNW Security, then?"

Roy ignored my question. "I'm trying to get you extracted from the situation before it spirals out of control."

"It already has."

A good spy did her preparation (Rule Number 35). I needed to see for myself what was so important in the Spoon. "What if I let someone into the museum or went in myself?"

"The consequences will have a far-reaching impact."

"Can you be more specific?" Dad had drawn a sketch of the museum. Why hide it?

"You have to trust us and obey the command." He hung up and I was left alone to live with my choices. I grabbed some of my not-secret spy gear from the bookshelf. It seemed I wasn't the most trusting or obedient kid in the world.

24

If you're working with a co-agent, never look for him/her. Never acknowledge the other agent unless it is appropriate to do so. When leaving an operation, never look back.

— Rule Number 19 from *Rules for a Successful Life as an Undercover Secret Agent*

We stood on the back porch of Le Petit Musée of Antique Silver Spoons, and Victoria spoke directly into her smartphone's camera. We were getting ready to break in, and all she cared about was how her hair looked. One thing was certain: Victoria would never make it working for the Agency. And the way I had been piling up the illegal activities, my future was none too bright, either.

Because of the way the ground sloped, the back of the old house was on raised brick pillars, about a foot and a half off the ground. The blinds were halfway down, yet I was sure I'd closed them on Sunday afternoon. That was the protocol. On the back window, there was a new sticker that proclaimed, *This business is guarded by PNW Security.* The words were printed over an outline of Mount Rainier. I touched the glass pane, but the sticker was on the inside. The security alarm's flashing red light pulsed every two seconds through the window. Victoria aimed the flashlight through the window, illumining a little white box, about two inches long and one inch wide with wires sticking out. One wire was connected to the glass and another snaked out of sight.

"OK, genius," Victoria said as she pointed to the other window, which also had a wired box on its inside frame. "How are we getting in without setting those off?"

I clicked on my headlamp. "Watch and learn," I said as I walked down the steps and knelt next to them. I parted a massive clump of three-foot-tall western sword ferns, which grew sporadically around the museum. I'd never shown anyone this trick before, not even Stanley. I was saving it for a day when he really needed cheering up.

The last time Stanley and I sat on the Spoon's back porch, he'd photographed the ferns and wondered how anyone with pteridophobia (he informed me that meant a morbid fear of ferns) could live in the Pacific Northwest since ferns thrived in the sodden, dark, and mild climate. I wished Stanley was here now. Instead, all I had was Rule Number 21 to guide me: *Assume every agent is a double agent.* I was going into an unknown situation with an agent of unknown loyalty.

The steps were hollow underneath, so I removed the small plywood boards that kept animals out. I dropped onto the cold, damp ground, squeezing my way under the back steps.

"Seriously?" Victoria said as she knelt.

"It's the only way in without setting off the alarm," I said.

"This is too realistic," Victoria said as she followed me in. "Make sure you show the dirt on my legs." She kept stopping to brush the dirt off her hands, which was ridiculous since we still had lots of dirt to crawl over.

I army-crawled under the museum until I was in the right area. I started pushing against floorboards until one popped up with a creak. The next two boards lifted up easily, making a hole about eighteen inches long and twelve inches wide.

Some of the original flooring had rotted away years ago. Whoever put in the new floorboards hadn't nailed them down. As a kid, my mom found that she could crawl under the museum and push the three short boards up, gaining entrance between two display cases. She'd showed me the trick once so we could scare Aunt Gertie. Luckily, silver spoons don't break when they're dropped.

"Nice," Victoria said when she saw how we'd be entering. "We're going to have to do that again so you can film me."

So we did. I took video of Victoria as she knelt next to the ferns, squished them down, removed the boards, and then crawled underneath the building. Then I had to inch my way in front so I could film her in the dark, enclosed space as she made her way toward the entrance. The ground was cold, and my hoodie wasn't warm enough. All the while, Victoria kept up a constant stream of comments: "I'm so scared. What's that noise? Oh, I hope I don't get caught. Yuck, I think that was a bug. Oh no, it slithered. It must be a snake." She timed her reactions perfectly. In fact, she was so convincing, I was starting to get seriously creeped out, even though I knew there wouldn't be any snakes out and about so late in the year.

I filmed Victoria entering the museum twice. The first time I was on the ground, so I got a great view of her legs going up into a dark hole. Then we had to film it with me already in Le Petit Musée so I could capture Victoria as she squeezed through the tight space where the floorboards had been.

While I felt guilty about disobeying Roy's direct command, I had things to take care of — namely, protecting Stanley and hiding the New Orleans collection.

Once inside, I double-checked the locks on all the doors — front, back, and the side office door, which opened up into the alleyway between the museum and the Star's Tale. The three deadbolts were all locked. All of the windows and doors had white boxes with wires on them.

Victoria picked up a bunch of spoons that were on display and tapped them on the glass case, making a *clank-tink* sound.

"Please don't move any of the spoons," I said. "I just arranged those by the harvest theme on Sunday afternoon."

"Mabel, chill. I don't give a rat's tail about some old spoons, no matter how fancy they are. Now give me my phone and stay out of my shot." Victoria started talking to her camera, making excited noises.

I grabbed an empty box from the office and lined it with paper towels. I opened up the New Orleans spoons display case and started placing them in the box, layering paper towels over each bunch of spoons. When all seventy-fives spoons were in the box, I stuffed more paper towels on top to prevent them clanking together. I also packed the info card. As quickly as I could, I rearranged the other spoon collections, spreading them out so it wouldn't appear like anything was missing from the display.

I carried the box into the office, struggling under its weight, and hid it behind rolls of paper towels in one of the cabinets. It wasn't the best spot, but it would have to do for now.

"Silverton sucks rotten eggs." Victoria marched into the kitchen, grabbed me by my arm, and pulled me to the other side of the big display room. "Nothing works in this town."

"What now?"

"See this," Victoria said as she stepped onto a chair, then climbed onto a tall black filing cabinet that was half-hidden in the back corner. She perched up there, legs crossed and smiling, perfectly positioned under the Spoon sign made of spoons.

Victoria snapped a photo of herself and then handed the phone to me.

"It's fuzzy," I said.

"Exactly. Which is why I want you to take it."

I stayed absolutely still as I snapped the photo, but when I looked at it, I found this one was also fuzzy. Not blurred like she had moved or out of focus like the camera wasn't working — just fuzzy.

"I can't believe this. First my computer cannot connect to the Internet, and now this." Victoria hopped down. "It's the perfect shot to prove I'm inside." She grabbed the phone from me, walked across the room, and snapped another picture. This photo of the Spoon sign came out fine. "Maybe it's too dark. Can we move the cabinet?"

I pulled on the handles of the filing cabinet. They didn't budge. "Mom lost the keys ages ago." *Hmm. The locks look small. Not small enough for the skeleton key on my pocketknife, but maybe small enough for the key I found next to the red case.* However, I'd left it in my desk drawer.

"Do you hear that?" Victoria tried to open the drawers too, but was unsuccessful. She leaned toward the cabinet, a puzzled expression on her face.

"Seriously? Save your 'I'm scared' bit for the camera," I said. I wasn't sure what her new game was, but I was too tired to play. Did she think I was that gullible?

Victoria placed her ear on the side of the filing cabinet. "Moppet, listen to this." She pulled me toward her so hard that I banged my head on the metal.

Then I heard it — a low humming sound. I moved around, listening from different spots. The lower I went, the louder the hum. "What is that?"

"Not old paperwork." Victoria straightened up. "Your museum, your problem."

I'd spent my whole life in and out of the museum, but I'd never noticed a humming sound. Was it new? Was it important? Would the small key fit the cabinet locks? I pressed my ear against the cabinet again. I had heard the soothing hum somewhere before. I closed my eyes to try to remember where. For some reason, I thought of the time in science class when Mr. Baker substituted. He had us build electrical circuits and then blow the fuses. We were supposed to use a wooden stick to press the button, but Emma H. used her finger, and instantaneously singed off her arm hair. The smoke detectors sounded, the sprinklers soaked us, and the fire trucks came. This hum seemed to be at the same frequency. But what would an electric circuit be doing in this filing cabinet?

While Victoria took more videos of herself, I pushed Mom's old wooden desk in front of the back door to act as an additional barricade. I also checked — again — that the deadbolts were firmly set. To block the front and side doors, I jammed chairs under their doorknobs, just like I had seen in the movies. Now, even with a key, there were physical barriers against intruders. The only way in or out of the museum was through the loose floorboards or smashing a window.

Our luck had held so far, but I didn't want to push it, so I said, "We should get back home."

"One more shot," Victoria said. Of course, she took three before finally jumping into the hole. I followed, pulling the wooden floorboards into place.

As we crawled out, Victoria kept up her patter about how afraid she was. I replaced the outside plywood boards, and the ferns sprung back, hiding all evidence of our covert ops. We walked the few yards to my back door in silence. The only light on the first floor was from the television room, so we sneaked in through the kitchen.

Once there, we waited until we heard Stella and Frank's guffaws drown out whatever show was on, then we tiptoed upstairs to my room.

We did it! I thought, my heart still beating double-time. My grin matched Victoria's. After changing out of our dirty clothes, we sat on my bed. Victoria plugged her phone into her laptop to transfer the videos, then replayed them, pointing out what she liked and didn't like about each take.

"You know your parents are going to be upset with you when they find out?" I whispered, not sure how I felt about what we had done.

"I know." Victoria shook her head. "I just like to remind them that I'm here."

"What are you talking about?" I said. "They're always saying how wonderful and precious you are."

"Because of you, or the principal, or your parents, or Aunt Gertie," Victoria said. "They try to act like a happy family when other people are around."

"So when no one else is around?"

"They ignore me. They're too busy with their own plans," she said. "Once I went three days without either of them saying a thing to me. Not even 'pass the ketchup' or 'close the refrigerator door.'"

While my parents didn't talk to me each day, it was because they *couldn't* as a matter of national security. And even then, they always — until this current mission — sent messages with Roy so that I never felt forgotten. When they were home, Mom and Dad always included me in discussions.

"Were your parents mad at you?" I asked, feeling sorry for my cousin.

"No, just busy." Victoria shook her hair — somehow still impossibly straight and smooth.

"I'm sorry. That sucks," I said.

"It doesn't matter. I have work to do now." She turned away from me.

I yawned as I watched Victoria watch the different videos. I didn't have the heart to kick her off my bed, so I just grabbed a pillow and curled up, pulling the cover over me.

25

Enjoy the small victories. They may be all you ever get.

— Rule Number 26 from *Rules for a Successful Life as an Undercover Secret Agent*

Victoria woke up extra cheerful Wednesday morning. For someone who was up most of the night before, she was way too upbeat. I felt like malicious fairies had glued sand in my eyes. Watching and re-watching the various videos of Victoria's adventure until three in the morning wasn't the brightest thing I'd ever done — along with breaking into the museum.

The weird thing was that I wasn't sorry. It was fun, but more than that, Victoria was sort of amazing — both at acting and at editing her video. She had talent. However, there was still a possibility she was a double agent, so I wasn't planning on spilling my secrets to her anytime soon.

Victoria bounded down the stairway and I followed. Frankenstella sat at the kitchen table in complete silence. The curtains were wide open, giving a clear view of the museum.

There was the smell of burned coffee, like it had been brewed hours before.

Stella clutched my mom's favorite big blue mug, looking as if she might rip it in two. "Mabel, the key or the code, now."

It was just one more day until their mystery visitor was supposed to come, and I could tell they were getting stressed. "I can't give you what I don't have," I replied curtly.

Victoria casually draped her arm around my shoulder. "She's right, Mom."

"There has to be a way in there." Stella's nostrils flared as she inhaled. She glared at her husband before turning her hard stare at me. "Do you know if all the windows are wired to the alarm?"

"Nope," I lied. A thought hit me. "Why don't you try opening one and see what happens?" I have to admit, I was curious to see if PNW Security would show up.

"No, we can't." Frank shook his head. "Does anyone else have keys?"

"No," I said, but a nagging doubt wiggled into my mind. I assumed no one else had keys or knew the security code, but I'd also assumed my parents hadn't found the red suitcase, and turns out, it had been sitting in our basement all this time. I guess I should've paid more attention to Rule Number 29: *Anticipate surprises. No one — not even a supergenius — knows all the facts.*

"Mabel, do you remember anything about the company that installed the security system?" Frank asked.

"Nope."

"Did PNW Security come from Silverton? Bluewater? Seattle?"

"I don't know." And I didn't know if PNW Security was my friend or foe. Right now, they were Frankenstella's foe, so that gave them points in my friendship book. Yet, it wasn't like I could trust PNW. I assumed they were a Cleaners' shell company, doing good work, but there was no way to know for sure. Roy had said that no agents were assigned to Silverton, but he could've been wrong.

"Is there anyone else your mom would have trusted?" Frank asked. "Like a neighbor or a friend?"

"Aunt Gertie," I said. "Why don't you ask her?"

Frank and Stella just looked at each other, their faces tense with worry.

"What's so important in there, anyway?" I asked. I enjoyed poking them, knowing they were going to lie to me.

"Yeah, Mom. It's just a bunch of old spoons." Victoria squeezed my shoulder. "What's so important in there?"

"Never mind," Uncle Frank said, shoving granola bars into our hands and ushering us toward the front door. "Isn't it time for the bus?"

26

If you panic, stop whatever you're doing. Breathe. Ask "Huh?" Or eat something as a diversion.

— Rule Number 24 from *Rules for a Successful Life as an Undercover Secret Agent*

My whole world was in disarray, but Bluewater-Silverton Unified Elementary School was the same as always. In first period, we had a reading quiz, which I'd forgotten about in yesterday's excitement. There was also a five-page math packet due in second period, which I had frantically completed on the bus. That meant that I wasn't able to talk to Stanley, even though his eyebrows had been wiggling up a storm as Victoria had dragged me to the back of the bus. I had to find out what he had learned about the unmarked topographic map, but not around Victoria.

If that wasn't enough, Grace K. managed to call me Moppet during the class meeting without Ms. Drysdale noticing. Stanley stared at me so hard that Victoria noticed and smirked at me. Fourth period was our PE fitness exams, so I ran a mile on an almost empty stomach and with little sleep. Apparently, sneaking into my aunt's house, setting off a fire alarm, and breaking into a museum weren't going to be the worst parts of my week.

By lunch, I was tired, sweaty, and really hungry. The smell of pizza and Emma G.'s funny story about her teeth being played like a harp by the orthodontist distracted me so much that I didn't hear the loudspeaker announcement.

Victoria did. She slapped me on my arm and repeated the message for me to go to the principal's office right away. I handed my untouched slice of pizza to Emma G. and shrugged apologetically.

Sheriff Baker sat in front of her husband's desk. Principal Baker also had a slice of untouched pizza on a tray. My mouth watered.

"Mabel, have a seat," Principal Baker said as he gazed at his Wall of Art. Because of Rule Number 19 — *when leaving an operation, never look back* — I knew better than to look at my sunflower picture, which now hung a little differently than before, and sat in the empty chair.

"I've got bad news for you, Mabel," the sheriff said.

My heart started racing. I wasn't hungry anymore. I wasn't anything anymore. I'm not even sure how I managed to keep breathing.

"Mabel, look at me." Sheriff Baker waved her hand in front of my face. "It's not that bad."

I hate surprises — always have. "Just tell me."

"I can't find a trace of Gertrude in the system."

"You lost my aunt?" I looked at Mr. and Mrs. Baker, and suddenly I realized they weren't any cleverer than me — just older. I didn't feel bad at all about not trusting them. "Isn't she supposed to be in the state jail in Yakima?"

"There was no record of her being transferred there," Sheriff Baker said as she glanced down at her small notebook. She looked up and continued, "Or of the judge's order to move her from Silverton."

"But you said you'd talked to a judge," I said, failing to control the shrillness in my voice.

"Yes," the sheriff said, maintaining eye contact with me. "At least I spoke with whom I thought was the judge. I called his office today, and he had no memory of speaking to me last Friday. The phone number I thought was his is now out of operation."

"Do you believe me now that Inspector Montgomery isn't a good guy?"

"I'm sure this is just a big miscommunication," Principal Baker said. "There's no reason to panic."

I could think of many reasons to panic. "What are you going to do?"

"I know this is upsetting news, but Ted is right. We have to remain calm," Sheriff Baker said. "I have reached out to my contacts in the state trooper headquarters. Let the professionals do their jobs."

By now, I really hated the word 'professional.' "Sure. Because they've been doing an A-plus job so far." Did all adults really think a few meaningless phrases would comfort kids when it was obvious things weren't going well? *How about less talk, more action,* I thought. Like breaking into the Spoon and hiding silverware from Frankenstella, which was just following Rule Number 15: *Be in control. Act. Be the one who chooses the time and place for action.*

"Well, Mabel, you can help us with another matter."

Sheriff Baker took out a small notebook, just like the inspector's. "Let me ask you again. Where are your parents?"

To keep from blurting out "Paraguay," I rolled my eyes and looked to the principal for assistance as I said, "I'm hungry." He handed over his pizza slice without a word.

After the first bite, my hunger took over and I gobbled my food.

Principal Baker wordlessly handed me a paper napkin.

"You didn't answer my question." Sheriff Baker's tone wasn't mad. It was sort of sad, actually.

I really wanted to tell them everything, but I couldn't. It would be against the rules. In fact, I couldn't even tell them it was against the rules, because that would be against the rules. And, of all the people on Earth, a principal and a sheriff should understand following the rules. So all I could do was stare back at them until Principal Baker finally let me go for the last few minutes of lunch recess.

I needed to wash my hands, so I stopped in the restroom. Three HEGs (both Hannahs and Grace K.) cornered me not even a minute later, and the Queen Bee asked, "Mabel, how are you?"

In truth, I felt terrible about my parents and Gertie. But hiding the New Orleans spoon collection had at least made me feel like I had some type of control over the crazy situation. That was too long and complicated an answer, so I just said, "OK."

"No. Really? How are you *really*?" Grace K. asked. "You have purple under your eyes and they're puffy, like you've been crying. Have you been crying?"

"No," I said, aware that those questions were the most

Grace K. had said to me in ages. "I just didn't sleep a lot last night."

"You're worried about your aunt Gertie in jail," Princess Bee Hannah said, a kind smile on her face. "That must be tough. My mother said she'd be so scared if she ever went to jail, even if she was innocent."

"Aunt Gertie is innocent," I said.

"*Of course* she is," Princess Bee Hannah said. "Have they found your parents yet?"

Why are they asking about my parents? I wondered. *Do they suspect something? Are the HEGs double agents?* Oh, snap out of it, Sunflower! They were just being their normal nosy selves.

"When will the Star's Tale reopen?" Grace K. asked.

"Soon, I hope," I said.

"I miss the Star's cinnamon buns," Grace K. said. "And the Spoon — can you open the museum for my uncle?"

"Grace K.!" Princess Bee Hannah's disapproval echoed through the restroom. "Mabel's family is going through a lot right now. This is not the time to ask favors."

"It's not like I'm asking her to let us in for free," Grace K. said. "We'd pay."

"Admission is a dollar," I said.

"Great," Grace K. said. "So today?"

"I don't know," I said.

"Tomorrow?" Grace K. asked, ignoring the searing look from the Hannahs.

What is up with Grace K.'s uncle? I thought. Her questions left an uneasy feeling in my gut.

"When is Victoria's birthday?" Princess Bee interrupted before I could speak. "I want to mark it down. And what is her favorite color? For Halloween's hair ribbons."

"I don't know," I said, realizing how little I actually knew about my only cousin.

"The most important question is," Queen Bee Hannah said, "what do you want to eat for your birthday dinner?"

"Pizza?" I said, but it came out like a question.

The door swung open, and Victoria rushed in. "There you are, Mabel."

"I was just asking about visiting the museum," Grace K. said as she was cut off by the bell ringing. Recess was over.

"We'll let you know when it's convenient," Victoria said as she placed her hand on my right arm, not too rough for once, and dragged me out of the bathroom.

27

Trust your instincts. Your gut wants you to stay alive. Listen to it.

— Rule Number 3 from *Rules for a Successful Life as an Undercover Secret Agent*

The day had come — Thursday, October thirtieth, the date Frankenstella had slated to sell the New Orleans Silver Spoon Historic Collection for a very hefty profit of $14,500. Of course, any amount would be a profit since it wasn't their property.

Victoria had been glued to my side ever since our museum break-in on Tuesday night. She insisted that I watch every version of her video. Depending on how she ordered the recordings, sometimes she seemed afraid the whole time. Others were funny. The best one was a mix of funny and scared. I had no idea where she got the groaning and creaking sound effects from, but they made it totally spook-tacular.

I finally managed to break away at seven p.m. last night, taking *An Abridged History of the United States* and its hidden phone with me into the bathroom. I ran the water to cover up my conversation with Roy, but it turned out that he had no news to report. "Hang in there, Sunflower," he said before hurrying off the phone. When I came out of the bathroom, Victoria was waiting in the hallway, so I decided to give up spying for the night. I didn't go into the museum to try the little key from the basement. I figured the spoons were as safe as they could be in their plain brown box. I never had a chance to study the liberated pages hidden in *The Definitive Northern Italian Cookbook*. And I never had the chance to talk to Stanley, who I knew had been hanging out in my backyard because I found three pinecones on my windowsill when I woke up in the morning.

At breakfast, Stella wasted no time with pleasantries. "Moppet, we are running out of time."

"Stella." Frank stood next to the stove, scrambling a large pan of eggs. "Remember our plan this morning?"

As I grabbed some flatware to set the table, I whispered in Victoria's ear. "Did you finish editing the video?"

"Not yet. I'll do it today, and then upload it at school."

"Mop — I mean Mabel." Uncle Frank plopped the pan of eggs onto the table. It was a slimy, unappetizing mess, but I dug in anyway. "I heard from my sister early this morning."

The food stuck in my throat. "Aunt Gertie or my mom?"

"Jane. She wants me to hire an attorney for Gertrude."

"Oh?" I didn't believe him for a second. Roy would have told me if the Agency had been in contact with my parents.

"We have to raise funds," Frank said. "Understand?"

Here it comes, I thought. *Why make it easy for him?* I wasn't going to be outright rude. I did know Rule Number 10, after all: *Try to be pleasant to the enemy.* I was trying.

"My sisters need money," Frank went on. "Stella and I

would be happy to pay for it ourselves, but unfortunately, all our cash is tied up in Alaska."

I glanced at Stella, who didn't look pleased at all. No one said a word and I knew to follow Rule Number 22: *He who talks first loses.*

After a minute of meaningful glances between Stella and Frank, he said, "Your mother sent a fax, authorizing us to sell some spoons in order to pay a lawyer to help get Gertrude out of jail."

Wow. The audacity of Frank's lie was so huge, I could barely conceal my amazement. "Can I see the fax?"

"Of course, Mabel." He handed me two pages. On the top of each, there was the receiver fax number of Gloria's Mini-Mart, but the sender's number was conveniently smudged.

I skimmed the handwritten paragraph on the first page:

I, Jane Baies Pear, do hereby authorize Frank E. Baies to sell up to one hundred spoons at his discretion in order to pay attorney's fees for our sister, Gertrude Baies.

Underneath was Mom's signature and yesterday's date, October twenty-ninth. The second page read:

Mabel,

Please assist your uncle Frank and aunt Stella. They will need to sell the New Orleans spoon collection to help your aunt Gertrude. We will return home from our trip as soon as we can arrange a flight. Be a good girl and listen to your uncle and aunt. Secondly, please help Inspector Montgomery search the Spoon for the red suitcase. I'll explain later.

Love,

Mom and Dad

I examined the pages. These were excellent forgeries. Whoever wrote them had mimicked my mother's handwriting down to her crooked *Ts*. The problems the forger made were in the language, grammar, and content.

Mom was one of the few people who called me Moppet — and I didn't mind . . . much. She always capitalized titles like "Uncle" and "Aunt." She's never told me to be a good girl. One of her favorite sayings is "Well-behaved women seldom make history." She calls her sister Gert or Gertie — never Gertrude. If Mom had wanted Montgomery to have the red suitcase, she would have just said, "It's in the basement in the Valentine's box wrapped up in a blue blanket." She would never have used the term "secondly" where it was used in that letter, since it was the third instruction. And finally, Mom hated the nickname "the Spoon." She always, *always* referred to the museum by its full name or Le Petit Musée at the very least.

I knew that calling out Frankenstella as liars and forgers wouldn't get me very far. Fishing for information, I asked, "Who are you going to sell them to?"

"That's not your business," Stella said in a very unpleasant tone.

Frank patted her arm. "What your aunt means is that you shouldn't concern yourself with adult troubles." He cleared his throat, folded his hands in front of him, and looked me straight in the eye. "I know these last few days must have been very unsettling for you, Mabel. We all have said things that could have been misconstrued. Let's put that behind us now and work together for Gertrude's sake."

Is this Frank's idea of an apology? I wondered. Someone needed to go back to kindergarten to learn the simple formula of: "I hurt you. I'm sorry."

"If you care about your aunt Gertrude, you'll help us get into the Spoon," Stella said. "Remember, your aunt is counting on you."

I couldn't believe they were playing on my feelings. So I asked, "Why don't you fax Mom back and ask her for that information?"

"Moppet, that's a great idea," Victoria said as she put on her coat and gathered her school books. "Let's go to school now."

"Vicky-girl, I heard you tossing and turning last night," Stella said. "Why don't you stay home today and rest?"

"Maybe because I want to go to school and see my friends." Victoria stamped her right foot, like a toddler about to have a fit. "Maybe I like living here now and don't want to leave. Maybe I am looking forward to the sleepover on Friday night. And trick-or-treating with my *friends*." She gripped my arm in her iron fist. "Come on, Mabel."

Victoria likes Silverton? I thought. *That's new.* I wasn't sure how I felt about her change of heart.

Frank looked at his wife and daughter, who were locked in a silent battle of the wills. "Just be ready to leave school early," he said.

"Are you going someplace, Uncle Frank?" I asked.

"We, um, may go visit Gertrude."

"Should I be ready to leave school early too?" I asked.

"No." Stella broke off her eye contact with Victoria. "There won't be room in the car if we're able to bring Gertrude home."

Another lie. Mom's car seats five easily.

"Fine. Later." Victoria stomped out of the house, dragging me across the lawn to the school bus stop.

Not even a minute later, Frankenstella slammed the front door shut and drove off in Mom's car.

At that moment, I knew I had to act. I had to find out what was in the red suitcase that was making these adults act so irrational. "I'm not going to school today," I told Victoria.

"Look, Mabel," Victoria said, her voice soft and kind. "My parents have been waiting too long in this wet, dreary state to let you stop them now."

"You've been here four days," I said.

"I wish," Victoria said.

So I had been right! "You weren't living in Alaska, were you? You've been hiding out near here." The mountains nearby were full of abandoned cabins.

"Give Moppet a gold star." She smiled. "Be careful. I'll tell the teacher you're out sick today."

Victoria's warning wasn't in vain. As I walked through the front entryway and into the kitchen, I heard a voice — a terrible, familiar voice drifting from the back of Le Petit Musée. I opened the back door a crack.

"Listen to this, Madison," Montgomery said into a cell phone. "Helena gave me an ultimatum today. Right? Who does she think she's dealing with?" He laughed in that fake, forced way adults do when something isn't funny. "Trenton's greedy and getting impatient."

I knew I should hide, but I wanted to eavesdrop. Maybe if I brought more information to Sheriff Baker, she'd be able to do something. I opened the door wider and stood in the doorway. I chanced peeking out and caught a glimpse of the inspector. His mouth was downturned and he was shaking his head.

"If they go in with the wrong code, the alarm will sound,

bringing everyone in this town running. I can't risk that until everything else is in place." Montgomery paused to listen, then continued. "We are too close to Jefferson City to misstep now."

Man, was Montgomery wrong. Jefferson *County* was far away — on the other side of Seattle and the Puget Sound, in the Olympic Mountains. There's no Jefferson City in Washington State. It's the capital of Missouri. Any fifth grader knew that.

"Get Cheyenne ready. She has to verify the signature's authenticity before we sell." He paused again for a moment. "We're not changing the game plan now. We will —"

Cheyenne? I thought. *As in the capital of Wyoming?* From my spy work, I knew that there were no such things as coincidences. Carson, Raleigh, Jefferson City, Madison, Montgomery, Jackson, Helena, Trenton — they were all state capitals. I gasped. The inspector *was* a phony, and Montgomery was his code name. I'd known it from the beginning. He was an odd sock. Why hadn't I insisted that my spy sense was right?

"I'll be there in ten," Montgomery said. He looked like he'd eaten a pile of lemons for breakfast, the way his mouth scrunched up in disgust. Ranting something about "incompetent" and "greedy," he got into his blue Ford and peeled out of the driveway.

28

Assume every agent is a double agent.

— Rule Number 21 from *Rules for a Successful Life as an Undercover Secret Agent*

I figured I had at least thirty minutes, probably a bit more, if only because Silverton was fifteen minutes away from anything. Fortunately, I had the *Rules* as a guide. In this case, Rule Number 16: *Always have a Plan B. And a Plan C. A Plan D would be good too.*

Today I had a long list of plans. One: Open the red suitcase. Two: Open the Spoon's humming file cabinet. Three: Contact the Agency to tell them to get here *now.* Four: Decode the topological map and the blueprint. Five: Share all intel with Sheriff Baker to see if she'd listen to me again.

First things first — the red suitcase. I made sure the basement door was firmly shut behind me. As I peered around, I had the same uncomfortable feeling I was being watched. *Keep calm, Sunflower.* Inspector Montgomery knew about my parents' weird travels, but he couldn't possibly know they were Cleaners, could he? The only thing I knew for certain was that Montgomery wanted the red suitcase.

A floorboard creaked from above. Startled, I froze. I waited for a minute, but no other sound came. *It's just an old house, Sunflower. Wooden floors make sounds.*

I moved the pile of giant plastic containers until I got to my parents' hidden stash. With the lantern turned on, I examined the combination lock. Even though I was no expert, I could clearly see that the lock looked modern and the suitcase was old. Really old. Antique, my parents would say. The leather handle flaked a little when I touched it.

My parents must have installed the new lock. They never used the same numbers, such as birthdays, that could be easily guessed. Instead, their system for making up codes was to use the telephone touch pad, but base it on the object in question. Since this was *the* red suitcase and a six-digit lock, I used the first three letters of each word to make the six-digit code. Red suitcase = red sui = 733784.

I rotated the digits on the lock and tried that combination. Nothing.

I remembered Dad had mentioned he'd also flip the numbers once in a while, so I tried them in reverse: 487337. *Click.* The lock opened, and I exhaled in relief.

It wasn't a suitcase after all. It was a silverware case from Monticello, Virginia, according to the stamp on the red velvet lining. On one side were sixteen soup spoons. Nothing fancy, except that the handles were gold. I picked one up. It felt pretty heavy, which meant that they might be real gold, not just plated. The initials TJ were inscribed on the back.

These were the gold-handled spoons Montgomery had questioned me about.

The spoons and the red suitcase were connected the whole time! I sat back on my heels as I tried to recall everything I'd heard about them. If Frank knew about the red suitcase from when he was young, that would mean his parents (my grandparents) did too. Montgomery had also tied the gold-handled TJ spoons to the suitcase. *How did he know about it?* I wondered. *And how much did my parents know?*

On the other side of the silverware case were several ancient letters. The paper was yellow and brittle. Barely breathing, I opened the top letter and could hardly read the fancy script. I made out a few words and phrases: "Martha is well," "my opinion," "our government must," and "I am concerned with Britain's navy."

Monticello? TJ? Martha? Concerns about Britain's navy?

Oh! I swallowed my victory yell. I had been right. So very, very right.

These spoons must have belonged to Thomas Jefferson, the third president of the United States and the guy who actually wrote the Declaration of Independence. This was serious history we had hidden in our basement, next to inflatable reindeer and beach buckets.

At first I couldn't believe my parents hadn't told me about this, but then doubt crept in. What if it wasn't my parents who had hidden this suitcase here? What if it had been Aunt Gertie? She was in and out of our house all the time. The Spoon was a perfect transfer place for stolen goods, especially when my parents were out on a mission and I was in school.

Aunt Gertie had a motive too. Frank had stolen her money and left her alone to raise their baby sister. Had she been picking up spy tips from Mom and Dad? What if Aunt Gertie was a criminal like her parents had been? What if the inspector was who he said he was? The unpleasant realization that Montgomery could be telling the truth hit me with great force.

Get it together, Sunflower! It was possible, but not probable. I shook my head. Aunt Gertie was neither a thief nor a smuggler. There had to be a reasonable explanation for why we had valuable American antiques hidden in our basement.

The spoons were no doubt very valuable. I wasn't sure about the letters, but I guessed they had historical value, if nothing else.

I carefully put Thomas Jefferson's gold-handled spoons and letters back where I found them, making sure to spin the digits on the lock.

Questions about my parents, Aunt Gertie, and the red suitcase swirled in my head, but I'd never find out the answers by just sitting around. As I restacked the containers, a creak sounded. Then another. Footsteps.

Friend or foe?

Tiptoeing up the stairs, I pressed my ear to the basement door. The footsteps were coming from the kitchen.

"Mabel," said a very familiar voice. "Are you here?"

I pushed the basement door open. Stanley jumped and let out a sharp, "Oh!"

"What are you doing?" I asked.

"Trying to help you."

"How did you get here?"

"When you didn't get on the bus this morning, I called my mom and told her I wasn't feeling well. She let the bus driver drop me off back at home."

He took out the topographic map with no markings and then the same one with markings. "I found the spot, not even five miles from here. It's almost all dense forest, except for this." He pointed to a landmark. "Tim Chamberlain's old warehouse."

"That's where Aunt Gertie thought we were going when Montgomery was eavesdropping on Saturday," I said. "What could be there?"

"It's supposed to be empty," Stanley said.

Tim Chamberlain, who had died just two years before, was famous in Silverton as a wilderness guide. He used to lead hikes on the mountains, and he flew helicopters, which he kept in the huge old warehouse. In his will, he stipulated that the land and the warehouse be sold for one dollar to the National Forest Service.

"We'll go there later today," I said. "Do you have your camera?"

"Always. I stopped at home to get everything we might need." Stanley patted his backpack. "But you should look at these again." He pulled photos out of his bag and spread them on the kitchen table. They were from our monthly hikes.

I glanced over the sets — trees with snow, trees with green leaves, evergreen trees surrounded by trees with autumn leaves. "Wait," I said. Something besides the seasonal changes was different in them. "The bat houses move around every month."

"I know. That can't be authorized," he said. "Bats need to hibernate, and it would throw off their senses to move them this late in the year. We have to tell the park rangers."

"Stanley, I don't think those black boxes are bat houses."

"Why not?"

"Bat houses don't need antennas, do they?" I said, pointing to the tall rod sticking out of the top of each one.

"No," Stanley said.

"Could they be some kind of signaling device? Maybe that's how Montgomery managed to walk off the path without getting lost." I turned to Stanley. "I need to see one of those black boxes up close."

"Let's go now," he said.

"Hang on, I need to get something from my room first, and then we'll stop at the Spoon for a minute," I said. If my gut was right, the small key I had found in the basement would open the Spoon's humming file cabinet.

My dash upstairs took fourteen seconds. It was another four seconds as I sped past my parents' bedroom and the bathroom. But I stopped short in the hallway. My door was closed and I knew that I'd left it open when Victoria and I had gone downstairs that morning.

That tingly feeling of unease set in as I twisted the knob and pushed the door open. The room was dark. I clicked on the overhead light. The curtains had been drawn shut. As I walked over to my desk to retrieve the key, that strange feeling of being watched crept up my back. I turned.

Inspector Montgomery stood in the corner, wearing the oddest-looking green goggles and holding a wall-penetrating radar gun just like my mother's. "Well, isn't this uncomfortable?" he said.

29

Recite Murphy's Law at least once a day: Anything that can go wrong, will go wrong. Be prepared.

— Rule Number 17 from *Rules for a Successful Life as an Undercover Secret Agent*

Wearing his green goggles, Inspector Montgomery looked like he was ready for Halloween.

"What are you doing in my room?" I asked.

"Searching." Montgomery pulled a piece of paper out of his jacket pocket. "Don't worry, I have a federally authorized warrant."

I was sure he did. I was also sure it was a fake.

Montgomery clicked on his headlamp, which glowed a familiar shade of blue — ultraviolet light. Beams of red also appeared. He closed the bedroom door and turned off the overhead light, making it pitch black. Then he pointed the radar gun at the wall.

"What are you searching for?" I clicked on the overhead lights again. I wasn't sure if that would make his ultraviolet light totally ineffective, but it was worth a shot.

"Hidden spaces. I've found three so far, two with boxes inside."

Whoa. My house has secrets! The blueprint of our house was a map — a real treasure map. Now I understood why Aunt Gertie had hidden it — and why Stella wanted it.

I glanced at the sunflower cipher, which had been moved. "Did you touch my flowers?" I asked.

He tapped the light yellow flower. "Didn't these used to be in your parents' room?" he asked as he snapped the lights off.

"How did you —" I stopped myself. *Of course, he had done recon* (spy word for examining a place really carefully for clues) *of my house.*

"Shouldn't you be at school, Mabel?" Montgomery tilted his head down, the UV beam catching the globs of ink I'd spilled on the floor when I wrote the *Rules*. He glanced around the room, and the beam hit the *Rules,* which glowed. "What's this — *Rules for a Successful Life as an Undercover Secret Agent?*"

Before he could get there, I jumped onto my bed and yanked the *Rules* off of the wall.

"Give me that," Montgomery said. "Right now."

"No." I tilted the frame so that I could unhook its backing.

Montgomery grabbed the metal framing, almost pulling me off my bed, but I leaned back to counterbalance him. Holding firmly to the frame, I managed to take off the backing. Then I lifted up the piece of paper with the sunflower where I had written the *Rules*. Montgomery twisted the metal frame and the glass fell to the floor, shattering into hundreds of tiny, sharp shards.

"Give me that paper now!" he thundered.

"Never." I tore my precious work into shreds — the only way to save the *Rules* from falling into enemy hands.

Just then, Stanley opened the door. "What's going on in here?"

"Run!" I screamed. "Get help! Get Sheriff Baker!" I jumped off the bed, slamming the door closed to protect Stanley. Montgomery tried to open it, but I stood in front, blocking it. Within a few seconds, the front door slammed, meaning Stanley had gotten away.

"He'll make it to the sheriff's office in three minutes," I said. "And then she'll arrest you."

"No, she will not." Montgomery removed his high-tech goggles. "You are the most meddlesome child I have ever met."

"You should meet the HEGs," I said as I flipped the lights on.

"No, thank you."

"How do you —" I started to ask when another odd sock moment fell into place. "You're Grace K.'s uncle, aren't you? That's why she's been bugging me to let her *uncle* into the museum this week."

"Honorary uncle. Her father and I go way back. Grace likes to talk."

"That's how you knew my nickname was Moppet in the café on Saturday."

"You have very finely tuned instincts, child." He nodded in approval. "Hone them, and you will go far in life."

"Thanks, I think." I looked at him. "Wait a second. Grace K. has been spying on me?"

He smirked. "Maybe." He shut off the lights and

resumed scanning the room with the radar gun. There was nothing left to hide, so I didn't bother to turn them on again. Plus, if Montgomery was busy here, that gave Stanley more time.

The memory of Montgomery talking about Sheriff Baker popped into my head. "You said that Silverton was the same as it was thirty years ago."

"True. Same four blocks of Main Street."

A good thing about living in a small town was that everyone knows everyone else. But Montgomery was a stranger. "Then why don't I know you?"

"I left and didn't come back for thirty years," he said as he swept the radar gun up and down the wall like a paintbrush.

A tingly feeling crept up my arm, so I blurted out my question: "Did you know my grandparents, Carl and Mabel Baies?"

"You are quite perceptive," Montgomery said, impressed.

My eyes adjusted to the dim light. "Does Frank know you were in the same criminal gang as my grandparents?"

"How do you know about that?"

"That's why you're looking for the red suitcase," I said. He didn't deny it, so I continued with my hypothesis. "Do you have a buyer for it?"

He looked like he was going to say something, but didn't.

"Why was Grace K. asking if you could visit the museum?" I went on. "You've already been there."

"I like looking at spoons, but I'd prefer to not set off an alarm while doing so."

I knew he wasn't telling the truth, but I didn't bother telling him that whatever he was looking for was long gone. *Let him waste his time searching the wrong places,* I thought.

"Miss Pear," he said, "your questions are much too good for my comfort. Didn't anyone ever tell you that curiosity killed the cat?"

Working hard to keep my voice steady, I said, "If you're a criminal, you're not a real government agent."

"Oh, I am." He moved over about two feet and started examining a new section of the wall. "You know the game."

"What game?"

"Your parents, Fred and Jane Pear. I have been tracking their travels for the past year — Turkmenistan, Estonia, Nepal, and Laos, to name a few."

"Where?" I asked, trying to sound naive. I don't think I fooled him.

"And of course, all of their domestic travel — usually Virginia or Massachusetts, but also Louisiana a few times. Considering the official limitations of their job mission, those domestic destinations are rather odd, don't you agree?"

I didn't know what to think. Montgomery had just named many of the places my parents had been, either for official Cleaners missions or the Great Reverse Heist. How did he know? I wanted to ask, but knew better than to say anything that might betray them.

"I don't know what racket your parents are running here, but they're pros, working both sides of the law." Montgomery said. "Maybe I'll team up with them someday, if it's mutually beneficial."

"They're not crooks." *How dare he accuse my parents of being criminals*, I thought, anger bubbling up inside my stomach. Then again, it was better than him figuring out the truth.

"You don't have to pretend with me, Miss Pear." Montgomery's voice was kind. "I know what's going on. They're off on another dangerous mission, this time in Paraguay."

How does he know about those places? I wondered. But it didn't matter. I had to keep him talking. Surely Stanley had gotten to Sheriff Baker by now and they would be back soon.

"How thrilling for them — adventures in foreign lands. And how lonely for you, especially with your eleventh birthday coming up tomorrow. Frank and Stella would be so jealous if they only knew how exciting your parents' lives actually are."

"What do they know?" I asked.

"They still believe your parents' silly cover stories." His laugh was sharp. "Idiots."

Where is the sheriff? I wondered. "What's your real name?" I asked, stalling.

"You don't think Montgomery is my real name?"

"I had to memorize the list of state capitals for history class," I said.

"It's best if you continue to call me Inspector Montgomery."

"Who do you work for?"

"Me," Montgomery said. "And the Agency."

"What agency?" I asked, failing to keep my voice calm.

"*The* Agency. The one that sent your parents to Paraguay."

He knew it all! I thought. Montgomery knew where my parents were and what they did. *Deny! Deny! Deny!* rang in my head so loudly, I was sure he could hear it too. "What are you talking about?" I asked.

"On Saturday afternoon, your parents closed the Spoon early and the three of you came into this house," Montgomery said, this time aiming the radar at the ceiling. "Then, about an hour later, they received a phone call. Correct?"

The only way for Montgomery to know that was if he had been spying on us. I didn't want to confirm or deny, so I said nothing.

"Their orders sent them to Paraguay," he continued. "They obeyed, since everything was legitimate. All correct Agency codes and clearance intel checked out."

"You said my parents were in Vietnam when we were in the principal's office."

"I lied, Mabel," Montgomery said. "Your parents are on an actual Cleaners job."

My curiosity was killing me, but all I said was, "Actual?"

"In fact, the orders they received have since been erased, so it appears your parents have gone off on their own, without Agency authorization." He paused. "And the call they received will be traced back to your aunt Gertrude's home phone, which won't raise suspicion since your mother and her sister call each other several times a day. The fact that their only communication came from Gertrude's phone does, however, cast grave doubt on their story of receiving new orders to go to Paraguay."

"What? Why?" I blurted out.

"Time. I'm buying time for myself. The Agency does not like it when their Agents go off on their own. Therefore, your parents will be arrested, held in a secret location, and investigated." His tone turned malicious. "By the time the higher-ups in the Agency figure out that your parents weren't going rogue, I'll be gone, like a ghost."

"You set them up," I said. "You're a total fraud."

Montgomery clapped in slow motion. "Bravo, Miss Pear. Bravo. It is an actual pleasure to work against you." Tapping his nose with his index finger, he furrowed his brow as if deep in thought. "Now what shall we do with someone as curious, brave, and clever as you?"

"Let me go," I said, wondering where Sheriff Baker was.

"We both know that's not possible." Montgomery walked toward my open closet door. "What's this?" The radar gun had found something under the floorboard.

My heart sank.

He had to put the radar gun down on the ground to move my shoes out of the closet. He started pressing down on one of the floorboards. It squeaked.

"What's in there, Moppet?" he asked as he kept pushing on the floorboard.

"Nothing." Nothing that I knew about, anyway. Since he was occupied with pressing the floorboard, I opened the curtains, yanked the window up, grabbed the wall-penetrating radar gun, and dropped it out the window.

"Hey," Montgomery said. "That radar gun is expensive."

A pinecone sat on the sill. *When had Stanley tossed that up here?* I wondered. I threw the pinecone at Montgomery's head, but it bounced off harmlessly. Next, I grabbed the sunflowers out of their vase and tossed them at him flower by flower to distract him.

"Stop it. That's annoying," Montgomery said as he batted them away. "You are feisty, I'll give you that." He picked up one of the scraps of the *Rules* from the floor, flashing the ultraviolent beam in it. "What's this? *Everyone overlooks the qu*—" He looked up at me with a vengeful gleam in his eyes. "What are you up to, Mabel Opal Pear?"

I pulled *An Abridged History of the United States* off my shelf, removed the secret spy phone, and chucked the book at him. It hit Montgomery in the stomach, but it didn't slow him down.

"What's in your hand?" he asked.

I shoved the phone into my pocket. To distract him — and to escape — I looked around for something heavier than the pinecone, flowers, and book. The glittering baby pumpkin was my only option, so I threw it at him as hard as possible.

Montgomery ducked out of the way, and the pumpkin exploded when it hit the wall behind him, showering him with stringy orange pumpkin guts.

"Yuck!" Montgomery exclaimed, wiping off his arms.

While he was distracted, I put a foot on the windowsill, leaned out, grabbed a branch on the apple tree, and swung toward the trunk.

"I don't have time for your antics," Montgomery said. "Come back here right now."

"Over here, Sheriff Baker!" I yelled as I shimmied down the tree. "He's upstairs." From inside I could hear Montgomery rushing out of my room and thudding down the stairs. Within thirty-eight seconds, a car engine roared to life and tires squealed as it sped away.

I exhaled and hugged the tree trunk. What Montgomery didn't know was that I wasn't actually calling to the sheriff. Besides some crows flying overhead, there wasn't anyone there to hear me.

30

Use technology, but don't count on it. Batteries die. Signals fade. Web pages can be faked. Email can be hacked.

— Rule Number 13 from *Rules for a Successful Life as an Undercover Secret Agent*

I didn't know why Stanley hadn't returned, but whatever the reason, I was sure it couldn't be good. Celebrating my small victory of faking out Montgomery would have to wait.

Keeping off the main highway, I jogged the three blocks to the sheriff's office. The sheriff's cruiser was parked outside. As soon as I opened the door, I heard voices coming from the office. As I went through the second set of double doors, I saw why the sheriff and Stanley hadn't come to my rescue.

He was talking to her, pointing to his nature photos, which he had spread out across her desk. The sheriff, however, was on the phone, looking none too pleased.

"Stanley, why didn't you come back?" I asked.

"I've been trying to convince Sheriff Baker there's something terribly wrong. She still doesn't get it," he said.

"Mabel's here," Sheriff Baker said into the phone as she shot an icy glare at me. Then she hung up.

"He escaped," I said. "Montgomery got away, and you didn't help me."

"Mabel, tell me what is going on." Sheriff Baker held up a hand to Stanley. "Do not mention bat houses or mammal hibernation to me again."

I took a deep breath and tried to figure out what I could tell the sheriff. *My parents are Cleaners and they've been sent on a mission by Agent Montgomery?* No, that wouldn't work. *I have Thomas Jefferson's gold spoons in my basement?* True, but that would lead to a whole lot of questions, which we didn't have time for. *Frankenstella are up to something devious?* Also true, but I didn't have enough compelling details to convince her of it. Instead, I thought of something she could take care of. "Stanley and I figured out where Aunt Gertie is."

"Tell me," Sheriff Baker said.

"Tim Chamberlain's warehouse," I said. "The road is closed for the winter, so no one is supposed to be there, but since there hasn't been any permanent snowfall yet, it is probably drivable. And the line of black —"

"That's enough, Mabel," Sheriff Baker said. "No talking about bat houses."

"You'll check it out?" I asked, relieved she was listening to me again.

"I don't have jurisdiction, but I will get the park rangers to go over there." True to her word, the sheriff called, putting in a distress code with a warning so the park rangers would know to be careful as they approached the warehouse. "It might take a while."

"Why?" I asked.

"Both the White River Wilderness Information Center and the Sunrise Visitor Center are closed for the off-season, so there aren't any rangers stationed nearby. In the meantime, I want you kids to stay here," she said.

"Where are you going?" I asked.

"I'm going to pay a visit to Inspector Montgomery's hotel room," she said as she put on her hat. "Do not leave this office."

"You know where he's staying?" I asked.

"At the Inn-Between," she said. The Inn-Between was a couple of guest cabins located in between Silverton and Bluewater.

"But he's probably at the warehouse now," I said.

"I can't legally search there, but I can search in Silverton," the sheriff said. "Don't step one foot out of this building until I come back."

The doors squeaked as she walked outside, leaving Stanley and me alone. "What do you want to do?" he asked as he gathered all his photos, taking care to put them in the right monthly order.

"Find my aunt," I said. "She can't wait hours."

"Let's go." He smiled and placed the photos in his backpack. "And we can examine those bat houses on our way."

We walked out of the sheriff's office and up the road we'd hiked just a few days ago. I felt confident that Sheriff Baker would know exactly where to search for us whenever she returned. I tried calling the Agency a few times on each phone as we walked, but no one answered. *Stupid spy agency.*

Neither of us talked much as we hiked at a very brisk pace. When we had been walking for about thirty-eight minutes, we reached Stanley's favorite tree grove, seven minutes faster than usual. He took out a photo for guidance. "Look," he said, pointing to a Douglas fir about twenty feet away. Sure enough, there was a black box with a large antenna.

We walked through the underbrush until we got to the tree. There were no branches to climb. "How can we reach it?" I asked.

"The same way your dad climbs telephone poles," Stanley said as he took out a set of climbing spikes. Stanley strapped them onto his heels so the two-inch spurs were aimed inward. He placed his arm through a coil of rope and pushed it up on his shoulder, then took out a long, thick belt. He wrapped it around the tree trunk, placed his right foot at about six inches off the ground, and tapped the spur into the tree. He leaned back, just like I'd seen my dad do, using the belt for balance. Then, like Stanley was walking on air, he lifted his left foot, tapped that heel against the tree, and started climbing up. Right, left, right, left. He was at the black box in no time.

He pulled the black box off a hook, tied it around himself with the rope, and descended the trunk.

"When did you learn to climb trees?" I asked, impressed.

"I get bored," he said, handing the box to me. Whatever it was, it wasn't a bat house. There was no entrance hole. The antenna was about four feet long and an inch in diameter. The box was made of metal, heavy for its size, and emitted an electronic hum, like the noise in the file cabinet.

Is this connected to my parents' job as Cleaners? I wondered. "Put it back," I said.

"OK." Like always, Stanley didn't waste time with questions.

When we resumed walking, he offered me water and a

granola bar from his backpack. I didn't feel hungry, but my legs were starting to ache. I knew I'd be no help to anyone if I didn't have energy, so I ate. While the route from Silverton to Stanley's favorite tree grove had a very slight incline, from the tree grove onward, it became much steeper until it was obvious we were heading up the mountain.

We soon reached the end of the paved path and the gate, which had a sign saying:

ROAD CLOSED FOR WINTER

KEEP OUT

NO TRESPASSING

After about ten minutes, the dirt path met an old gravel logging road. Stanley pointed to black boxes in trees every five minutes or so, taking pictures as we went. I was nervous about what we might find at the warehouse, and more nervous that we would find nothing.

The gravel road narrowed as we walked. Freshly crushed grass on the sides of the road indicated that a car had been there recently. The trees became denser and the undergrowth thicker. We followed a turn in the road, and Tim Chamberlain's warehouse — as large as my house and the museum together, metal, and dirt brown — appeared. Montgomery's car was parked at the end of the road. Stanley had read the topological map correctly.

The huge sliding doors were partially opened, letting out the sound of clanking and an undercurrent of voices. I couldn't understand the exact words, but they sounded rushed. I turned to Stanley with a finger on my lips, and was surprised to see that he was making the hush sign at me too. He motioned for us to go through the undergrowth and around to the back of the warehouse. I nodded, following him through the trees until we reached the back.

In just a few years of disuse, weeds had popped through cracks in the cement of the helicopter landing pad. But they hadn't prevented a Robinson R22 Beta II from landing here. The blue helicopter was small yet agile, with room for a pilot and one passenger. Dad loved flying them, which was why I recognized it on sight. Mom could pilot one too. All Agents could; it was standard training. My heart sunk. Was it possible Montgomery really was an Agent? *Doesn't matter, Sunflower. Focus on the mission: Find and rescue Aunt Gertie.*

I continued my recon. Vines crept up the back of the warehouse's corrugated metal siding until they reached the large windows, which were propped open. Stanley touched me on the shoulder, then pointed to a nearby tree — another black box. We were hot on the trail of . . . something.

In back of the building there were no bushes around to hide behind if anyone was on patrol, but I decided to take a chance. I walked up to the back wall of the warehouse and pressed my ear to the metal. Some type of machinery was in use — *clang, whoosh, clang, whoosh*. Stanley joined me, his eyes closed, eyebrows wiggling, and mouth open.

"We don't have all day," Montgomery said. I flinched at the sound of his voice. I whipped my head around, but he wasn't outside. He must have been standing really close to the wall inside. "I don't know where your troublesome niece went, and I don't want to be here when she figures it out."

"You worry too much. What can Moppet do?" That was Frank. "She's just a girl."

I can figure out the suitcase's code, which unlocked Thomas

Jefferson's gold spoons, I thought. *And break into the museum without setting off the alarm. And track you to a remote location.*

They spoke some more, but their voices and footsteps grew fainter as they walked away from the window, making it difficult to make out their words.

"Once the print job is complete, we're leaving," Montgomery said. "And you're coming with me."

Print job? Was that the *clang, whoosh* sound?

"Just tell me where you put the red suitcase, Gert," Frank said.

I was right. Aunt Gertie was being held here. *Where are the park rangers?*

"I've never seen a red suitcase. Our parents didn't have one. We never traveled anywhere." Aunt Gertie's voice sounded hoarse and tired. "Frank, if I knew where it was, I would tell you."

I thought about the size of the warehouse. Big enough to park six school buses — three rows of two deep — inside. Since I could hear them clearly, that meant Aunt Gertie and the men were at the back. *How can I get Aunt Gertie out of there without Frank and Montgomery noticing me?*

"Sad about leaving the warehouse, Frank?" Montgomery's tone was joking. "Are you going to miss this place?"

Frank grunted in reply.

"It was a good setup for you — rent-free with no one bothering you," Montgomery continued. "Wouldn't you agree, Frank?"

I couldn't hear Frank's answer.

"True," Montgomery continued. "Living in the woods is fine in the fall with its warm, sunny days. Winter, especially up here on the mountain, gets downright frosty at night."

A memory fell into place. Victoria had smelled of the woods that first morning when she'd taken video of me sleeping. *This must be where Frankenstella had been living, plotting against my family.* No wonder they wanted to take over my house.

"So, leaving you here — all tied up — wouldn't do, Ms. Baies," Montgomery said. "Tell me where the red suitcase is, and I'll release you before I leave the country."

"I still say we should just leave her," Frank said. The *clang, whoosh* sound stopped. "It's done."

"She knows too much," Montgomery said. "I'll bring her with me. She'll talk."

"No, I won't," Aunt Gertie said. "Because I don't know anything."

"They all talk eventually," Montgomery said.

"I want what's mine," Frank said.

"The suitcase has been hidden for thirty years. A few more days won't make a difference," Montgomery said. "Pack the car, Frank. We're leaving now."

"Why the car?" Frank asked. "We're taking the helicopter."

Not all three of you, I thought.

"It's a two-seater," Montgomery said, "and you don't know how to fly it. We'll meet at the rendezvous in three days."

(Rendezvous was a French [and spy] term for an agreed upon meeting spot.)

There was the sound of a chair being dragged on the floor and more talking, but the voices had moved away again.

I couldn't let Montgomery take Aunt Gertie in the helicopter. With the Robinson R22 Beta II's range of two hundred and fifty miles, he could fly almost anywhere. The Canadian border was about two hundred miles north. The Pacific Ocean was less than one hundred and thirty miles west, and who knew if he had a boat waiting for him in international waters? I tugged Stanley's arm and led him into the undergrowth. "You go to Silverton and tell Sheriff Baker what we've discovered."

"What are you going to do?" he asked me.

"Stop Montgomery from getting on that helicopter," I said.

"The park rangers should be here soon," Stanley said. "I'll make sure Frank won't be able to drive anywhere."

"How?" I asked.

Stanley pulled out his pocketknife. "Can you disable the helicopter?"

"I'm too short to reach its engine," I said. "I'll just have to keep them here."

"Be careful," he said. We walked together around the side of the warehouse. I stood next to the open doors, but out of sight from the inside.

Stanley ran to the car, slashing the first tire with a quick cut. He darted around until all four were cut. I could hear the *hiss* of air from where I stood. I watched Stanley running down the path. When he was no longer visible, and the car's tires were flat, I walked into the warehouse's open doorway.

"Hi," I said to three very startled adults.

31

Never leave a fellow agent behind. You're in this together. Go team Secret Agent!

— Rule Number 25 from *Rules for a Successful Life as an Undercover Secret Agent*

"Run!" Aunt Gertie yelled.

Frank stared at me, slack-jawed.

Montgomery merely sighed. "Miss Pear," he said. "Someone really should put a tracking device on you. A bell, at the very least."

Aunt Gertie stood barefoot between the two men, her ankles tied together with rope and her wrists handcuffed. When she saw that I wasn't going to run, she asked, "What are you doing here?"

"Rescuing you," I said. I walked into the warehouse, hoping they would follow me. "What's that?" I asked, pointing to a large industrial machine. Waves of heat rolled off of it. I picked up a piece of paper from the ground. "Who is Judge Phoenix and why does he or she have so many different signatures?"

"Never you mind," Montgomery said, approaching me.

I darted away before he could snatch the paper or me. I needed to keep Montgomery away from the helicopter and Frank away from the car as long as possible. As soon as the slashed tires were discovered, Montgomery's survival training would kick in and he would try to escape. I needed to keep them there until the park rangers came.

I walked closer to the industrial machines, passing sleeping bags and a camping stove. The footsteps behind me let me know that my plan to stall them was working.

Computers and what looked like a giant printer took up an entire corner of the warehouse. Stacks of paper in various sizes were laid out on a table. Oddities from the past few days fell into place. The warrant, the judge's order, my guardianship papers were fakes. Counterfeits. If they'd produced them here, it was a big-time crime.

"OK, Miss Pear," Montgomery said. "What do you want?"

"Why are you asking her?" Frank said before I could answer. I waited a few seconds, still stalling, to see if the inspector would say anything, but he was focused on me.

"A trade," I said directly to Montgomery, ignoring Frank. "You release my aunt, and I'll tell you exactly where the red suitcase is."

"She's lying," Frank said. "Bluffing. Stella searched her room. It wasn't there."

I waited a few more beats before addressing Montgomery again. "If you promise that you can guarantee that he," I said, pointing to Frank, "never bothers us again, I'll even tell you the case's code so that you don't have to smash an antique."

"There really is a red suitcase?" Aunt Gertie's shoulders sagged. She looked from her brother to me and back. For once,

I couldn't read her expression. "Mabel, what do you know about my parents?"

Mom had omitted the truth so that Aunt Gertie wouldn't have the burden of knowing their parents were criminals. But wasn't it worse to be the only one who didn't know the truth? I had been keeping so many secrets (good, important secrets), I had almost forgotten I could trust my family and friends. *Choice time, Sunflower.* Either I lied, keeping this secret and betraying Aunt Gertie, or I broke my promise to Mom. *Sorry, Mom.*

I had to reveal the Great Reverse Heist, and I didn't have any time to waste. "Your parents dealt in stolen goods," I said to my aunt. "Thirty years ago, Montgomery here was a carrier for their criminal gang. He delivered the suitcase to the house several months before your parents died. The museum was used as a place to store stolen property before it could be sold. All of the jewelry you thought was your mom's was actually stolen. I'm sorry."

"The statute of limitations is past," Frank said. "That suitcase and everything in it is mine."

Montgomery looked at me, and I could've sworn he was fighting a smirk. He turned to Frank. "There is no time limit on stolen property. The spoons will forever be considered stolen, which is why we must be discreet when trying to sell them."

I knew the Thomas Jefferson spoons were stolen! I thought.

"That's absurd," Aunt Gertie said, but her voice wavered. "Our parents would never have done that."

"All of the spoons *displayed* in the museum are legitimate," Montgomery said. "I had some of my people check it out during the summer. The Pear house, however, has many interesting hidden treasures."

"How long has Jane known?" Aunt Gertie asked.

I couldn't answer that, so I just shrugged.

"You never wondered how our parents paid for everything?" Frank asked.

Aunt Gertie shook her head.

"Do you remember that Christmas before they died, Gertrude?" Frank asked. "We each got one present — a lousy pair of new shoes. Then, in the spring, Mom and Dad suddenly had enough money to not only fill in the cracks in the walls of the house, but to add a second floor, a basement, electricity, and indoor plumbing. Where do you think they got the money from?"

"I never did think about that," Aunt Gertie said, confused.

"You inherited everything — the house, the museum, all the goods," Frank spat.

"You left." Aunt Gertie shook her head, her voice rough. "You ran away in the middle of the night, two weeks after Mom and Dad died. You stole all the money in their bank account — I could barely buy food."

"I was searching for the red suitcase."

"For thirty years?" Aunt Gertie laughed bitterly.

"I tried to give you and Jane a chance to share with me last summer," Frank said, "but you refused. There are a lot more things hidden. There are other boxes with things to sell."

"I had to raise our baby sister all by myself, Frank! I didn't go away to art school. I barely graduated from high school." Aunt Gertie used her special glare that could freeze someone in their tracks. "I didn't find anything of value in the house."

"Don't lie. You must have sold some of it to build your own house and fund your stupid coffee shop."

"No, Frank. I borrowed money from Jane and Fred."

"Well, where did they get it from?" her brother asked.

Montgomery winked at me, as if he was enjoying sharing a secret.

Aunt Gertie glanced at me, panicked. There was no good answer to that question without giving away that Mom and Dad had other jobs besides Mrs. Museum and Mr. Telephone. "They saved their pennies."

"Ha." Frank sneered.

"This lovely reunion is not helping me achieve my objective: collect the red suitcase and get out of town," Montgomery said. "Nor yours, Frank." He turned to me. "When you're on a mission, Mabel, you have to focus. If you can remember your goal, you'll be able to measure your success rate."

"Why are you talking to Moppet like that?" Frank asked.

Montgomery shrugged. "She's got potential, unlike others."

"Well, Montgomery," I said. "What about my offer?"

"If Moppet is lying to us about where the suitcase is," Frank said, "and if we go to get it and it's not there, we'll end up with nothing."

"Good point," Montgomery said. He turned to me. "Prove it."

"It has letters from Thomas Jefferson in it." I held my breath.

The two men exchanged a look. "Hold on, Baies." Montgomery walked toward me, a genuine smile on his face. "Well, well, Mabel Opal Pear. Where did you hear that?"

"Nowhere. I saw them when I opened the silverware case."

"I am impressed." Montgomery did that slow-motion

clapping thing again. "Maybe I should have hired you for my organization."

"Which is what, exactly?"

Montgomery grabbed me by the arm and started pulling me toward the door.

"Where are you going?" Frank asked.

"To retrieve the elusive red case that neither you nor your wife seems to be able to find."

"No." Frank walked up to us and grabbed my other arm. "If the sheriff sees you in town with the kid, she might question you. I'll take her since I'm her legal guardian. No one can say a thing if they see me driving her home."

"You're not really, legally, her guardian. You understand that, right?" Montgomery asked. "I made up the document, I'm the boss, and I'm taking Miss Pear, since you've had days to complete the assignment and you failed."

Frank raised his hands in defeat.

Montgomery and I took two steps toward the door. I couldn't risk getting in the helicopter, but if we went near the car, he'd discover the slashed tires. *Think, Sunflower.*

A swoosh of air from behind us should have warned Montgomery what was coming, but grown-ups never do pay attention when they're in a hurry. Montgomery fell to the floor with a low moan. Frank stood behind, his hand still clenched in a fist.

"I was king of the boxing ring in high school." Frank waved his hands high in the air like a champion. "Who's the boss now?" His belly jiggled in joy.

"Not you." Montgomery spun his legs around, knocking Frank down with a kick. The two grown men went at it, just like the fifth-grade boys at recess.

I ran to Aunt Gertie and pulled out my pocketknife. I opened it to the tiny skeleton key and inserted it in the handcuff lock. I twisted the key — *click* — and the cuffs fell off. Aunt Gertie wiggled her fingers. I opened my knife to the saw blade and cut through the rope in no time. Bruises circled her ankles where the ropes had been tied too tightly.

By this time, Frank was sitting on Montgomery's torso, screaming, "It's my silver! It was my idea!"

"You morons would still be living in that flea-infested, rundown motel in Nome if it wasn't for me," Montgomery shouted, punching Frank's stomach.

Holding the handcuffs gave me an idea. Approaching them as I would a bird — quiet and unseen — I cuffed Montgomery's right ankle. "Hey!" he shouted.

Frank snorted. "Stupid kid." He stood up. "That does no good."

Montgomery took the opportunity and kicked him in the back of his knees. Frank fell forward with a thud.

I grabbed hold of Frank's right ankle and cuffed it, then jumped away from the wiggling mess of angry men.

Frank stood up and tried to walk, but Montgomery's weight prevented him.

Montgomery staggered up, fists clenched. "You're gonna pay for that."

But before Montgomery could do anything to make Frank pay, Frank jerked his leg, making Montgomery fall down again. This time Montgomery stayed down, eyes closed.

"Are you OK, Aunt Gertie?" I asked.

"I'm fine, child," Aunt Gertie whispered. "Are they?"

Frank groaned on the ground. I checked Montgomery's vital signs. His pulse was strong and his breathing was steady.

Using the rope that had been around Aunt Gertie's ankles, I bound Montgomery's hands behind his back. Frank grunted, so I left him sitting on the floor, cuffed to Montgomery. "The park rangers should be here soon to get them," I said. "And Sheriff Baker knows we're here." For good measure, I took Montgomery's key ring out of his pocket.

"Well, we'll wait for rescue, then," Aunt Gertie said. "There are lots of chips and soda, if you're hungry."

"We can't wait. Stella could be ripping apart the Spoon right this very minute." *What if she found the New Orleans collection hiding in the cabinet?* I thought. *And was selling it?* "We have to start walking now."

"You have the inspector's keys, right? I'll drive."

"Umm . . . we can't. Stanley slashed the tires so they wouldn't be able to get away."

"I don't have shoes," she said. "Even if I did, I'm too tired to walk."

I held up my cell phone, which was supposed to be a direct link to Roy. I punched in the numbers, but nothing happened. I tried again. "The batteries must be dead."

"No. The mountain prevents any service coming through." Aunt Gertie put her hand on my shoulder. "If you have to go, there's an old mountain bike over there." She motioned to the corner with Frankenstella's camping gear.

"Help should be on its way soon."

"Not soon enough," Aunt Gertie said. "Go."

32

Double-crossing a double agent makes double the work. Don't do it, unless there is no other choice.

— Rule Number 33 from *Rules for a Successful Life as an Undercover Secret Agent*

After riding the too-big bicycle on a bumpy gravel road that was filled with potholes and tree roots, I realized why I preferred hiking with my own two feet.

With aching legs and hands that hurt from gripping the handlebars so tightly, I rode into Silverton. Everything appeared normal. The clock over Mai's Diner read 4:15. My bike ride had taken more than thirty minutes, which meant that Aunt Gertie had been watching over Montgomery and Frank for that long. I had to hurry.

Just as I was passing by, the doors to Mai's Diner swung open, and the HEGs rushed out. Typical. I'm not in town for sixty seconds and I know the first people I see.

"Mabel, there you are," Queen Bee Hannah said. "Victoria said you're sick and that's why you missed school. Are you feeling OK?"

"Why are you riding a bike?" Emma H. asked.

"Stanley wasn't in school, either," Grace L. said. "Are you contagious? Grace K. went home early too. She'd been crying."

"That bike is too big for you," Emma Z. added. "How did you get up on it?"

"You don't look good at all," Princess Bee Hannah said. "You need to rest."

"Where's Emma G.?" I asked.

"She had something to do," Princess Bee Hannah said.

"Why did Victoria leave school early today?" Grace T. asked.

"Both Grace K. and Victoria left early?" I repeated. The HEGs nodded. "That's bad."

"Is this connected to your aunt Gertie?" Emma Z. asked.

"Grace K. thinks she did something wrong," Grace L. blurted out. "She said she didn't mean to hurt you, Mabel."

"What did she do?" I asked. *Spy on me? Report on my movements to the man who sent my parents away on a mission that might endanger their careers? Did she just say the wrong thing at the wrong time?*

"I'm not sure, exactly," Grace L. said, aware that for once, she was the center of attention. "In the bathroom at morning recess, she told me that she and her mom may have been gossiping about your family, Mabel, and her father's old friend may have overheard it. He might have misunderstood and was going to use the gossip against you. She's real sorry."

"I have to see Sheriff Baker now," I said, "but I need your help."

"Sure," Queen Bee Hannah said. "Anything."

The HEGs circled around me.

"Could you all go to Grace K.'s house and tell her that I'm not angry?" I figured no one could get through a wall of HEGs.

"Of course," Princess Bee Hannah said. "What else?"

I didn't want to endanger them, so I said, "Just hang out there for a few hours. Don't let her go anywhere. I have to talk to the sheriff about Aunt Gertie."

Like a migrating herd of elk, the HEGs took off toward Grace K.'s house on the outskirts of Silverton. Knowing Montgomery wouldn't stay unconscious for long, I pedaled down the street to the sheriff's office.

I let the bike clatter to the ground and ran inside, yelling for Sheriff Baker. The lights were off, but I didn't know if that was a good or bad sign. Stanley should have made it back. Just as I was wondering if we could have missed each other going in opposite directions, I heard a noise from somewhere in the dark.

"Mmmmmp."

"Who's there?" I called out.

"Mmmmmp!" said the voice again.

But another sound, higher-pitched, said, "Tssss."

I felt my way to the wall and ran my hands along it until I came upon a light switch, which I flipped on immediately. I glanced back and forth, covering the entire room, but didn't see anyone.

"Mmmmmmp," a deep voice growled from the far corner.

I whipped my head around. Inside the last cell were Sheriff and Principal Baker, with tape covering their mouths.

"Are you all right?" I asked. Stupid question.

Their arms were behind them. Handcuffed together, I imagined. Their legs were shackled to the bed. I tried to slide open the cell door. It didn't budge. Apparently, whoever did this didn't trust the sheriff and her husband to wait patiently. I put my arm through the bars. They were too far away to reach.

"Did Stanley tell you what we saw at Tim Chamberlain's warehouse?"

The sheriff nodded vigorously.

"Did Montgomery do this to you?"

They shook their heads in unison.

"Frank?"

Sheriff Baker tried again to say something.

"The fake state troopers who came with Montgomery — Carson and Raleigh?"

The sheriff nodded to confirm my suspicions.

"Did Stanley get away?" I asked.

They both nodded.

Relieved to hear that Stanley was safe, I began searching for the large key ring that the sheriff normally kept on her desk. "They took the keys, didn't they?"

They nodded.

"I'll call for help." I dialed 911.

Almost instantaneously, the other phone started ringing. I tried ignoring it, but the sheriff started making a noise like, "Ffffff," so I hung up the phone I was holding and picked up the other one.

"Hello. This is the sheriff's office." No answer. "Hello." I tried again. "This is the sheriff's office." Still no answer, so I hung up and went back to the original phone.

I redialed 911. Again, the other stupid phone began to ring. I looked at the sheriff and Principal Baker. They seemed to be laughing under the tape covering their mouths.

"What's so funny? 911 isn't answering. Someone's prank calling the sheriff. And —" I hung up the phone. The other one stopped ringing. "I was calling myself, wasn't I?"

Sheriff Baker and her husband both nodded.

"Seriously, Aunt Gertie needs help now." Neither the sheriff nor the principal could help me until I found a way to help them. "Who should I call to rescue the town sheriff?"

Sheriff Baker tried to tell me, but the tape prevented any words from getting out.

Think, Sunflower. Who'd show up whenever someone got injured or lost near our part of the mountain? I visualized the yellow and red rescue vehicles with their bright blue letters. "Pierce County Sheriff!"

Sheriff Baker nodded in agreement, relief on her face. She motioned her head toward her left. I looked down at my left. Nothing, but on my right, there was a contact list next to the phone.

I quickly called the Pierce County sheriff's office. Unlike Silverton, they had actual staff to answer their phones. The operator didn't believe that Sheriff Baker was physically tied up and unable to speak at first, but I managed to convince her by reading all of the sheriff's contact list over the phone to her. In case the park rangers hadn't been able to make it yet, I pleaded with her to send an ambulance and officers to Aunt Gertie at Tim Chamberlain's warehouse. I asked for help for Sheriff Baker and her husband. And finally, I requested backup for myself.

The front doors squeaked. "Sheriff Baker." I recognized Emma G.'s voice at once.

"Something terrible has happened at Mabel's house." That was Stanley.

"We're in the back," I shouted. "What's wrong?"

Stanley, red-faced and huffing from exhaustion, burst through the second set of doors. "Emma G. said your aunt took Victoria out of school early today. When I was warning the sheriff, two guys came in."

"Why aren't you locked up?" I asked.

"Once I saw they had Mr. Baker in handcuffs, I hid, then ran out before they noticed me." He inhaled sharply.

Emma G. hugged me. "Mabel, thank goodness you're OK." She breathed in deeply. "I was bringing you your homework when Stanley showed up outside your house."

What was this obsession about my homework?

"Your front door was open," Emma G. said, "so I went upstairs. Your room was a mess." She held up what was left of my decorated baby pumpkin — half of the rind, one googly eye, and three spider legs. And glitter. "Someone smashed it." She held back a sob. "I think you've been robbed." Emma G.'s eyes grew wider when she noticed the sheriff and principal tied up in the holding cell.

"Do you know where Victoria and her mother are?" I asked.

"No, I don't." Emma G.'s skin paled, like she was going to faint. I pushed her into a chair before she could fall.

I picked up the telephone, handing the receiver to her. "Call your parents. Tell them to come here." She nodded.

"Mabel, there's something else," Stanley said. "The museum alarm was shrieking."

Just as I had feared — Stella had broken in. Now that I was in the middle of Silverton, I tried using the cell phones. No one answered them, no matter how many times I dialed or how long I let them ring.

"I have to go," I said. "Will you two stay with the Bakers?"

"Of course." Emma nodded. "My parents are on their way here." She clutched the smashed baby pumpkin, rocking it for comfort. Tears rolled down her cheeks at an increasing rate.

"Mabel, I should go with you," Stanley said. "In case you need help."

"Emma G. needs you more," I said. And I didn't know if the fake state troopers were coming back anytime soon.

I looked at the sheriff and her husband. "You'll be OK?" It wasn't like I could do anything more to help them.

They both nodded.

I had one more mission — save the spoons — and not a lot of time.

33

Float like a butterfly, sting like a bee.

— Rule Number 23 from *Rules for a Successful Life as an Undercover Secret Agent*

The front door of Le Petit Musée of Antique Silver Spoons was wide open. Victoria and Stella's shouts were louder than the frantic buzzing of the alarm. A large shattered glass pane from a side window was the obvious point of entry.

By the sounds of it, Stella and Victoria were either cheering for their favorite hockey team or tearing down the museum. Victoria needed me. She had helped me when she didn't have to. Now it was my turn to return the favor.

I stood outside Le Petit Musée for a moment, listening to their shrieks of fury. The fading sounds of stomping feet and slamming doors led me to think they had moved their fight into the small kitchen, closer to where I had hidden the New Orleans spoons. I inched into the doorway. On the first display case, Victoria's purple smartphone lay forgotten. I had an idea.

"You don't care about me," Victoria yelled in the kitchen. "I have friends here. They like me. I'm going to a sleepover on Friday, and they're making me a special hair ribbon. I don't want to leave."

I couldn't hear Stella's reply. Whatever it was, it riled Victoria even more. The crash of breaking glass was followed by the unmistakable *tink* of silver spoons hitting each other. *Tink. Tink.* Lots of spoons.

Mom was going to be so angry if she came home. *When,* I corrected myself. *When she comes home.*

The kitchen door swung open. I was caught like a deer in hunting season.

"You." Stella grabbed me under my armpits and lifted me off the ground. "You lied." She wore multitudes of rings, bracelets, and necklaces. The diamond and sapphire clusters were back in her earlobes.

"I wasn't the first." I tried to kick her, but my legs swung harmlessly, missing her. Stupid short legs. "Plus, you've been stealing my mother's jewelry this whole time."

"As the oldest, Frank should have inherited them."

"They're from my dad's side of the family," I said.

With her pink and purple sweater ripped to pieces, Victoria stood behind her mother. She held one of the floorboards I had popped up. "Put Mabel down, Mom."

"Yes, put me down," I said, earning a hard shake from Stella.

Stella carried me between two smashed-in display cases. "Stay out of this, Vicky-girl. This doesn't concern you." A large green duffel bag was opened on the floor, filled with silver spoons and, I'd bet, the rest of my mother's good jewelry.

"It never does," Victoria said. "Nothing you do is ever for me. Or about me. I'm just another inconvenience in your life."

"Vicky," Stella's voice wavered. "Everything I've done is to make your life better."

"How did camping out for months in a drafty old warehouse in the middle of the woods with no running water make my life better? No school. No friends. No flush toilet." Victoria shouted. "Tell me that, Mother. How is my life better?"

"If you let me deal with Mabel, our sacrifices will be worthwhile," Stella said. "Then you can get everything your heart desires."

"Like what?" Victoria asked. "You don't even know me."

Next to the duffel bag sat the red suitcase. The lock for the silverware case was intact, thank goodness. Thomas Jefferson's gold-handled spoons were safe for the moment.

"I'm calling Dad." Victoria walked to the first display case.

"And will you tell him that you broke into the museum and filmed yourself? All so you can be on some television show?" Stella's voice was icy.

"It's a web series, Mom," Victoria said with disdain. "Where's my phone?"

"Don't bother calling. Your father is busy."

"With what?"

"A job."

"He's unemployed." Victoria rolled her eyes. "Your stupid schemes don't count as actual work."

"Victoria, this is not the time." Stella focused on me. "Mabel, if you want to see your aunt Gertrude again, you will do exactly what I say."

"Or what?" I asked. "You'll eat my food and wear my mother's jewelry?"

"I'll do worse than that this time." Stella motioned to the red suitcase. "Open it."

"Can't," I said. "I don't know the code."

"Don't lie to me, Mabel Opal Pear." Stella pointed to a small gray monitor, which I had never seen before. "I had the whole house under surveillance with infrared wireless cameras. I just watched the video of you opening it in the basement."

That explained the creepy feelings I'd had. Someone *had* been watching me.

"Don't listen to her, Mabel," Victoria said. "The video is fuzzy, like the photo of me in front of the Spoon sign. Mom didn't see anything useful."

"I saw enough," Stella said.

How much is enough? I wondered. I crossed my arms and tried to stretch out the conversation. It seemed like my whole day had consisted of stalling while waiting for help to come. "You're working with Montgomery."

"Very good." Stella snatched the floorboard away from Victoria. "Now open the suitcase."

"Aunt Gertie is innocent." I stalled, hoping the Pierce County officers would arrive soon. "Can you think of one thing she did wrong?"

"No." Stella swung the board like a baseball bat. "She's an upstanding member of the community, just like your mother and father." She smashed the top of a glass case. Then she scooped up the Pennsylvania Dutch Country horse and buggy spoons.

"When was the last time you talked with your husband?"

"Stop wasting time." Stella cracked open another case to take spoons of the World's Fairs. "Or I will have to do this the hard way."

"Mom." Victoria grabbed her mother's arm and tried to wrestle the floorboard away from her. "The cases are unlocked — you don't have to break everything."

"But I can," Stella said as she shook her arm out of Victoria's grasp.

Victoria lost her balance, which caused her to trip over one of the bags. She landed with a hard *thud* on the floor.

"Are you OK?" I asked my cousin.

"Not really." Victoria inhaled quickly, as if she couldn't catch her breath. "You've got the silver, Mom. Why are you making such a mess?"

"I'm going to count to three," Stella said to me. "That red suitcase better be open."

I touched the combination lock.

"One."

Victoria crawled behind her mother. She stared intently at me, not with snark or judgment. Victoria looked eager, a bit afraid, but mostly, she looked hopeful.

In that instant, I remembered all the things Victoria had done to me — and for me — during the past week. She'd taken video of me sleeping, but she'd also brought me food when Frankenstella hadn't let me come to meals. She'd blackmailed me into breaking into the museum, but she had also covered for me when I left the house without permission. Most importantly, she'd reminded me that the HEGs were my friends.

Victoria's eyebrows lifted in question.

"Two." Stella gripped the bat.

Friend or foe? Agent or double agent? What role had Victoria chosen? Could I trust her?

I started spinning the numbers. I stared back at Victoria, raised an eyebrow in reply, and hoped that she read the answer — *Yes, I trust you* — on my face.

"Three!" Stella cried.

I picked up the red suitcase and swung with all my might.

Smack! The silverware case slammed into Stella's legs. She tumbled backward over Victoria.

"Freeze!" came a voice out of nowhere.

34

Luck counts too.

—Rule Number 31 from *Rules for a Successful Life as an Undercover Secret Agent*

County sheriff's officers swarmed the museum once they heard the crash. Stella had a few warrants out for her arrest, which didn't surprise me at all. Apparently, she liked to use other people's credit cards.

"My aunt Gertie is hurt, and she's at the abandoned warehouse outside of town," I said to one of the officers. "Do you know if help has reached her yet?"

"He'll know," the officer said, pointing to a guy in a blue suit.

The man in the suit looked more like a college student dressed up in his father's clothing than a police professional. With short black hair pointing in different directions and a huge grin on his face, he walked right up to me. "Gertrude's en route to the hospital. Frank Baies and Montgomery have been taken into custody. Other members of Montgomery's organization were arrested this afternoon." His deep voice was so familiar.

"Roy?" I asked.

"Tweedledee," he whispered.

I breathed in deeply. "Tweedledum." I handed Victoria's purple smartphone to Roy. "I recorded everything."

"Sunfl—" Roy started to say. He glanced over at Victoria sitting on the museum floor amid shards of glass. He led me outside to the front porch. "Mabel. I am so proud of you. Your parents will be so proud of you."

"You found them?" I asked.

"Thanks to you," he said. "Yes, we did."

The bewildered look on my face made Roy laugh.

"The phone your mother hid in the basement is actually a tertiary emergency distress beacon," he said. "Like a third wall of defense."

"A what?"

"When other systems fail — which they did this time — that phone automatically calls for help when you dial the Agency's normal operative number for dependents," Roy said. "Your father rigged that phone so that it not only activated the Agency's highest priority distress signal, it also began the emergency extraction protocol for your parents."

"What took so long?" I asked.

"It was rather weird," Roy said. "Once the beacon started the emergency extraction protocol, someone — we don't know who yet — tried to stop it. However, your father had a password protection on the computer code so the beacon immediately kicked itself up to the top commander of the Agency. And the commander wanted answers before she'd send us, especially since your parents were not supposed to be in the field."

"Montgomery did it," I said, feeling certain, even without a shred of evidence. "He's a double agent."

Roy looked confused, so I repeated myself.

"Montgomery said he works for the Agency. He claims he sent Mom and Dad to Paraguay and then somehow erased their orders so that it will look like they went on their own accord. And he said he knew Grace K.'s father from a long time ago."

Before he could question me further, Roy's phone rang. As he listened to the person on the other line, his shoulders sagged. After hanging up, Roy said to me, "Montgomery, or Cedric Hawkins from the fingerprints, is the mastermind of an international smuggling organization that deals primarily in early American artifacts."

A sheriff's officer wrapped a quilt around Victoria and escorted her out of the museum.

"Victoria, wait. Where are you going?" I asked. I may not have been her biggest fan in the past, but she was family now.

"Just to the hospital," she said, pointing to cuts on her arms and knees. "Relax. I'm not being arrested."

"You're right, Mabel," Roy said once Victoria was out of hearing range. "He's a double agent. Instead of working for another government, he was working for himself."

"That's terrible," I said.

"Gets worse," Roy said. "Somehow, just minutes ago, Montgomery escaped from custody."

"What?" I almost shouted. "I practically handed Montgomery over to the authorities — handcuffed and tied up — and they let him escape?"

"They thought he was unconscious, and they assumed he was a Washington State Border Patrol Officer named

Al Montgomery," Roy said, "so they uncuffed him to lay him on the hospital gurney. He was gone without a trace within seconds."

"How?"

"Cedric Hawkins is a known mastermind of escape — he's broken out of three maximum-security prisons without ever leaving a clue behind."

"Whoever he is, he told me that he was part of the gang my grandparents, Carl and Mabel Baies, belonged to. He said he was a courier at the time. That's why he came back to Silverton. He was looking for forgotten items."

"And now he's the boss," Roy said.

"What about the helicopter?" I asked. "After you dust it for fingerprints, can you track its registration to the Agency or one of its shell companies?"

"What copter?" Roy asked.

"The blue Robinson R22 Beta II behind the warehouse," I said.

Roy got back on his phone. Within a minute, he was shaking his head. "It's gone."

I tried to recall exactly what Montgomery looked like so that I could describe him to a sketch artist, but I had a feeling capturing him again would be difficult even so — especially if he was an Agency-trained spy. "What else do you know about him?"

Roy looked at his little flip notebook. "Montgomery was known to make counterfeit copies of rare letters that he would sell to private collectors for extra profit."

"Mementos from presidents." I pointed to the red suitcase. "Thomas Jefferson's gold-handled spoons are in there. And some of his letters."

"How many?" Roy asked.

"Sixteen spoons."

"No. Letters. How many?"

I shrugged, trying to recall the wad of papers. "Maybe ten or fifteen."

Roy let out a low whistle. "If they're authentic, each letter might sell for $100,000 at auction."

I felt a little lightheaded for second. "I used more than a million dollars worth of American history to hit Stella?"

"You saved more than a million dollars worth of American history." Roy grinned.

"Why was the silverware case in our basement in the first place?"

"Your dad found it a few months ago in your attic when he was installing —" Roy stopped talking suddenly.

"The satellite dish." A thought hit me. "Dad installed a second dish on the Spoon's roof in July, mumbling something about better reception."

"Did he?" Roy looked uncomfortable. "The silverware case was hidden in your rafters for decades."

"And there's more stuff in our house too." The blueprint would pinpoint all of the secret nooks. "It's from my grandparents, right?"

"Tracking the last known legal owners has been a low priority item for the Agency," Roy said. "Your parents received permission to do it during quiet periods and return the goods as unobtrusively as possible."

The Great Reverse Heist.

Montgomery must have been waiting to get his hands on the stuff all this time. He'd even used Grace K. to track my movements. That must've been how Frankenstella knew that I'd jumped off the bus. I owed Victoria an apology.

"The important thing is that you kept the museum safe from prying eyes," Roy said.

Did I? I wondered. "When Victoria and I were in the Spoon, she couldn't take a clear photograph next to the black file cabinet. It buzzed, like a transmitter."

Roy said nothing, but thoughts churned in my head. "The museum's satellite is for that, not television shows," I said. "All of those black boxes that lead to the warehouse — it's all connected to Mom and Dad's work for the Agency, right?"

Roy looked at me in amazement.

"That's why the Agency didn't want anyone in the Spoon," I said.

"I can't tell you much, except it's a top secret prototype of a brand new way to transmit highly classified intel. The computer software was designed by your father."

"I was in the Spoon all summer long and never noticed it," I said. "How long has it been there?"

"Your parents began testing it about eight weeks ago," Roy said. "There's a transmitter — looks like a weathervane — on top of that supposedly abandoned warehouse."

That's what the topological map was really showing — Dad's work for the Agency.

"The transmitter didn't appear to be the target of Frank and Stella's theft," Roy said. "Montgomery's smuggling ring, however, could have recognized it for what it was."

"What's his real name?"

"That's the question, isn't it?" Roy shook his head. "Not Cedric Hawkins, even though he's used that for years. Is Montgomery real or code? Who knows? We should all be grateful he didn't discover the transmitter. With his Agency training, he could have used it for his own illegal operations."

And I was the one who came close to doing just that. "How does the transmitter work?"

"That's classified," Roy said. "Way above my level."

"How did Frank and Stella get involved with Montgomery?" I asked.

"Montgomery is clever. He ran into Frank some years back and must have realized Frank didn't know where the red suitcase ended up. More than anyone else alive, Montgomery knew the museum, or the house — had unknown gems. After the June visit, which was instigated by Stella's greed, Montgomery investigated your parents. Their odd traveling schedules tipped him off that they were smugglers like him. Or Agents. He must have been straddling both worlds for a long while."

"And no one ever noticed that Montgomery was an odd sock?"

"I guess not," Roy said.

"My parents —" I paused, not sure exactly what I wanted to ask.

"Montgomery sent them on a real Agency mission, which they successfully completed. He just wanted them out of the way for a while so he could install Frank and Stella in the house."

"The documents giving Frankenstella legal guardianship over me and the warrant for Aunt Gertie's arrest were counterfeit, right?"

"First-class forgeries." Roy whistled again. "We're going to learn a lot from this case. Sunflower, you played a huge role in cracking this smuggler's ring wide open. And it will lead us to Montgomery — whoever he really is."

"How will we explain this to the sheriff?" I asked. "And Victoria? And my friends?"

"Stick as close to the truth as possible," Roy said. "Frank and Stella Baies were trying to steal the museum's silver spoon collections with help from Montgomery."

"Who's PNW Security?" I motioned to the control panel, which someone had finally ripped out of the wall, making the alarm stop.

Roy scratched his head. "I don't know. Local company, maybe?"

"If PNW Security isn't from the Agency, and it wasn't Montgomery, then who is it?"

"You can ask your parents when they return from their *Monaco* spoon-buying trip." Roy winked. "In fact, they are on a plane right now."

"They'll be here by tomorrow?"

"On your eleventh birthday." Roy grinned. "Happy early Halloween."

35

The enemy of my enemy is my friend. Well, my not-enemy for today, at least.

— Rule Number 32 from *Rules for a Successful Life as an Undercover Secret Agent*

On Saturday afternoon, Aunt Gertie sat up on her hospital bed, chatting with Victoria. Containers from Mai's Diner covered the small rolling hospital table. My aunt stretched her arms out to me.

I hugged her as gently as possible, not sure where she was sore. "I tried to hurry on Thursday."

"Don't worry about me," Aunt Gertie said. "I was just a little dehydrated. Doctors say I'm as good as new." She patted my hand. "I'm just sorry I wasn't able to make you cinnamon buns for your birthday breakfast, Mabel."

"That's OK, Aunt Gertie."

Victoria nibbled thoughtfully on a piece of fried chicken.

"Any more drumsticks?" I asked. They were my favorite.

"Sorry." Victoria pointed to the trash. "I ate them all."

"So tell me about your birthday," Aunt Gertie said.

What could I say in front of Victoria? I couldn't reveal that early yesterday morning, way before the sun peeked out on the horizon, Roy brought me to Sea-Tac International Airport. I'm not ashamed to say I threw myself into my parents' arms. Mom and Dad said they were very proud of me, and that I was one of the best agents-in-training they'd ever seen. Roy, driving crazier than Bus Driver Mark, got me to school before the first bell.

Admitting Monaco was a cover story wasn't an option. I certainly couldn't tell them that Dad said we'd rewrite *Rules for a Successful Life as an Undercover Secret Agent* with a brand new type of invisible ink and new parchment. He even bought a frame with unbreakable glass.

I guess the only thing I could say out loud was, "Mom and I went grocery shopping after school and we made the traditional birthday carrot cake with cream cheese icing. I saved some for you."

"That's so sweet," Aunt Gertie said. "How was Halloween?"

"Fun! We trick-or-treated with the HEGs and Stanley," I said. "Hannah was the Pied Piper and we were her rats."

Victoria rolled her eyes, but she didn't fool me. She had a great time parading around Bluewater and loved it when people took pictures of us.

We didn't stay for the sleepover. That would've been like diving into a pool of glitter without a safety rope securely fastened. My excuse was that we had to drive Stanley back home. Really, I wanted to be in the same house as my parents, for a change. Who knew when they'd be called upon to save the world — or pick up a document — again.

"Victoria and I have good news for you, Mabel." Aunt Gertie took Victoria's hand in her own. "Your cousin is going to stay with me for the rest of the school year. And maybe longer."

"Oh." I had been so happy to get my parents back, I hadn't considered what would happen to Victoria. The thought of her staying didn't upset me at all, like it would have a week ago. In fact, knowing Victoria was going to be around gave me a warm, bubbly feeling, like I wanted to laugh for no particular reason. "Welcome to Silverton, Cousin."

"Thanks, Cousin," she said as she spread butter on a biscuit.

I poked around the containers. "Any more biscuits?" They were my second favorite thing.

"Nope." Victoria took a bite. Aunt Gertie pushed Victoria's bangs out of her eyes.

I settled for some coleslaw, which wasn't my favorite, but I couldn't begrudge Victoria a hot meal. She had lived in that warehouse for months without heat or running water.

My parents were in the hospital lobby, filling out paperwork for my aunt's release. While Montgomery (or Cedric Hawkins or whoever he was) was on the run, his state capital gang had been rounded up by the good guys. Hopefully, the Agency would find Montgomery soon and deal with one of their own gone bad. Frankenstella, my archenemies, were in police custody.

My plans for this Saturday evening — after we got Aunt Gertie and Victoria settled at her house — included my favorite meal: tuna noodle casserole, steamed broccoli, and more carrot cake.

Except for the fact that I still didn't know who or what PNW Security was, everything seemed normal again. I was too happy to deal with the far-reaching impact of Victoria living full-time in Silverton. Maybe we would be friends, even if our parents were foes. I could wait a while to see how things would be. I wasn't ready to trust her with all my secrets, but I didn't *distrust* her, either. She had been there when I'd needed her, after all.

"I have a question," I said to Victoria. "I thought you hated Silverton."

"That's a statement, not a question, Moppet."

"What made you change your mind?"

"I will be a famous actress someday." My cousin nodded. "I want to live in Los Angeles, just not right now. It's nice being somewhere with decent food. And family." She squeezed Aunt Gertie's hand.

"You belong here with us," Aunt Gertie said.

"Plus, all the girls in the class — the Hannahs, the Emmas, and the Graces — have been so welcoming and kind." Victoria patted the orange and black hair ribbon on her head, just like the one I was wearing, courtesy of the HEGs. "They make me feel like I've lived here forever, Moppet." She reached for the last chocolate chip cookie, but I got it first.

Victoria exhaled, raised an eyebrow in question, and looked like someone had replaced her favorite breakfast with a row of dead fish. Remembering Rule Number 32 — *The enemy of my enemy is my friend. Well, my not-enemy for today, at least* — I broke the last cookie in half.

Assume every agent is a double agent.

Coincidences do happen, just not that often. When in doubt, check it out.

Act natural. Be consistent in your cover story. Simple, true statements work best. Don't get fancy.

Anticipate surprises. No one — not even a supergenius — knows all the facts.

Never leave a fellow agent behind. You're in this together. Go team Secret Agent!

Enjoy the small victories. They may be all you ever get.

Rules for a Successful Life as an Undercover Secret Agent.

1. Live in a quiet and remote small town where everyone thinks they already know the real you. Don't give them a reason to change their minds.

2. Just be around a lot. The enemy will get so used to seeing you, they'll no longer notice you.

3. Trust your instincts. Your gut wants you to stay alive. Listen to it.

4. Everyone else could be the enemy. Or they could be working for the enemy. Or they could be under the influence of the enemy. Or they could just not like you.

5. Never blow the cover of a fellow agent. Deny all knowledge of their work. Deny all evidence. Deny, deny, deny.

6. Don't stand out. Follow the crowd. Never call attention to yourself. Shop, eat, and act like the locals.

7. Act natural. Be consistent in your cover story. Simple, true statements work best. Don't get fancy.

8. Change up your routine so that the enemy has a harder time tracking you. They will follow you, but make them work for it. Don't ever rush. Unless you have a bus to catch. Then run.

9. Any operation can be terminated at any point. If something feels wrong, stop. Remove yourself from the situation.

10. Try to be pleasant to the enemy. Don't be rude. Use polite manners.

11. Never trust anyone who works hard to befriend you. Watch carefully for anyone who does special, unasked favors. Try to figure out what they might want from you.

12. Always have an escape plan. Always.

13. Use technology, but don't count on it. Batteries die. Signals fade. Web pages can be faked. Email can be hacked.

14. Most people believe what they want to believe, despite overwhelming evidence to the contrary. Don't be most people.

15. Be in control. Act. Be the one who chooses the time and place for action. Only retaliate if absolutely necessary. Know the difference between reacting and responding.

16. Always have a Plan B. And a Plan C. A Plan D would be good too.

17. Recite Murphy's Law at least once a day: Anything that can go wrong, will go wrong. Be prepared.

18. If captured by the enemy, play along and be agreeable. Lie if you have to. You will not get in trouble.

19. If you're working with a co-agent, never look for him/her. Never acknowledge the other agent unless it is appropriate to do so. When leaving an operation, never look back.

20. If your contact doesn't make contact at the agreed upon time, assume the worst. Go immediately to Plan B. Or Plan C. Or whatever is the next plan. Just go.

21. Assume every agent is a double agent.

22. He who talks first loses.

23. Float like a butterfly, sting like a bee.

24. If you panic, stop whatever you're doing. Breathe. Ask "Huh?" Or eat something as a diversion.

25. Never leave a fellow agent behind. You're in this together. Go team Secret Agent!

26. Enjoy the small victories. They may be all you ever get.

27. Keep your friends close and your enemies closer. Invite your archenemies over for tea and cookies. It will confuse them.

28. If all else fails, beg like a puppy, making big eyes. But don't whimper. No one likes a whiner.

29. Anticipate surprises. No one - not even a supergenius - knows all the facts.

30. Everyone overlooks the quiet ones. Gather your ordinariness like an invisibility cloak and make some serious mischief.

31. Luck counts too.

32. The enemy of my enemy is my friend. Well, my not-enemy for today, at least.

33. Double-crossing a double agent makes double the work. Don't do it, unless there is no other choice.

34. If you find yourself behind enemy lines and your cover holds, use this golden opportunity to observe the enemy at close range. Then escape as soon as possible.

35. Successful spying consists of 50 percent preparation, 30 percent inspiration, 20 percent perspiration, and 10 percent action, which adds up to 110 percent because a great spy gives it her all and then some.

36. Coincidences do happen, just not that often. When in doubt, check it out.

Author's Note

Mabel's inspiration for *Rules for A Successful Life as an Undercover Secret Agent* came from her parents' copy of *The Moscow Rules.*

The Moscow Rules are real. Well, maybe. At least lots of people think they are real. If you're interested in learning more about them, the International Spy Museum in Washington, D.C. posts *The Moscow Rules* online: http://www.spymuseum.org/exhibition-experiences/online-exhibits/argo-exposed/moscow-rules

The Moscow Rules

1. Assume nothing.
2. Never go against your gut.
3. Everyone is potentially under opposition control.
4. Don't look back; you are never completely alone.
5. Go with the flow, blend in.
6. Vary your pattern and stay within your cover.
7. Lull them into a sense of complacency.
8. Don't harass the opposition.
9. Pick the time and place for action.
10. Keep your options open.

I don't remember when I first learned about *The Moscow Rules*. In a childhood spent reading obsessively, I picked up lots of useless but fun information, like the fact that Thomas Jefferson had no middle name.

Mabel's Rule Number 23: *Float like a butterfly, sting like a bee* is a quotation from Muhammad Ali, the Greatest of All Time.

The expression "odd sock" came from the ABC TV show *Castle*. The ruggedly handsome Nathan Fillion (he'll always be my captain!) played the titular character Richard Castle, a mystery writer.

Love nature?

Mabel and Stanley love hiking on Mount Rainier. Wherever you live, you can visit its website at https://www.nps.gov/mora/index.htm, or find out more about America's best idea at https://www.nps.gov/index.htm, the National Park Service website.

If captured by the enemy, play along and be agreeable. Lie if you have to. You will not get in trouble.

Anticipate surprises. No one — not even a supergenius — knows all the facts.

Try to be pleasant to the enemy. Don't be rude. Use polite manners.

Always have an escape plan. Always.

Float like a butterfly, sting like a bee.

Be in control. Act. Be the one who chooses the time and place for action. Only retaliate if absolutely necessary. Know the difference between reacting and responding.

Acknowledgments

Writing is a solitary activity; revision takes a village, lots of coffee, and a neverending supply of chocolate.

Val Moses read an early draft of Mabel Opal Pear with a fine-toothed comb and gave invaluable suggestions. Corina Linden (my fancy artist friend) and Tatiana Linden read the manuscript and gave constant encouragement. Kelly Delaney offered great revision notes. Many thanks to Jolie Stekly and her marvelous University of Washington's Writing for Children class (2013-14), Wendy Terrien, Jude Bloom, Kevin Wolf, Wendy Heipt, and the generous and wise members of SCWBI, especially the Western Washington region.

The people who make up my writers' village are Allison Conner, Jessica Petersen, Amy Nibert, and Arlene Bolton. Thank you all for making Tuesday evenings the best.

Every book needs its champion, and agent extraordinaire Steven Chudney found MOP a perfect home. Eliza Leahy, your editorial guidance has made MOP a better, kinder, and richer story. Thank you both.

Thank you to Ira Sluyterman van Langeweyde for bringing Mabel and Silverton to life. And a giant thank you to Capstone's editorial, marketing, and design teams for their enthusiasm and support.

My family — Andrew, Anne, and Susu — I could not have done this without all of you. Thank you for reading and listening, for understanding why I write, for sharing in the struggles and the joys. I love you all more than . . .

This book is for the ancestors: my mother Jane, grandmother Dorothy, the great-aunts: Eleanor and Anne Faulkner, godmother Annie, and grandma Amelie, who let me play with her amazing collection of collectible spoons. Aunt Sue and Aunt Blizzie, thank you for taking over grandmother duty for my girls.

Last, but not least, in loving memory of Beetle J. Cat, who spent the last months of her 22 years curled on my lap while I wrote Moppet.

About the Author

Amanda Hosch loves writing, travel, and coffee. She lived abroad for almost a decade, teaching English as a Foreign Language. A fifth-generation New Orleanian, Amanda now lives in Seattle with her husband, their two daughters, and a ghost cat.

4

If captured by the enemy, play along and be agreeable. Lie if you have to. You will not get in trouble.

7

Anticipate surprises. No one — not even a supergenius — knows all the facts.

9

Always have an escape plan. Always.